Ilse Aichinger — The Greater Hope

Ilse Aichinger

The Greater Hope

Translated from the German
by Geoff Wilkes

Königshausen & Neumann

Bibliografische Information der Deutschen Nationalbibliothek

Die Deutsche Nationalbibliothek verzeichnet diese Publikation in der Deutschen Nationalbibliografie; detaillierte bibliografische Daten sind im Internet über http://dnb.d-nb.de abrufbar.

© Verlag Königshausen & Neumann GmbH, Würzburg 2016
Gedruckt auf säurefreiem, alterungsbeständigem Papier
Umschlag: skh-softics / coverart
Umschlagabbildung: Das Foto wurde von Ilse Aichingers Tante Klara Kremer aufgenommen und wird mit der Genehmigung von Aichingers Schwester Helga Michie und deren Tochter Ruth Rix veröffentlicht.
Bindung: docupoint GmbH, Magdeburg
Printed in Germany
ISBN 978-3-8260-5921-6
www.koenigshausen-neumann.de
www.libri.de
www.buchhandel.de
www.buchkatalog.de

The Great Hope 7

The Quay 27

The Holy Land 43

In the Service of a Foreign Power 67

The Fear of Fear 83

The Great Play 102

The Death of the Grandmother 127

Dream of Wings 149

Marvel Not At This 175

The Greater Hope 198

Translator's Note 221

Family Tree 222

Afterword 224

Coda: Geliebtes Helgilein: *Christmas 1945* 248

Acknowledgements 252

The Great Hope

All around the Cape of Good Hope, the sea was turning dark. The shipping routes blazed with light one more time, and died out. The aerial routes disappeared, as if they were out of place. The groups of islands drew together anxiously. The sea overflowed all the lines of longitude and latitude. It laughed at the world's knowledge, and nestled itself like heavy silk against the bright land so that the southern tip of Africa could be no more than sensed in the twilight. The sea smoothed out the shredded-looking coastlines and deprived them of their purpose.

The darkness made landfall and moved slowly northward. Like a great caravan, it travelled up through the desert, broad and unstoppable. Ellen pushed her sailor's cap to the top of her head and raised her eyebrows. Suddenly she placed her hand on the Mediterranean, a small hot hand. But nothing would be any use. The darkness had entered the harbours of Europe.

Heavy shadows sank through the white windowframes. In the courtyard, water splashed in a fountain. Somewhere a laugh ebbed away. A fly crawled from Dover to Calais.

Ellen was freezing. She tore the map from the wall and spread it out over the floor. And she folded her ticket to make a white paper boat with a broad sail in the middle.

The boat set sail from Hamburg. The boat was carrying children. Children who had something or other wrong with them. The boat was fully laden. It sailed along the west coast, taking on children all the time. Children with long coats and very small knapsacks, children who had to flee. Not one of them had permission to stay and not one of them had permission to go.

Children with the wrong kind of grandparents, children with neither a passport nor a visa, children who had no-one left to vouch for them. That's why they were leaving at night. No-one knew about it. They avoided the lighthouses and made great

7

detours around the ocean-going liners. When they encountered fishing boats, they asked for bread. They didn't ask anyone for sympathy.

In the middle of the ocean, they stretched their heads over the side of the boat and began to sing. The song about the busy, buzzy bumble-bee, "It's a long way to Tipperary –," the one about the bunny in his burrow, and lots more. The moon laid a strand of silver Christmas tinsel across the sea. He knew that they had no helmsman. The wind blew helpfully into their sails. He felt what they were feeling, he too was one of those who had no-one to vouch for them. A shark swam along beside them. When he had asked, they had granted him the right to be allowed to protect them from people. When he felt hungry, they gave him some of their bread. And he felt hungry quite often. He had no-one to vouch for him either.

He told the children that he was being hunted, and the children told him that they were being hunted, that they were travelling secretly and that it was very exciting. They had neither a passport nor a visa. But they intended to get to the other side at any price.

The shark comforted them as only a shark can. And he stayed alongside them.

A submarine surfaced ahead of them. They were very frightened, but when the sailors saw that several of the children were wearing sailor's caps they threw them oranges and didn't harm them.

As the shark was just about to tell the children a joke, to distract them from their sad thoughts, a dreadful storm broke out. The poor shark was swept a long way off by a huge wave. Horrified, the moon snatched back the Christmas tinsel. Coal-black water splashed over the little boat. The children cried out loudly for help. No-one had vouched for them. Not one of them had a lifebelt.

Tall and bright and unreachable, the Statue of Liberty arose from amid the fear. For the first and for the last time.

Ellen cried out in her sleep. She was lying right across the map and tossing uneasily back and forth between Europe and

America. With her outstretched arms, she reached Siberia and Hawaii. In one fist, she was holding the little paper boat, and she was holding it tightly. The white benches with the red plush cushions ran in an astonished circle. The high, gleaming doors trembled gently. The brightly-coloured posters were turning dark at the sight of this pain. Ellen was crying. Her tears moistened the Pacific Ocean. Her sailor's cap had fallen from her head and was covering part of the South Polar Sea. This world was hard enough to lie on. If she hadn't had the little paper boat!

The consul lifted his head from his work.

He stood up, walked around the desk and sat down again. His watch had stopped and he had no idea what time it was. It had to be almost midnight. It wasn't today anymore and it wasn't tomorrow yet, that much was certain.

He slipped into his coat and switched off the light. Just as he was about to put on his hat, he heard it. The hat stayed in his hand. It was the crying of a cat; helpless and insistent. It made him angry.

Possibly it was coming from the room where the people sat during the day, waiting to be turned away. Those crowds and crowds of people with white, expectant faces, who all wanted to emigrate, because they were afraid, and because they were clinging to the fact that the world was round. Impossible to explain to them that the rule was an exception and the exception wasn't a rule. Impossible to make clear to them the difference between God the Father and a consular official. They wouldn't stop hoping, weighing the unweighable in their hands and calculating the incalculable. They simply wouldn't stop.

The consul leaned out of the window again and looked down. No-one there. He locked the office door behind him and put the key in his pocket. He passed through the anterooms with long strides. More anterooms than rooms, if you counted them all up. More hope than you could fulfil. Much too much hope. Really, too much?

9

But the silence hurt. The night was black within black. Woven warmly and tightly into each other like a suit of mourning. Have hope, you people, have hope! Weave bright threads in between! A new pattern must appear on the other side.

The consul walked more quickly. He looked straight ahead and yawned. But before he could put his hand to his mouth, he fell headlong. He had tripped over an obstacle.

The consul jumped up. He had a little trouble finding the switch. When he turned on the light, Ellen was still sleeping. Her mouth was open. She was lying on her back with her fists balled. Her hair was cut like a pony's mane, and the front of her cap bore the inscription *Training Ship Nelson* in little, golden letters. She was lying between the Cape of Good Hope and the Statue of Liberty and couldn't be moved. That was what you could make out more or less with a bump over your left eye. The consul was about to say something unfriendly in a loud voice, but pressed his hand to his mouth. He picked up his hat from the floor and smoothed everything down. And he approached Ellen quite slowly. She was breathing deeply and rapidly, as if every breath was diverting her from something much more important.

The consul tip-toed around the map. He bent down, lifted Ellen gently off the hard world and laid her on the plush cushions. Eyes still closed, she sighed and buried her head in his light grey coat – it was a round head, and quite hard. When both his feet had gone to sleep, the consul took Ellen into his arms, unlocked all the doors again and carried her carefully to his room.

One o'clock struck, the hour at which no clock in the world could be induced to say more. The hour at which it's either already too late or still too early, the hour after twelve. A dog barked. August. People were still dancing on a roof-garden. Somewhere a night-bird cried out.

The consul waited patiently. He had put Ellen down in an armchair. A cigar between his fingers, his legs stretched out fully, he sat opposite her. He was firmly resolved to be patient. In all his life, he had never received a more relaxed visitor.

Ellen's head was lying on the arm of the chair. Boundless trust was reflected in her face, revealed by the standard lamp. The consul lit one cigar from the stub of another. He took a big piece of chocolate from the cupboard and put it on the smoker's table in front of Ellen; he also got a red pencil ready. And he found a pile of brightly-coloured brochures too. But none of that could induce Ellen to wake up. At one point she turned her head to the other side – the consul sat up eagerly – but she was already asleep again.

Two o'clock struck. The water was still splashing in the fountain. The consul was tired to death. The picture of the deceased president smiled down on him with a surprised expression. The consul tried to meet the president's gaze. But he was no longer able to.

The instant Ellen woke up, she noticed that the map was gone. No chance that a piece of chocolate and a sleeping consul could console her for the loss. She frowned and drew her knees up to her chest. Then she climbed over the arm of the chair and shook the consul by the shoulders.

"Where have you put the map?"

"The map?" the consul said confusedly, straightening his tie and rubbing his hand over his eyes.

"Who are you, little girl?"

"Where's the map?" Ellen repeated threateningly.

"I don't know," the consul said, annoyed. "Or do you think I've hidden it?"

"Maybe," Ellen murmured.

"How can you think that of me?" the consul said, stretching. "What kind of person would want to hide the whole world?"

"You don't know much about grown-ups," Ellen answered, humouring him. "Are you the consul?"

"I'm the consul."

"Then –," Ellen said, "then –"; her lips trembled.

"What do you mean, then?"

"Then you really did hide the map."

11

"What's the meaning of this nonsense?" the consul said angrily.

"You can make it right." Ellen was rummaging in her schoolbag. "I brought my sketching board, and a pen. In case your desk is already locked."

"What am I supposed to do with them?"

"The visa." Ellen smiled anxiously. "Please write out the visa for me! My grandmother said: It depends on you, all you have to do is sign. And my grandmother is a clever woman, you can believe me!"

"Yes," he said, "I believe you."

"Thank God!" Ellen smiled. "But in that case, why did you deny me the visa? My mother can't cross the sea alone. Whose hair should she brush and whose socks should she wash? Who should she tell a fairytale to in the evenings, if she's alone? Who should she peel an apple for, if I can't go with her? And whose ears should she box when it gets too much for her all of a sudden? I can't let my mother go alone, Mr Consul! And my mother is being expelled."

"It's not as easy as that," the consul explained, buying some time.

"And," Ellen said, "it's all because no-one will vouch for me. The person who's vouching for my mother won't vouch for me. It's a question of money, my grandmother says, it's ridiculous, my grandmother says, one little bird more or less, my grandmother says, the child's not staying, the child's getting away from here, it's all the consul's fault!"

"That's what your grandmother says?"

"Yes. No-one can pay for me. Every ice-box finds someone who'll offer a guarantee for it, it's only me that has no-one. My grandmother says: that's correct, no-one can vouch for me, but anyway, who can anyone vouch for if they're alive, my grandmother says. The shark and the wind, they don't have anyone vouching for them either, but of course the shark and the wind don't need visas!"

"Should we try talking like sensible people now?" the consul said impatiently.

12

"Yes!" Ellen was more than ready to. And she began to tell him the story of the shark, of the children without visas and of the great storm. She paused sometimes to sing him a song, too. Then she took up the story again. Her voice sounded loudly and anxiously from the depths of the big armchair. She was sitting right back, and the patched soles of her shoes stared pleadingly into his face.

When she reached the end, he offered her chocolate.

"Might it be possible that you dreamed it all?" he asked cautiously.

"Dreamed?" Ellen called out. "Not a chance! Because then I would also have dreamed that the children in our building don't want to play with me, then I would have dreamed that my mother is being expelled and I have to stay here alone, then I would have dreamed that no-one will vouch for me, then I would only have dreamed that you've hidden the map and that my visa has been denied!"

"All the children are sleeping," the consul said slowly, "except for you."

"At night there are fewer people in the consulate," Ellen explained, "at night you don't need a number, at night everything happens much more quickly, because there are no business hours!"

"Good idea!"

"Yes!" Ellen laughed. "The cobbler in our building, the Czech cobbler, you know, he said: Go to the consul, the consul is a good man, the consul vouches for the wind and the sharks, the consul will vouch for you too!"

"How did you get in here?" the consul asked more keenly.

"I gave the porter an apple."

"But maybe you were dreaming after all? You have to go home now."

"Home," Ellen insisted, "that's always the place where my mother is. And tomorrow my mother is crossing the sea, and the day after tomorrow she'll already be at the place where everything turns blue, where the wind lies down to sleep and the dolphins leap around the Statue of Liberty!"

"The dolphins don't leap around the Statue of Liberty," the consul said, interrupting her.

"That doesn't matter." Ellen laid her head on her arms. "I'm tired, I should've been asleep by now, because I'm crossing the sea tomorrow."

Her trust was imperturbable. It moved like a desert wind through the chilly room.

"The visa!"

"You've got a fever," the consul said.

"The visa, please!"

She held the sketching board right under his nose. A white page was stretched on it, bearing the heading "Visa" in big, awkward letters. Pictures of brightly-coloured flowers were drawn around it, flowers and birds, and underneath there was a line for the signature.

"I brought everything, all you have to do is sign. Please, dear Mr Consul, please!"

"It's not as easy as that." He stood up and closed the window. "Not as easy as writing lines in school. Come with me," he said, "come with me now! I'll explain everything to you in the street."

"No!" Ellen cried out, rolling herself into a ball in the armchair. Her cheeks were burning. "Please, the cobbler said, the cobbler really did say: The man who vouches for the wind and the sharks will vouch for me too!!"

"Yes," the consul said, "yes, the man who vouches for the wind and the sharks will vouch for you too. But I'm not that man."

"I don't believe a word you're saying," Ellen whispered. "And if you don't sign now –." She was trembling. The cobbler had lied. The cobbler had said: the consul – but the consul was pushing the job onto someone else. And her mother was sitting at home and couldn't pack the bags, because she was afraid. And it was the last night.

"If you don't sign now –," Ellen was searching for a serious threat. Her teeth were chattering. "Then I'll be a dolphin. Then

I'll swim along beside the liner and then I'll leap around the Statue of Liberty, whether you like it or not!"

She fell silent. The chocolate lay on the round smoker's table untouched, the brightly-coloured brochures lay untouched. "I'm freezing!" Ellen murmured. Her mouth was open. She didn't move. When the consul approached her, she kicked out at him. He tried to grab her, but she swung herself over the arm of the chair with lightning speed. He ran after her. She slipped through underneath the desk, knocked over two chairs and clung onto the oven with both arms. Throughout it all, she kept repeating her threat to turn herself into a dolphin. Tears coursed down her face.

When he caught hold of her at last, he felt like she was glowing. Heavy and hot, Ellen hung in his arms. He wrapped her in a blanket and put her back in the armchair.

"The map, please, the map!"

He went into the anteroom, took the map from the floor, smoothed it out and brought it back. He spread it out on the smoker's table.

"It's turning!" Ellen said.

"Yes," he said, smiling uneasily, "the world rotates. Haven't you learned that in school yet? The world is round."

"Yes," Ellen answered faintly, "the world is round." She groped for the map.

"Now do you believe that I haven't hidden anything?"

"Please," Ellen said one last time, "please sign the visa!" She lifted her head and propped herself on her elbows. "That indelible pencil there, that will be enough. If you sign, I'll never steal apples again. I'll do everything I can do for you! Is it true that you get oranges at the border and a picture of the president, is it really true? And how many lifeboats are there on the big liners?"

"Everyone is their own lifeboat," the consul said. "And now I've got an idea!" He took the sketching board onto his knees.

"You have to give yourself your visa. You have to sign it yourself!"

15

"How can I do that?" Ellen asked mistrustfully.

"You can do it. When you get right down to it, every one of us is their own consul. And every one of us decides if the wide world really is wide."

Ellen stared at him in surprise.

"You see," he said, "all those crowds of people I've issued visas for, they'll all be disappointed. The wind doesn't go to sleep anywhere."

"Not anywhere?" she echoed unbelievingly.

"Someone who doesn't give themself their visa," the consul said, "can travel around the whole world, but will never get to the other side. Someone who doesn't give themself their visa will always remain a prisoner. Only someone who gives themself their visa will find freedom."

"I want to give myself my visa," Ellen was trying to sit up, "but how am I supposed to do it?"

"You have to sign," he said, "and the signature stands for a promise which you give yourself: You won't cry when you say goodbye to your mother, quite the opposite: you'll comfort your grandmother, who'll need comforting. You won't steal apples again under any circumstances. And whatever happens, you'll always believe that somewhere there's a place where everything turns blue! Whatever happens."

Feverishly, Ellen signed her own visa.

The morning was dawning, creeping up the windows like a skilful burglar. A bird began to sing.

"Listen," the consul said, "he's not setting any conditions either."

Ellen no longer understood him.

Milk carts were rolling along the streets outside. Things were becoming distinguishable from each other again. And in the big parks the first autumn flowers were emerging colourfully and casually out of the mist.

The consul went to the telephone. He put his hands to his temples and stroked back his hair. He shook his head, rocked back and forth three times on his toes, closed his eyes and opened them again quickly. He lifted the receiver, dialled a wrong number and dropped it again.

Footsteps were clattering across the courtyard. The water was still splashing in the fountain. The consul wanted to write something down, but couldn't find his notebook. He went over to Ellen and took her school student's identity card from her coat pocket. Then he sent for his car, righted the overturned chairs and smoothed out the rug. All around the Cape of Good Hope, the sea was turning light. The consul folded the map, wrapped the chocolate in it and opened Ellen's schoolbag. Once again he held the sketching board right under his eyes: stars, birds and brightly-coloured flowers, and Ellen's signature in big, sloping letters underneath. The first real visa during his entire time in office.

He sighed, buttoned up Ellen's coat and put her cap carefully on her head. Her face was wild and dark, but above it the golden inscription *Training Ship Nelson* could be seen again quite clearly.

The consul blew very gently on the visa once again, as if to make it complete and give it life. Then he pushed it into the schoolbag, which he closed and hung over Ellen's shoulder. He took her into his arms and carried her down the stairs, made her comfortable in the back of the car and gave the chauffeur the address. The car turned the corner.

Suddenly the consul put his hand over his eyes and ran up the staircase again with long strides.

The moon was turning pale.

Ellen grabbed for her mother's face. With both arms, she grabbed for the hot face which was burning with tears under the black hat. For this face which had given the world truth and warmth, for this face which had been there from the first moment, for this one face. Once again Ellen grabbed pleadingly for the beginning of all things, for the hiding place of all secrets, but her mother's face had become unreachable, retreated and turned as pale as the moon at the dawn of the morning.

Ellen cried aloud. She cast off the blanket, tried to sit up and grabbed at emptiness. With her last remaining strength, she pushed down the guard-rails. She fell out of the bed. And she fell into the depths.

No-one made any attempt to catch her. Nowhere was there a star for her to cling onto. Ellen fell through the arms of all her dolls and of all her teddy bears. Like a ball through a hoop, she fell through the ring of the children in their building who wouldn't let her play with them. Ellen fell through the arms of her mother.

The half-moon caught her, rocked deceitfully like all children's cribs and slung her into space again. No chance that the clouds were comforters and the heavens a blue vault. The heavens were wide open, fatally open, and as Ellen fell it became clear to her that there was no up or down anymore. Did they still not understand this? These poor grown-ups, who called falling downwards jumping and falling upwards flying. When would they get it?

Falling, Ellen broke through the pictures in the big picture-book, through the acrobats' net.

Her grandmother picked her up and put her back in her bed.

Like temperature charts in a hospital, the sun and the moon, the days and the nights climbed unstoppably, hot and high, and fell in upon themselves again.

When Ellen opened her eyes, she propped herself on her elbows and said:

"Mother!"

Her voice was loud and friendly. Then she waited.

The oven crackled and hid itself further back behind the dark green tiles. Otherwise everything remained quiet. The grey thickened.

Ellen shook her head slightly, felt dizzy and fell back onto the pillows. Through the upper part of the window she saw a formation of migratory birds, as neatly arranged as in a drawing. Then they were rubbed out again. Ellen laughed softly. Just like in a drawing!

But you're rubbing out too much! the old teacher would have said warningly to God the Father. You'll end up with a hole!

But my dear, God the Father would have said, that's just what I wanted. Look through it, please!

I apologise, now I understand everything!

Ellen closed her eyes and opened them again quickly, shocked. The window hadn't been cleaned for a long time. It was hard to see through it. Long grey streaks ran down the panes like dried-up tears. Ellen drew her feet back under the blanket. They were ice-cold and seemed not quite to belong to her. She stretched. She must have grown. Mostly she grew overnight. But there was something wrong about this spring morning. Maybe – maybe it was autumn. And maybe it was approaching evening.

All the better. Ellen was in complete agreement. Anyway, her mother had gone shopping. To the greengrocer's, around the corner.

I have to hurry, you know! Ellen is at home alone, and you never know what might happen. I'd like a few apples, please! We'll bake them, that's what Ellen likes best, and I've also promised to light a little fire for her, it's already turning cold. What do I owe you? I beg your pardon? How much? No, that's too much. Too much!

Ellen sat bolt upright.

It had been like a shout. It was as if she had heard it with her own ears, this stifled: Too much! And the greengrocer's face loomed like a threat, red and distorted, out of the twilight.

"Hey!" Ellen said, and let her legs dangle threateningly over the side of the bed. "You'll be in trouble if you ask for too much!" The greengrocer gave no answer. It became even colder.

"Mother," Ellen called out, "mother, give me stockings!"

Nothing moved.

Oh, they'd all just hidden. They were playing a bad joke on her yet again.

"Mother, I want to get up!" That sounded more urgent.

19

"Then I'll just go barefoot. If you don't give me any stockings, I'll just go barefoot."

But even this threat proved in vain.

Ellen climbed out of the bed. She was rather uneasy. Staggering, she ran to the door. There was no-one in the next room either. The lid of the piano was open. Aunt Sonja must have just been practising. Maybe she'd gone to the movies. Since it had been forbidden, she'd been going to the movies much more often. Ellen pressed her cheeks against the cold, smooth windowpanes. Over there, in the old apartment building, on the other side of the freight-train line, the old woman was holding the child up to the window. Ellen waved. The child waved back. The old woman was guiding its hand. Everything was normal so far. You had to buy some time, you had to think quite calmly.

Ellen walked from one end of the apartment to the other, and turned around again. She'd be in trouble if her mother found her like this, barefoot and in her nightgown!

The walls stared at her, hostile. Ellen struck a note on the piano. The sound echoed. She struck a second note and a third. None of the sounds sustained itself. None dissolved itself into the next one. None comforted her. It was if they didn't want to be heard, as if they wanted to fall silent, as if they were concealing something from her.

If my mother knew, her heart would burst in her body! That's what it said in the old fairytale book.

"Just wait, I'll tell my mother!"

Ellen threatened the silence, but the silence kept its own counsel.

Ellen stamped her foot, heat rose to her temples. Down in the street a dog was barking, children were shouting. A long way down. She put her hands to her cheeks. It wasn't the dog and it wasn't the children. It was something else. And it was raging. Ellen beat with both fists on the keys, on the white ones and on the black ones, beating wildly as if on a drum. She threw the cushions off the couch, tore the cloth off the table and slung the wastepaper basket at the mirror like David slung his stone at Goliath. Like David against Goliath, she fought against the horror of abandonment, against the new terrible realisation that was rearing its head like an ugly sprite out of the turbulent waters of dreams.

How could they leave her on her own for so long? How could her mother stay away for so long? It was cold, they had to light a fire, it was cold, it was cold!

Ellen ran through all the rooms. She tore open the cupboards, prodded the clothes, threw herself onto the floor and looked under the beds. But her mother was nowhere to be seen.

She had to disprove it, she had to prove the exact opposite, she wanted to choke the gaping maw of reality, she had to find her mother! Nowhere to be seen, that just wasn't possible! Nowhere?

Ellen was running in circles. She had torn open all the doors and was running after her mother. They were playing tag, that was it! And her mother was running very fast, she was running faster than Ellen, she was running so fast that really she had to be just behind Ellen again, because they were running in circles. In a moment she'd have caught up with Ellen, she'd lift her up and swing her round and round.

Ellen stood still suddenly, turned around very quickly and spread her arms wide. "The game's over!" she cried out despairingly. "The game's over, mother, the game's over!" On the table lay the visa: birds and stars and her signature.

"Late final edition!" the newspaper boy shouted across the intersection. He was shouting at the top of his lungs, freezing and excited to death. He jumped onto the running boards of the trams, snapped up the coins with his left hand, panted and couldn't keep up. He was doing good business, oh, it was the most wonderful business in the world: "Late final edition!"

They couldn't get enough of them. They would all have paid much more for them. They were as greedy as if he wasn't selling them the war news and the cinema program, they were as greedy as if he was selling them the breath of life itself.

"Late final edition!" the newspaper boy shouted.

"Late final edition!" came a whisper close behind him. Yes, again. His stand was on the stone island in the middle of the great intersection. Beside the stand, a blind man was leaning. He had his hat on his head and didn't want any favours. He was simply standing there, and no-one could forbid him to. From time to time he said: "Late final edition." But he had nothing to sell. He said it quietly and didn't ask any money for doing so. Like a forest, he threw all the newspaper boy's shouts back to him. He looked as if he didn't regard this whole thing as a business.

The boy circled the stand like a bird of prey. He looked over mistrustfully to the blind man, who was standing there as if he wasn't the only blind man in the middle of the great intersection at all.

The boy was thinking about how to get rid of him. The blind man was mocking him, the blind man was making all his loud shouts into soft calls for help, the blind man had no right to do that.

"Late final edition!"

"Late final edition!"

Cars rushed by, with blue glass over their headlights. Quite a few of them paused so that the newspaper could be pushed in through a side window. Just as the boy was working out how much time it would cost him to lead the blind man to the pavement, Ellen crossed the intersection against the traffic signal. She walked unsteadily and looked straight ahead. She was carrying the sketching board under her arm, she had pulled her cap down over her face.

Cars stopped, the trams' brakes squealed. The policeman in the middle of the intersection waved his arm indignantly.

In the meantime Ellen had made landfall on the stone island. The drivers' angry shouting ran off her like seawater. "Hey, you –," the newspaper boy said to the blind man, "here's someone who could take you across quite safely!" The blind man straightened up and grabbed into the dark. Ellen felt his hand on her shoulder. By the time the policeman joined the newspaper boy on the island, she had disappeared with the blind man in the confusion, submerging them in the fearful, blacked-out city.

"Where should I lead you to?"

"Lead me across the intersection."

"We're already across it!"

"Really?" the blind man said. "Isn't it the great intersection?"

"Maybe you're thinking of another one," Ellen said carefully.

"Another one?" the blind man repeated. "I don't believe so. But maybe you're thinking of another one?"

"No," Ellen cried out angrily. She stopped walking, let go of his hand and looked up at him anxiously.

"Just a little further!" the blind man said.

"But I have to get to the consul," Ellen said, taking his arm again, "and the consul lives in the other direction."

"Which consul?"

"The one for the great ocean. The one for the wind and the sharks!"

"Oh," the blind man said, "that one! In that case, just walk on with me!"

They had turned into a long dark street. It led uphill. Silent houses stood on the right-hand side, foreign embassies with diplomats who were too diplomatic to say anything. They walked along beside a wall. The blind man's stick tapped crisply and monotonously on the pavement. Leaves fell like heralds of what had not been said. The blind man walked faster. With short quick steps, Ellen ran along beside him.

"What do you want from the consul?" the blind man asked.

"I want to ask what my visa means."

"Which visa?"

"I signed it myself," Ellen explained uncertainly, "it's got flowers around it."

"Ah!" the blind man said respectfully. "Then it's just what you need."

"And now I want to get it stamped," Ellen said.

"Didn't you sign it yourself?"

"Yes."

"What is there for the consul to stamp?"

"I don't know," Ellen said, "but I want to be with my mother."

"And where's your mother?"

"Over there. Across the great ocean."

"Do you want to cross it on foot?" the blind man said.

"You!" Ellen was trembling with anger. "You're just laughing at me!" Suddenly it seemed to her, exactly as it had seemed to the newspaper boy, as if the blind man wasn't blind at all, as if there was a light in his empty eyes flashing over the wall and beyond. She turned around, the sketching board under her arm, and ran down the street again.

"Don't leave me on my own!" the blind man called out. "Don't leave me on my own!" He stood with his stick in the middle of the street. His shape looked heavy and abandoned against the chilly sky.

"I don't understand you," Ellen panted as she joined him again. "My mother is over there and I want to be with her. Nothing's going to stop me!"

"There's a war on," the blind man said, "and there aren't many passenger ships sailing anymore."

"There aren't many passenger ships," Ellen stammered despairingly and gripped his arm more tightly, "but there'll still be one for me!" She stared beseechingly into the damp, dark air: "There'll still be one for me!"

Where the street ended, the sky began. Two towers reared up from the embassies like border guards.

"Many thanks," the blind man said politely, shook Ellen's hand and sat down on the steps of the church. He put his hat between his knees, as if nothing had happened, took a rusty mouth-organ from his coat pocket and began to play. The sacristan had permitted this for many years, because the blind man played so softly and so tunelessly that it only sounded as if the wind was groaning in the branches.

"So how do I get to the consulate now?" Ellen called out. "What's the quickest way from here to the consul?"

But the blind man paid her no further attention. He was leaning his head on the pillar, preoccupied with blowing into his rusty mouth-organ, and giving no more answers. And now it began raining as well.

"Hey!" Ellen said, tugging at his coat. She tore the tin instrument from his hands and put it back on his knees again. She sat down beside him on the cold steps and spoke directly and loudly to him.

"What did you mean, how do I get to the consul, what did you mean! Who'll take me across the ocean if there isn't a ship for me anymore? Who'll take me across then?"

Sobbing with anger, she struck at the blind man with her fist, but he didn't move. Feet widely planted, Ellen stood uncertainly before him and stared right into his face. He remained as unconcerned as the steps which led upwards.

Hesitantly, Ellen entered the deserted church, debating with herself until the last second whether it wouldn't be better to turn around. She felt humiliated and was revulsed by her own footsteps, which shattered the silence of this space. She snatched her cap from her head and put it back on, and she held the sketching board more tightly than before. Confused, she examined the saints' images on the side altars. To which of all these could she dare complain about the blind man?

His face clouded, the cross raised in his lean hand, standing on a burning peak to which yellow faces which were pleading for salvation surged upwards, Franz Xaver waited. Ellen stopped and lifted her head, but she realised that the saint was looking far beyond her into the distance. She tried to attract his gaze, in vain. The old painter had done his job properly. "I don't know why I've come to you in particular," she said, but it was difficult for her. She had never understood those people who enjoyed going to church, and who talked about it extravagantly as if it was a physical pleasure. No, it wasn't a pleasure. It was more like a sorrow, that led to more sorrow. It was like extending a finger to someone who wanted much more than the whole hand. And praying? Ellen would rather have done without it. A year ago she had learned to dive, and that was much the same.

You had to climb onto a high diving board to get down to the depths. And then you still had to decide to make the leap, to accept that Franz Xaver wasn't looking at you, and to forget about yourself.

But now a decision had to be made. Ellen still didn't know why she was turning with her request to this saint in particular, who the old book said had indeed travelled in many foreign lands, but had died just before reaching the most desired land of all.

She tried with all her might to explain everything to him. "My mother is over there, but she can't vouch for me, no-one is vouching for me. Couldn't you –," Ellen hesitated, "I mean, couldn't you inspire someone to vouch for me? And I wouldn't disappoint you either, if I could just reach freedom!"

The saint seemed surprised. Ellen realised that she hadn't said exactly what she meant. With an effort, she pushed aside what was dividing her from herself.

"What I'm saying is, I would never disappoint you – even if I had to stay here, even if I had to drown in tears!"

Again the saint seemed surprised, and she had to go even further.

"What I'm saying is, I wouldn't drown in tears. I'd always try not to blame you, even – even if I didn't find freedom."

Still nothing but wordless surprise on Franz Xaver's part, and the last door began to open.

"What I'm saying is, I meant – I don't know what has to be done for me to find freedom."

Ellen's tears came, but she felt that tears weren't appropriate to this discussion.

"I'm asking you: Whatever happens, help me to believe that somewhere there's a place where everything turns blue. Help me to cross the ocean, even if I have to stay here!"

The conversation with the saint had reached its end. All the doors stood open.

The Quay

"Let me play with you!"
"Take yourself off!"
"Let me play with you!"
"Just go!"
"Let me play with you!"
"But we're not playing."
"So what are you doing?"
"We're waiting."
"But what for?"
"We're waiting for a child to drown somewhere around here."
"Why?"
"Because then we'll save it."
"And then?"
"And then we'll have made it right."
"Have you done something wrong?"
"The grandparents have. It's our grandparents' fault."
"Aha. And have you been waiting for a long time?"
"Seven weeks."
"And do lots of children drown here?"
"No."
"And do you really want to wait until an infant comes floating down the canal?"
"Why not? We'll dry it off and take it to the mayor. And the mayor will say: Good, very good! You're allowed to sit on all the benches again, starting tomorrow. We'll forget about your grandparents. Thanks very much, Mr Mayor!"
"Don't mention it, a pleasure. Say hallo to your grandparents from me!"
"You did that very nicely. If you like, you can play the mayor, starting today."
"Let's do it again!"
"We've brought you a child, Mr Mayor!"

"What for?"

"We saved it."

"And how did that happen?"

"We were just sitting on the bank and waiting for –"

"No, you mustn't say that!"

"Right: We were just sitting on the bank, and it fell in!"

"And then?"

"Then it all happened very quickly, Mr Mayor. And we enjoyed doing it. Are we allowed to sit on all the benches again now?"

"Yes. And to go into the city park to play too. We'll forget about your grandparents!"

"Thanks a lot, Mr Mayor!"

"Wait, what should I do with the child?"

"You're allowed to keep it, sir."

"But I don't want to keep it," Ellen shouted in despair, "it's a useless child. Its mother has emigrated and its father has joined the army. And if it runs into the father anywhere, it's not allowed to talk about the mother. Wait – and there's a problem with the grandparents too: Two are the right kind and two are the wrong kind! A draw, it's most annoying, I can't accept it!"

"What are you talking about?"

"This child doesn't belong anywhere, it's useless, why did you save it? Take it back, just take it back! And if it wants to play with you, then let it, in God's name, let it!"

"Stay here!"

"Come on, sit down next to us. What's your name?"

"Ellen."

"Let's wait for the child together, Ellen."

"And what are your names?"

"This one here is Bibi. Four grandparents of the wrong kind, and a light-coloured lipstick she's proud of. She wants to go to dancing classes. And she thinks the mayor will let her once the baby has been saved.

"The third one, there, that's Kurt, who actually thinks that it's ridiculous to wait for the child. But he's waiting all the same.

He'd like to play football again once it's been saved. Three grandparents of the wrong kind and he's a goalkeeper.

"Leon is the oldest. Practises lifesaving with us, wants to be a theatre director and knows all the holds, four grandparents of the wrong kind.

"That's Hanna over there. She wants to have seven children and a house on the Swedish coast later on, she wants a pastor for her husband and she's always stitching away on a tablecloth. But it could also be a curtain for the nursery in her new house, couldn't it, Hanna? Too much sun is harmful. But still she waits like us and doesn't even go home at lunch-time or walk up the river, to where the gasometer makes a bit of shadow.

"Ruth, that's Ruth! She likes to sing and mostly songs about the golden streets after the sorrows of love. And although her parents have been given notice to leave in September, she's sure that there'll be a place to live in Heaven. The world is big and beautiful – we all admit that – but still! There's a catch, isn't there, Ruth? Something's not right.

"Herbert, come here, little one, he's the youngest of all. His foot is stiff and he's afraid. Afraid that he won't be able to swim with us to save the child. But he's practising hard and he'll be ready soon. Three-and-a-half grandparents of the wrong kind, that he all loves very much, and a red inflatable ball that he lends us sometimes, don't you, little one? He's a serious child!"

"And you?"

"I'm Georg."

"The saint who slays the dragons?"

"The closest I get to Heaven is with the kites I fly. Wait till October! Then Ruth will sing: Let your soul soar like a kite, or something like that. What else have I got? Four grandparents of the wrong kind and a butterfly collection. You'll have to find everything else yourself!"

"Shift closer. You see, Herbert's got some old opera glasses, and from time to time he runs an eye over the canal with them. Herbert's our lighthouse. And over there's the local railway, do you see it? And there's an old boat down there, it can carry one of us."

"If you walk a bit further, towards the mountains, you get to the merry-go-round with the seats that fly up."

"The seats that fly up are nice, you grab each other and let go again –"

"And then you all fly apart!"

"You close your eyes!"

"And if you're lucky, the chains break. The music is modern and the momentum will take you to Manhattan, the man in the shooting booth says. If the chains break! But who is that lucky?"

"Every year a man from the department comes and checks the merry-go-round. Useless, the man in the shooting booth says. Stops the people flying. But they like being stopped, the man in the shooting booth says."

"And there are also some seats where they stand on their heads!"

"That's when they finally realise that they're standing on their heads, the man in the shooting booth says."

They were all talking over the top of each other.

"Have you ridden a lot on the merry-go-round?" Ellen asked nervously.

"Have we?"

"Have we, were you thinking?"

"We've never ridden on it."

"Not ever?"

"It's forbidden, the chains could break!"

"Our grandparents would weigh too much."

"But sometimes the man from the shooting booth comes and sits down next to us. He says: Better to weigh too much than too little! He says: They're afraid of us."

"And that's why we're not allowed to go on the merry-go-round either."

"Only after the baby has been saved!"

"And if a child doesn't fall into the water?"

"If one doesn't?"

Horror took possession of the children.

"What do you mean? The summer will last for ages yet!"

"Why are you asking questions like that? You don't belong with us!"

"With two grandparents of the wrong kind! That's not enough."

"You don't understand. You don't need to save the child. You're allowed to sit on all the benches anyway! You're allowed to ride on the merry-go-round already! Why are you crying?"

"I –" Ellen sobbed, "I just thought all of a sudden – I thought of winter coming. And you're still sitting here, all next to each other, and you're waiting for the child! There are long icicles hanging from your ears, and from your noses and from your eyes, and the opera glasses have frozen solid. And you're looking and looking, but the child that you're wanting to save doesn't drown. The man from the shooting booth went home ages ago, the flying chains are surrounded by boards and the kites have already risen up. Ruth feels like singing, Ruth feels like saying: But still! But she can't open her mouth anymore.

"Across the water the people in the warm, well-lit local train press their cheeks against the cold windows: Look, look over there? Behind the canal, where the streets are becoming so quiet, look across the ice floating in the water, to the right of the gasometer, can't you see a little memorial in the snow there? A memorial? Who's that supposed to be for?

"And then I'll say: A memorial for the children with the wrong kind of grandparents. And then I'll say: I'm freezing."

"Be quiet now, Ellen."

"Don't be afraid for us, the child will be saved alright!"

A man was walking along the canal. The flowing water tugged at his reflection, folded it, and pulled it apart again, leaving it to itself only for a few seconds.

"Life," the man said, looking down and laughing, "life is a bracing cruelty." Then he spat in a wide arc across the dirty surface of the canal.

Two old women were standing on the bank and talking excitedly to each other.

They were talking as quickly as if they were reciting a poem.

"Look for yourselves in the flowing water," the man said as he walked past, "I think you'll look very odd." He was walking calmly and quickly.

When he saw the children, he began waving and walked even faster.

"I have made my way through the world now –," Ruth and Hanna were singing the hymn as a duet. "And the world was grand and fine." The other children were silent. "But still –," Ruth and Hanna sang. The boat swung on the thin rope which fastened it to the bank.

"But still!" the man called out, shaking each child's hand in turn. "But still – but still – but still?"

"That's Ellen," Georg explained quickly. "Two grandparents of the wrong kind and two of the right kind. Like a drawn game."

"That's what we all are," the man laughed and patted Ellen on the shoulder with his great hand, "you can be happy when the result becomes clear."

"I suppose so," Ellen said hesitantly.

"Be happy when the result becomes clear," the man repeated.

"If someone's laughing to your right and someone's crying to your left, which one will you go to?"

"The one who's crying," Ellen said.

"She wants to play with us!" Herbert called out.

"Her mother has emigrated and her father has joined the army."

"And where do you live?" the man asked sternly.

"With my grandmother," Ellen answered anxiously. "She's one of the wrong kind, but she's alright."

"Just wait till you find out how wrong what's right is," the man said morosely.

"Ellen's afraid," Georg said quietly, "she's worried that the child we want to save will never fall into the water."

"How can you think that?" the man shouted angrily, shaking Ellen. "How can you think something like that? The child

32

has to fall into the water if it wants to be saved, do you understand?"

"Yes," Ellen replied, shocked, and tried to twist herself out of his grasp.

"You understand nothing!" the man said, becoming even angrier. "No-one understands what's happening to him. Everyone wants to save themselves without falling into the water. But how can someone who doesn't fall into the water possibly be saved?"

The old boat was still swinging on its mooring rope. "It can only carry one of us!" Bibi was trying to distract the man.

"Only one at a time," he said more calmly, "only one at a time. And it's doing the right thing."

"A feeble boat," Kurt murmured contemptuously.

"Smarter than an ocean-going liner," the man replied. He sat down right next to the children. The water beat relentlessly against the wall of the quay.

"What about you?" Ellen said shyly. "I mean, your grandparents."

"Four of the right kind and four of the wrong kind," the man replied, stretching out his legs across the grey grass.

"No," Ellen called out, laughing, "eight grandparents!"

"Four of the right kind and four of the wrong kind," the man repeated, undeterred, as he rolled himself a cigarette with three fingers, "just like each of us."

Birds swooped low above the river. Tirelessly, Herbert scanned the water with the opera glasses. "And anyway, I'm just like God the Father," the man explained, to Ellen's astonishment, "I wanted to own the world, and I own a shooting booth."

"I'm very sorry," Ellen said politely. Then everyone was silent again. Attentively, the children stared across the canal. Late sun smiled deceitfully over their shoulders, but they didn't notice.

We're waiting for the unknown child, we're saving it from drowning and we're carrying it to the town hall. You've behaved well! the mayor will say. Forget your grandparents. Starting

33

tomorrow, you're allowed to sit on all the benches again, starting tomorrow, you're allowed to ride on the merry-go-round
again – tomorrow – tomorrow – tomorrow – "Leaping fishes!"
Herbert laughed, making the opera glasses dance in front of his
eyes.

"The lighthouse sees them, but they don't see the lighthouse," Ruth said thoughtfully. "You might think it's the
wrong way round. But still, that's how it is in one of those
songs."

"But still," the man from the shooting booth called out,
leaping up suddenly, "but still you'll ride on the merry-go-
round again, today!"

"You don't believe that yourself," Hanna said sceptically.
Bibi pulled her stockings up to her knees slowly.

"But do you know what you're risking, letting us play like
that?"

"There!" Herbert shouted, beside himself, "the unknown
child! It's drowning!"

Leon took the glasses from his hand. "It's a man," he said
bitterly, "and he's swimming."

"Come on," the booth owner urged, "I'm not joking. My
partner is away, it's your only opportunity. No-one wants to fly
at this time of the day. You'll be all by yourselves."

"We'll be all by ourselves," Georg repeated dazedly.

"Fine!" Bibi shouted, and it sounded as if a bird had
shouted.

"And Ellen?"

"Ellen doesn't have to ride it today," the man said, "after
all, she's allowed any time."

"I'll wait for you here," Ellen said unconcernedly. She
complied with this kind of justice without demur. She followed
them with her eyes.

The man from the shooting booth went ahead and they ran
behind him, towards the mountains. The water was flowing
towards them; this made it look as if they were running even
faster. They held each other's hands tightly. Dogs barked and

hung back, couples on the grey lawns rolled apart. Flat stones slapped onto the surface of the water.

The merry-go-round stood motionless in the late sun. The man unlocked the gate. The merry-go-round stood there between the gasometers, detached and as preoccupied as a clown before his make-up is put on. Long and serious, the chains hung from the brightly-coloured roof. The little seats were painted. Suddenly the sky and the sun were painted too.

The children laughed for no reason.

"Do you want music?" the man asked.

"Proper music?" Herbert called out excitedly.

"You're asking too much," the man replied.

Black and threatening, the gasometers loomed.

"Music is dangerous!" Georg said. "You can hear it a long way across water. The secret police are somewhere."

"The water is flowing past," the man said darkly.

"If they knew that we're riding on the merry-go-round!" Ruth shrank into herself, shuddering. The booth owner checked the seats silently. The sand gleamed hostilely.

"Music!"

"What if someone reports you?"

"Do you know what that means?"

"No," the man said calmly and strapped the children in. He started the merry-go-round as if he was testing it. The seats began to sway.

"Go!" Bibi shouted again. "Music!"

The roof began to revolve. Herbert's stiff foot jutted out anxiously into the empty air.

"Come back!" the horn of the loudspeaker growled, throwing its sound across the wall of the quay.

"I want to get off!" Herbert shouted. No-one heard him.

The children were flying. They were flying, defying the law of their heavy shoes and defying the law of the secret police. They were flying away from the centre, obeying the law of centrifugal force.

Everything grey-green remained far below them. The colours melted. Pure and dazzling, the light shimmered in praise of the unknown. The image yielded to the meaning.

Deep down below, the booth owner stood with folded arms. He closed his eyes. In this second, he had exchanged his shooting booth for the whole world. The children were shouting. They grabbed each other again and again, as people grab each other before flying even further apart. Everything was as they had imagined. "Come back!" the loudspeaker growled.

The children didn't hear. The radiant gleam of the most distant star had reached them.

A woman pushed her pram across the bridge. The child in the pram slept and lay and smiled. The child beside the pram ran and cried loudly.

"Are you hungry?" the woman asked.

"No," the child answered, crying.

"Are you thirsty?" the woman asked.

"No," the child answered, crying.

"Have you hurt yourself somewhere?" the woman asked.

The child cried much more loudly, and gave no more answers.

"Help me to carry!" the woman said, annoyed.

The steps slanted down to the water.

"Hold more tightly," she panted, "you hold everything too loosely."

Wind rose and tried to put a wave into her straggly hair. The child in the pram began to cry. The child beside the pram laughed. They walked along the river.

"Why are you laughing?" the woman asked.

The child laughed more loudly.

"We have to find a spot," she said, "a good spot!"

"Where there's wind," the child laughed, "where there are lots of ants!"

"Where there's no wind," the woman replied, "and where there are no ants."

"Where no-one has ever been lying down," the child laughed, "where the grass is still high!"

"Where the grass is trampled," the woman said, "where lots of people have already been lying down. Lying down is more comfortable there."

The child fell silent. In the distance you could hear the loudspeaker.

"Here!" the woman called out, "this is a good spot here! Someone must have been here just before us."

"Who's been here?" the child asked.

The woman took a blanket from the pram and spread it on the grass. "Little footprints," she said, "children like you."

"Really like me?" The child was smiling.

"Stop it now!" the woman said impatiently.

The child ran down to the water. It bent down, picked up a stone and weighed it in one hand.

"Does a stone float, mother?"

"No."

"But I want to make it float!"

"Do whatever you want. I'm tired."

"Whatever I want," the child repeated. The sun had disappeared.

"Mother, a boat, an old boat! And the train over there! It's moving so fast, the windows are lit so brightly! Which one shall I take, mother, which one will carry me on? The boat or the train? Are you asleep, mother?"

Exhausted, the woman had put her head on her arms and was breathing regularly. The infant lay beside her with his eyes open and watched the sky at play. The child ran up the slope again and bent over the little one. Stiff and black, the pram stood out against the haze.

"Do you really want to take that one, to travel on?" the child asked. "Isn't it much too slow?"

The little one smiled silently.

"Then you'll change onto the train later. But it makes far too many stops!"

The little one grimaced anxiously.

37

"No, no, you don't want to do that either! Hey! There's a boat down there. That'll keep moving, once you're in it! That'll keep going for as long as you want. You'll never have to get out, no-one will change your nappy. Do you want to? Come on!"

The woman was breathing deeply, she turned slowly onto her other side. The boat swung gently on its mooring rope.

The child grabbed the infant and ran with him down the slope.

"Isn't it like a crib?"

The infant screamed. He lay at the stern of the boat like a helmsman who had been tied up.

"Just wait, I'm coming!"

The child untied the boat. He stood with both feet in the water.

"Why are you screaming? Wait, wait! Why don't you wait?" The infant screamed more loudly. Big, dirty drops ran over his little face. The boat drifted towards the middle. It turned, swayed and seemed undecided. Smarter than an ocean-going liner. Smarter than –

Blinking sleepily, Ellen lifted her head above the wall of the quay. At that moment, the boat was gripped by the current. It tipped over.

"Come back!" A little further down, the loudspeaker broke off with a discordant sound.

"Have you had enough?" the booth owner laughed.

"Enough," the children answered, cheerfully and a little dazedly.

He unstrapped them.

"I don't feel sick at all," Herbert said, "I really don't."

"Thanks very much!"

They shook his hand. The man beamed.

"Tomorrow, again?"

"Never again," Georg answered seriously. "The secret police are two kilometres further down."

"Be careful!" the man said. "And if – I mean: There are good friends. Anyway: You've never ridden on the merry-go-round!"

"We've never ridden on the merry-go-round," Leon said.

A solid young man was leaning on the wall at the exit.

"How come you don't pay anything?"

"We did," the children called out and ran away. Quick, quicker! They were only a few steps away from their spot.

"Look!"

Their arms fell to their sides. All the blood drained from their faces. Frozen, they stood at the top of the slope, their silhouettes standing out black and stiff against the summer evening.

What they saw exceeded their high ideas about the injustice of the world and it exceeded their capacity for suffering: With drops splashing around her and the infant on her arm, Ellen was climbing out of the canal.

The child they had been waiting seven weeks for, the child they wanted to save so that they could justify their existence, so that at last they would be allowed to sit on all the benches again, their infant!

Holding her other child's hand, the mother stood on the bank, screaming in fear and joy. People flooded in from all sides. It was as if they were all emerging like spirits from the river, taking this one opportunity to prove that they possessed hearts which shared her feelings. Confused, Ellen stood in their midst. At that moment she recognised her friends at the top of the slope.

The woman tried to embrace Ellen, but Ellen pushed her back. "It's not my fault!" she cried despairingly, "it's not my fault! I tried to call you, but you were too far away, I tried –"

She pushed the people aside.

"Save your breath!" Kurt said icily.

"Where are my opera glasses?" Herbert called out. Hanna and Ruth tried without success to hold back their tears.

"We pay differently," Leon whispered.

Pale and despairing, Ellen stood before them.

"Come on," Georg said calmly and threw his jacket around her, "there are some benches higher up. And we'll all sit down on a bench now. One way or another."

Boots tramped down on the gravel, meaningless and as self-assured as only the walking of those who have lost their way can be. Horrified, the children jumped up. The bench tipped over.

"Your papers!!" a voice demanded. "Do you have the right to sit here?"

That voice. Ellen turned her face towards the dark.

"Yes," Georg said, petrified with fear.

Hanna fumbled in her coat pockets searching for some papers. But she didn't find any. Leon, who found himself outside the circle of light, tried to slip into the bushes, Herbert tried to follow him. His stiff foot made a dragging, rustling sound. They were both fetched back.

The soldiers stood in dull silence. The one in the middle seemed to be an officer. His silver epaulettes gleamed. Bibi began to cry and fell silent again.

"We've lost everything," Kurt whispered.

For several seconds, neither the soldiers nor the children moved.

The officer in the middle began to get impatient; he fingered his revolver indignantly.

"I asked if you have the right to sit here!"

Herbert swallowed twice, loudly.

"Are you Aryans?"

Ellen still stood frozen in the shadows, trying to step forward and then recoiling. But when the officer repeated his question sharply and more clearly, she stepped briskly into the circle of light, threw her short hair back from her face with a characteristic movement and said:

"You should know, father!"

Helmets seem to be created for the express purpose of hiding facial expressions. They have always served this purpose on every front.

The little, dusty park suddenly took on a breathlessness, a monstrous, loud silence. The two soldiers to the left and right didn't quite understand, but still felt nauseous and dizzy, as if they had been proved wrong. All the children did understand, and remained triumphantly in the dark.

This man here was the one who had asked Ellen to forget him. But can the word forget the mouth which has spoken it? He had refused to follow a thought to its conclusion. Now it was overshadowing him and surpassing him.

None of the children was thinking about fleeing anymore. All at once they were on the offensive, unfamiliar power was radiating from their powerlessness. The Tower of Babel shuddered in the gentle trembling as they breathed in and out. Damp wind heavy with rain blew from the west across the water, the liberating breath of the world.

Ellen tried to smile. "Father!" And she stretched out her arms to him. The man stepped back slightly. Now he was standing a little behind his companions, so that his movements were invisible to them. His eyes were fixed in torment and supplication on the child. He reached for his belt with his right hand, because that hand was trembling. Silently, in every way possible, he tried to influence Ellen.

But she was unstoppable now. Her confidence surged about her and enabled her to make landfall, in the barrenness of a country shorn of pretence, dead centre in the torment and bitterness of her disappointment. With one jump she was at his throat, and she kissed him. But he had already collected himself, removed her hands forcefully from his shoulders and pushed her away from him slightly.

"How did you get here?" he asked with some severity. "And in such company?"

"Oh," she said, "comparatively quite good company."

She turned around and waved her hand casually.

"You can go home now!"

A rustling sound began in the bushes, soft and ever louder, leaves crackled as they were pushed aside, clothing snagged on thorns which snapped as it was pulled away. For several seconds only Leon's whispering and the dragging of Herbert's foot could be heard, a soft, swift tapping and then all was quiet.

The two soldiers had turned around, disconcerted, but received no order, as Ellen was squeezing her arms around her father, enraged and conscious of her goal. She concentrated her whole being on him, not letting him speak. She was hanging onto his epaulettes like a small, annoying animal.

She was thinking: 'Herbert has a stiff foot, Herbert needs more time.' That was all she was thinking. She was crying and her tears were making spots on the uniform. Her body was shaken with sobbing, but at intervals she laughed, and before her father managed to free himself she bit him on the cheek.

He took out his handkerchief, wiped his mouth and dried the spots on his tunic.

"You're ill," he said, "you should go now."

Ellen nodded.

"Will you find your way home on your own?"

"Yes," she said calmly, "I think so," but she didn't mean the grubby quarters where she lived with her grandmother and Aunt Sonja, but actually the remoteness which shrouded her. "I'm on duty," he said, calming down gradually. He could represent the whole thing to his superiors as a hallucination caused by fever.

"I don't want to keep you any longer," Ellen said politely.

Searching for a gesture of finality, he placed his hand hesitantly on the rim of his helmet. Ellen wanted to say something else, wanted to see his face once more, but didn't move. The ball of light abandoned her. She remained in the dark.

She turned back to the bench. "Georg!" she whispered.

But Georg wasn't here. No-one was here. They had all fled.

At that moment, the wind pushed the clouds aside. Ellen ran down the steps, standing beside the water now. The moon cast its shadow towards the other bank like a bridge.

The Holy Land

If you can't establish your identity, you're lost, if you can't establish your identity, you're doomed. Where should we go? Who will establish our identity, and save us? Who will help us become ourselves?

Our grandparents have failed: Our grandparents don't vouch for us. Our grandparents have handed down their guilt to us. We're guilty of being alive, we're guilty of growing night by night. Forgive us this trespass. Forgive us our red cheeks and our white foreheads, forgive us ourselves. Are we not gifts from one hand, fire from one spark and guilt from one transgression? Our guilt is passed down from the adults, the adults' guilt is passed down from the generations before, and the guilt of the generations before is passed down from the first generation. Is it not like the pathway to the horizon? Where does it stop, the pathway of this guilt, where does it reach its end? Does any one of you know?

Where do the people who have been wake again? Where do they lift their heads from their graves and bear witness for us? Where do they shake the earth from their bodies and swear that we are ourselves? Where does the mocking laughter end?

A hundred years back, two hundred years back, three hundred years back? Is that what you call establishing our identity, and saving us? Keep counting back! A thousand years, two thousand years, three thousand years. Back to where Cain vouches for Abel and Abel for Cain, back to where your head spins, back to where you begin to murder because you too don't know what else to do. Because you too are not vouched for. Because you too are only witnesses of the flowing blood. Where shall we meet again, where does what has been created become itself? Where are all of our identities established, where is our salvation written on the heavens? That's at the place where the molten bells toll for the beginning and the end simultaneously, that's at the place where the seconds are unveiled, that can only,

only be at the place where everything turns blue at last. Where the last farewell ends and the reunion begins. Where the last cemetery ends and the fields begin. If you've forbidden us to play in the city park, then we'll play in the cemetery. If you've forbidden us to rest on the benches, then we'll rest on the graves. And if you've forbidden us to wait for what is to come: Still, we're waiting for it.

One, two, three – coming, ready or not, we're playing hide-and-seek. If you find yourself, you're pronounced innocent. There, the white gravestone! That's where a space turns into a refuge. That's somewhere we play a game, elsewhere we are fair game. One, two, three – coming, ready or not, the dead people play too. Do you all hear it? Did you hear it? Establish our identity, stand up, raise your hands and swear that you're alive and you'll vouch for us! Swear that we're alive like everyone else. Swear that we're hungry!

"No, Leon, that's not allowed. You're cheating, you're peeking through your fingers! And you can see where we're running to!"

"I can see where you're running to," Leon repeated softly, "I'm looking through my fingers. And I can see you disappearing between the graves, I can see that alright. And then I can't see anything. Don't run away now!" he implored. "Let's stay together! It'll be dark soon."

"Keep the game going! The cemetery will be closed in an hour. Let's use the time!"

"Make sure that you don't lose yourselves," Leon shouted, beside himself, "make sure that you're not buried by mistake, all of you!"

"If you make so much noise, the watchman will throw us out and we'll have lost the last place we can play!"

"Make sure that they don't get you mixed up with the dead people!"

"You're mad, Leon!"

"If you hide now, it could be that I never find you again. I walk between the graves and call your names, I shout and stamp my feet, but you don't answer. Suddenly it's not a game anymore. The leaves rustle, but I don't understand what they're trying to tell me, the wild bushes bend over me and touch my hair, but they can't comfort me. The watchman comes running from the mortuary and grabs me by the collar. Who are you searching for? I'm searching for the others! Which others? The ones who were playing with me. And what game were you playing? Hide-and-seek. That's how it happened! The watchman stares into my face. Suddenly he begins to laugh. Why are you laughing? Where are my friends? Where are the others? There are no others. They hid in the graves and have been buried. They didn't establish their identity, and save themselves, but that was a long time ago.

"Why were you playing hide-and-seek? Why do you play hide-and-seek all your lives? Why do you only start searching for yourselves in the cemeteries? Go! Run away from here, the gate is being closed! There are no others. The watchman is threatening me. He has an angry face. Go! I don't go. So you belong with them? So you haven't established your identity and been saved either? So there's no you either. Suddenly the watchman has disappeared. The white pathway turns black. To the left and right there are graves, graves without names, graves of children. There's no us anymore. We've died and no-one has established our identity!"

"Leon's right!"

"Are we playing hide-and-seek now, or aren't we?"

"Let us think, Georg!"

"No, I won't let you think, I want to play, I know the best spot! Should I tell you where? Over there – where the oldest graves are! Where the gravestones are already leaning to one side and the mounds are settling down as if they had never existed! Where no-one is crying anymore, where everyone is waiting. Where the wind becomes quieter, like someone who's listening. And where the sky above is like a face – none of you will find me there!"

"In a hundred years we'll find your white bones!"

"Leon has infected you all."

"Why are you all asking?"

"So why are you hiding?"

"Stay here!"

"Let's stay together!"

"Who knows whether we're here at all," Leon said.

"We don't have any dead people to prove that we're here. Our grandparents are contemptible, our great-grandparents aren't vouching for us."

"They refuse to."

"They've come from far away and they've gone far away."

"They're being harried like us."

"They're uneasy."

"They won't be found where people search for them."

"They're not lying quietly under the gravestones!"

"People insult them!"

"People hate them!"

"People persecute them!"

"It looks like our dead people aren't dead," Leon said. The children grabbed each other's hands. They formed a circle and leapt around the stranger's grave.

"Now we know, now we know, the dead people aren't dead!" Like a shower of sparks, their shouts flew into the grey sky. Into the sky which was like a face above them, like a stranger's mercy, like light which conceals itself as it falls. Into the sky which sank heavily and ever more heavily over them like wings which are too big.

"Our dead people aren't dead."

"They're just hiding."

"They're playing hide-and-seek with us!"

"Let's go and search for them," Leon said.

The others lowered their arms, standing still suddenly.

"Where should we go to?"

They pushed close together, putting their arms on each other's shoulders. With heads lowered, they sat on the silent grave. Motionless, their weak, dark figures stood out against the white stone. In the distance, the dome on the mortuary floated like a sad dream in the twilight. Across the gravel path, the last golden leaves danced at the feet of the unknown.

"My days shall be as leaves before your feet," Ruth said anxiously, "it's from one of those songs too."

Where do the leaves drift to? Where do the chestnuts roll to? Where do the migratory birds fly to?

"Where should we go to?"

The lines of graves extended out of sight to the west. Removed from all intentions, they disappeared into the invisible.

Divided again and again by low red-brick walls, now organised only by denomination, the other cemeteries extended between the last cemetery and the city. And the ranks of graves extended to the south as well, like a silent army which is contemplating an attack on two fronts.

The road lay to the north. From there you could hear the rattling of the tram, which didn't stop at this last cemetery, driving past so rapidly as to suggest that it was afraid, that it wanted to turn away its head as the people do. If you climbed onto a mound and pulled yourself up a little on a gravestone, you could see the tram's rapid, red lights, back and forth, back and forth, like restless eyes. And if you liked, you could laugh about it.

This last cemetery was deep with despairing secrets, with curses, and its graves were badly neglected. It had little stone houses with strange writing on them and benches for mourning, but there had also been butterflies and jasmine for as long as summer had lasted, and a multitude of things unsaid and of bushes growing over every grave. Playing here was painful, and every spontaneous, exuberant shout was immediately transformed into a bottomless longing. The children yielded willingly to the white arms of the gravel pathways, to the open hands of little round lawns. "Where should we go to?"

Like the last hurdle in the great race, a black, low hedge to the east divided the cemetery from the expanse of the fields, which ran on with a limitlessness which proved the curvature of the earth and was proved by it. Wasn't it round, this earth, to be without limit? Wasn't it round, to rest in a single hand?

But which of all the pathways is it? How shall we catch up to the dead people? How shall we call them to account? Where will they establish our identity?

Isn't it the place where what's near is far, and what's far is near, isn't it the place where everything turns blue? All the way along the road, beside the fields between fears and fruits?

"Where should we go to?"

Despairingly, the children thought about it. Their eyes drank the silent dark like the last provisions on a journey.

An aeroplane hummed high above them. They lifted their heads from the graves and followed it with their eyes. Crows were startled into flight. Their shapes mixed together indistinguishably in the darkness and disappeared. The plane and the crows. Not us. We don't want to disappear without an identity.

On the other side of the hedge a small fire was burning, and three goats were grazing.

"It's time for you to go home," the old man said. He said it tenderly; but he said it to the goats.

"And for us," Leon murmured.

Bibi jumped up and ran towards the hedge, with the others following her.

Fog shrouded the fields. The old man with the goats was gone. Dispirited, they walked back to the stranger's grave. Their arms were hanging down. Their feet were heavy. It was turning colder gradually. From far off you could hear the pounding of a train.

"To get away from here!"

"Across the border, secretly!"

"Quick, before it's too late!"

But how little luggage you had to possess so that you could ride a little way on a locomotive's whistle. Less than yourself. This way of travelling was more exhausting than you thought. And where should you go to?

Hadn't they already used up the last of their money buying platform tickets every time a *Kindertransport* had left for a foreign country, and hadn't they used up the last of their smiles wishing their more fortunate friends even more good fortune and all the best for the journey? And didn't they already have lots of practice in waving big handkerchiefs and staying behind, in the flickering light of blue, darkened station lamps? But that was all a long time ago.

For now they had long known that you put yourself in the wrong in this world whenever you go in search of what's your right. They had learned to sell their furniture and to accept kicks without flinching. They had watched through the skylight as the temples burned. But the day after the sky had been blue again.

No, they didn't trust this shiny, cheerful sky anymore, nor the falling snow nor the swelling buds. But their awakening senses and the searing, dangerous river of unshed tears were probing for a way out. And the river was digging its bed.

"Away!"

"To a foreign country!"

Wasn't it already too late? The last *Kindertransport* had left long ago. The borders were closed. There was a war on.

"Where should we go to?"

"Which of all the countries will still take us?"

Not the south and not the north, not the east and not the west, not the past and not the future.

So it can only be a country: Where the dead people come to life again. So it can only be a country: Where the migratory birds and the shredded clouds have an identity, so it can only be a country –

"Where the goats get their identity from," Herbert said, "the white goats, the leaves and the chestnuts, we'll get our identity too."

"Be quiet, little one! Don't tell us any fairytales!"

"He's right," Leon said thoughtfully. "A country where the wind has an identity and the birds in the air, that's where we'll have an identity too. But where is it?"

"The man who vouches for the wind and the sharks," Ellen called out, "he will vouch for us too, the consul said."

"But where is the man?"

Leon jumped up.

"We ought to go to Jerusalem!" he said suddenly.

"Do you mean the holy land?" Ellen called out.

The others laughed.

"I've heard," Leon said, leaning on the white gravestone, "that they harvest lots of oranges there. With their hands!"

"And how are you going to get there?" Kurt asked mockingly.

"If we just get across the nearest border," Leon said. "Maybe it won't be so difficult from there."

"But how are we going to get to the border?"

"Who's going to help us?"

"The fog," Leon said, "someone or other, maybe the man with the goats will help us too."

"The man with the goats!" Bibi began to laugh.

The laughter shook them.

"And if they catch us at the border?"

"And if they send us back?"

"I don't think that'll happen," Leon said calmly.

"Be quiet!" Kurt shouted. "You're making fools of all of us! Come on, everyone, we're going now."

"Where to?"

"Stay here! Let's stay together."

"Together!" Kurt jeered. "Together? When you don't even know the direction? Straight across the graves? How do people get to the holy land?"

"I really mean it," said Leon.

Again, in the distance behind the little wall, you could hear the rattling of the trams. White smoke rose behind the hedge, where the fire had been. Fearfully, the evening star stayed behind the fog. Like something decided long ago, which no-one knows yet. Heavy twilight concealed the contours as if they were an error.

"There's someone standing over there!" Leon said.

"Where?"

"Over there, where the pathway goes to the gate."

"Do you see him?"

"Someone who's listening!"

50

"Do you see him now?"

"Yes, I see him."

"Right next to the crooked gravestone!"

"It's a bush," Hanna said.

"A young bush, quite a young bush," Kurt said mockingly. "Shooting up from the earth within ten minutes, an enchanted prince!"

"So save him!"

"Now he's moving."

"He heard everything!"

"We said nothing at all."

"All our plans!"

"Why are you talking so loudly?"

"Ellen shouts the moment she has anything to say."

"You were all shouting too!"

"Now he's standing still again."

"He's a visitor to the cemetery, one of the people who are left behind!"

Wind stirred the bushes. The last leaves struggled not to fall.

"And if there's no-one there?"

"If he reports us?"

"He didn't hear anything."

"He heard everything!"

"That's the end of your plan," Kurt said mockingly.

The children fell silent suddenly.

From the grave where they were standing, the pathway continued a little further and then turned the corner towards the cemetery buildings. Partly obscured by bushes and benches, it became visible again near the wall, where it joined a wide, black gate like a river of which it was impossible to say whether it had its beginning or its end there. On this pathway, a funeral was moving from the mortuary in the children's direction. Although in recent years more people had been buried in the last cemetery than before, this was still a very late funeral. The gate had to be closing quite soon. At first you could only make out something dark creeping slowly along the pathway like a caterpillar, and disappearing behind the bushes as if to shed its cocoon. As it moved around the corner and into view again, it became clearer. Be happy when it becomes clear, the booth owner had said.

It really was a funeral. The pallbearers were moving as quickly as they could, but their speed was still slow. The boards of the bier made reluctant cracking sounds.

Lord, abide with us, fast falls the eventide!

The pallbearers were eager to get home. They felt the same great eagerness to get home as the dead man in the coffin.

The children jumped off the grave, dust and leaves swirled up. For a moment the whole thing seemed like a cloud which was prepared to carry them away, to dissolve them into something else. But this dust was cursed too, and forced to settle down again.

They moved aside. The pallbearers hurried past with the coffin without paying any further attention to them. The coffin was made of raw wood, a long, light-coloured coffin. Dependent on the movements of the pallbearers, it yet had a floating quality which made it appear free again. It seemed intent on proving that a kind of mute, floating and final independence lay within this last dependency, like the kernel within the fruit.

No-one followed the coffin. None of those sobbing, always and unwittingly somewhat ridiculous mourners who wanted to follow without being able to follow and who, not looking through their dark veils, tripped over their own feet. No-one followed the coffin?

Which of the children had been the first? Had it been Herbert, Ellen or Leon? And what had moved them to do it? Had it been fear, fear of the bush next to the crooked gravestone which wasn't a bush? Or had it been a burning longing, a longing for the holy land?

They walked behind the stranger's coffin; behind the unknown dead man, the only man they could turn to here, the only man who could protect them now, who gave them a purpose and an identity: Herbert, who was dragging his stiff foot a little as usual, between Ellen and Georg, Ruth and Hanna, whose light-coloured, straggly hair, matching the lightness of raw planks used to make poor men's coffins, was blowing in the autumn wind.

The further the children walked, the more their movements fitted in with the bearers' movements, troubled by hesitation and impatience, but troubled to the same extent, suspended among the others. Guests, not funeral guests. It seemed like they were helping with the work of carrying. Was this the pathway to the holy land? Not a single light was burning on the graves. The official bearers panted angrily. Their official duties were hard enough. Their official duties were no joke, at this hour in late autumn.

"Hey, you children, what do you think you're doing back there?"

"We belong here."

"Children he's left behind?"

"No."

"Funeral guests?"

It was a dark evening. And it was difficult to turn around if you had a load to move forward in the dark. It was even more difficult to find the right words for getting rid of the guests who weren't funeral guests. The bearers walked more slowly and sped up again, they called threats and curses back over their shoulders. Finally they tried to make the coffin jump on the bier to frighten the children. But nothing worked. They walked steadily behind the coffin, borne on as if by a song by the floating brightness of what was being borne before them, with their eyes fixed confidently upon it. As if this was really the way to the holy land: not east and not south, not north and not west, not the past and not the future. The way, simply the way. Simply straight ahead. And straight ahead is everywhere.

The children were laughing quietly at the bearers' curses as they walked along like this. Unrecognised, the destination was reflected in their faces.

They weren't surprised that the way was so long. It would have been no marvel if they had gone on like this hour after hour, straight on through the fog, alongside the graves, and they wouldn't really have been surprised if the bearers with the coffin had suddenly jumped over the hedge to follow the three goats on their way home.

But the bearers stood still. They stood still and put the bier down. It seemed as if they had stood still purely and simply to make the children stop. It seemed as if the grave had been dug purely and simply for that reason.

The grave had been dug long before, what else would you expect? Thin black branches bent down over it, their ends touching the edge of the depths. The grave lay at the furthest end of the last cemetery.

The bearers stooped, removed the coffin from the bier and put the straps underneath, ready to lower it. The coffin swayed and disappeared rapidly into the dark.

Silently, the children stood around the cast-up earth. Suddenly it seemed to them that it was their last way out which was coming to an end here, the last way to get across the border, the last way to attain some kind of identity. When the bearers began to shovel the earth back into the grave, they turned hesitantly to leave.

The first of them could already see the walls of the mortuary in front of them when they noticed the stranger, who was approaching them with a slow, swinging walk on the white pathway. They broke and ran into the bushes, like startled game.

Ellen and Georg, adrift a little behind the others, didn't hear their warning calls. They began to run when the others disappeared, and ran right into the stranger's arms.

"Where are you off to in such a hurry?"

With his head bent on one side, he stood on broad legs in the middle of the pathway, not letting them past.

"Where to?"

"Who are you?"

"Not a bush and not a spy."

He was, as it soon turned out, the coachman who drove the hearse. And he had heard everything.

"You want to get to the holy land?"

"It was a joke," Georg said. They held themselves rigid, not trying to flee anymore. He took them by the shoulders and walked with them towards the gate. They felt his cold, loose grip.

"And why do you want to get to the holy land, of all places?"

"That's what we played," Ellen replied.

"But that's nonsense," the coachman said angrily. "The holy land is too far away, do you hear me?" He bent his head closer to the children. "There's a border quite nearby, it's quite simple to get across! And you don't have to move on from there at all. There's any amount of toys there, you'll get everything back there –"

"The fowls in the yards there are already roasted," Ellen smiled gently, "it's like in a fairytale!"

The coachman looked at her angrily.

"There's a border, near here," he repeated urgently.

"And lots of border guards," Georg said.

"There aren't guards everywhere," the coachman replied. "And I don't only drive hearses."

"What do you want for it?"

He named a sum.

"Money," Ellen said.

"What did you expect?"

"And when would you leave?"

"The day after tomorrow. I could do it the day after tomorrow."

"You'd be ready by the day after tomorrow?" Georg said.

"Quickly or not at all," the man replied.

"And if we got the money together?" Suddenly, they were eager.

"Do whatever you want," the coachman said. "If you're there, I'll be there too."

They had reached the gate. The caretaker rattled his keys. "Do you people belong with the ones who went along there?"

"No," the coachman said.

"Yes," the children called out, but they had already passed through. The gate closed behind them.

"The day after tomorrow, towards evening, starting from the last cemetery. I'll be waiting by the wall."

"The day after tomorrow," the coachman repeated for the last time. The day after tomorrow. It's not a mistake? Living for the day after tomorrow and dying for the day after tomorrow. Isn't it a doubtful rendezvous? Isn't it always like an arrangement with a coachman who's a stranger? Like the meeting place by the cemetery wall? Pleasure in the day after tomorrow and fear of the day after tomorrow? The day after tomorrow, that was the day when people were due to be removed from these quarters too. "Like being harried by dogs," the grandmother said.

And tomorrow, that was the day before.

On this last day, the children's quiet air of being miles away grew beyond all boundaries. And the grandmother blamed Ellen for the fact that the bookcase still wasn't sold. This old bookcase, with a value which was determined by the dreams of people who were growing and people who had died and a price which was determined by extortion. Who should you explain that to?

"We need the money for the resettlement," the grandmother explained before she went out. "The bookcase has to be sold."

"For the resettlement," Ellen repeated. "For what resettlement?" Left on her own, she crept restlessly through all the rooms like a betrayed traitor.

The carriage was waiting outside the last cemetery. The bookcase had to be sold. For what price do you sell what you love?

"You for money," Ellen explained to the bookcase, "and the money for the border. You have to understand me, you for the border!"

She tried to embrace the bookcase with both arms.

The first buyer left because he had no appreciation of the relationship between dreams and business, the second left because he discovered a spider in a corner of the old bookcase, and it was only with the third that Ellen could attempt to negotiate. It wasn't a bad negotiation, because it began with silence. When they had both been silent for long enough to get to know each other a little, Ellen urged her arguments, which gleamed like fairytales, on the disconcerted buyer. She spoke for the old bookcase.

"It creaks!" she said, putting a finger to her mouth and moving the ageing doors gently. "And if a train passes over there, the glass here begins to rattle. Do you want to wait until a train passes?"

The buyer sat down in an armchair, which promptly tipped over. He stood up again, but didn't answer. "It smells of apples," Ellen whispered, threateningly and helplessly. "There's a shelf missing right at the bottom, you can hide there!"

She was trying in vain to express the inexpressible in hard words. She completely forgot to say that the bookcase's doors had cut glass, as the grandmother had told her to do, and she forgot the inlay work on the two sides.

Instead, she announced triumphantly: "In the autumn it makes cracking sounds as if it has a heart!"

"Does one make cracking sounds in the autumn, if one has a heart?" the buyer asked. Then they were silent again, waiting for the train.

"The wind is blowing!" Ellen said, as if this fact ought to establish the bookcase's value too. "How much do you want to pay?"

"I'm waiting," the buyer said, immovable. "I'm waiting for the train."

The train came. The glass rattled.

"It's afraid," Ellen said, turning pale, "the bookcase is afraid of you."

"I'll take it," the buyer said. "Please tell me the price."

"Thank you," Ellen said, "but I'm not sure – it's afraid of you."

"It'll calm down," the buyer said.

"Can you pay for it?" Ellen asked anxiously.

"No," the buyer answered sadly, "no, I can't pay for it. It creaks and smells of apples. I'll remain in your debt." And he put five hundred marks on the table.

"No!" Ellen stopped him, confused. "The grandmother said: It's worth not less than a hundred and fifty!"

"Please tell your grandmother: Nothing's worth more than a profound dream." And the buyer left, and never sent to fetch the bookcase. He had bought the aroma of apples and Ellen's pale face.

The day after tomorrow becomes tomorrow and tomorrow becomes today. The days roll away like beads from a broken necklace. Throw yourselves to the ground and search – you won't find them anymore. Today becomes yesterday and yesterday becomes the day before yesterday, don't you permit it! Catch hold of Today! Make sure that you stay! Time is like the beating of wings around your ears, like the wild hunt outside your windows. Now and in the hour of our death. Isn't it part of it, Now in the hour of death, just as the hour of death is part of Now? They're murderers, the days, thieves! A band of smugglers across your borders. Don't you permit it, catch them! Catch hold of Today! But how do you think you can do that?

Haven't you posted guards on all the borders of your space, armed to the teeth? Then post guards on the borders of your time too, arm your ancestors and their ancestors, arm the dead people! And make them prove that today is today. Guards on all your borders, then nothing can happen to you.

What do you say? It's no use?

Speak more quietly. The secret police are somewhere about.

What do you say? Your guards won't stand still? They've deserted to another country, taking the days with them? Your great-grandparents have deserted and your borders are open? No-one can prove anymore that today is today?

Don't admit it. Go back. A hundred years, two hundred years, three hundred years. And then?

The *Ahnenpass* doesn't matter anymore. Isn't time round, isn't it round like your space? How could you stay? All your borders are open, proving that your life is fleeting. You flee, you're refugees, who walk and hide, walk and hide, moving on, always moving on. For you, time rolls on like a carriage, a black carriage.

"Get in!"

The coachman doffed his hat. Ellen pressed the money into his hand. He opened the door and bowed. His watch-chain rattled. The children hesitated. They held each other's hands more tightly.

It was a black, heavy carriage, battered, crouching low on its springs, the leather cracked by sunlight and dryness. It was a mourning coach. The horses' eyes shone dully, thin dark horses with weals which had formed scars. The street which ran beside the cemetery was empty at this hour, that is, at this hour its emptiness became clear, it revealed itself to its true being.

Tomorrow becomes today and today becomes yesterday.

"Hurry up!" The children jumped up. The door closed. The sound travelled clear to the gardens where the wreaths were woven for the dead people. It was like a bird's warning call.

The carriage set off.

Georg put the blanket over Ellen's knees. They were moving. Slowly at first and then faster, faster and faster, roughly in the direction of the railway and towards the border. The red wall of the cemetery, the white yards of the stonemasons' workshops and the grey-green gardeners' huts, that all stayed far behind. Far behind with the last flowers, the smoke from the chimneys and the cries of hungry birds. But perhaps the black carriage stayed behind too, and everything else was flying. Who could determine that with certainty?

The sky was made of blue glass, and the red beech trees by the wayside bumped their heads bloody. And not only the red beech trees. But the glass shattered the further they went, shattered into the grey of grey birds, filling the sky, which then darkened before the blackness of the black carriage.

"The border, where's the border?"

59

"Can't any of you see it? There, where the line runs between the sky and the earth, that's the border."

"You're laughing at us, coachman!"

"How could I?"

"You're taking us in circles!"

"Why are you all so mistrustful?"

"We're tired."

"That's the same thing."

"The line you're talking about is always the same distance away!"

"Stop, coachman, stop! We want to get off!"

"I'll take you across alright!"

"We want to go back home. We want to go back to the others."

"I want to go back!"

"I want to go back to my grandmother!"

But the coachman gave no more answers. Gradually they stopped shouting. They put their arms around each other and put their heads together. They yielded to the coachman who was a stranger, to the black carriage and the border which was always the same distance away.

"Ellen, Ellen, your head is getting too heavy for me! Ellen, where are we going to? Ellen, it's turning very dark, I can't protect you anymore, everything is spinning around – –"

"– – Everything is spinning around!" the man with the bagpipes called out, jumping up onto the back of the moving coach. "And how awful if would be if everything wasn't spinning around! You wouldn't be able to find the Pole anymore." He managed to open the door. He snatched his cap from his head, laughed and pulled at his nose. "Corpses, it smells of corpses!"

The coach raced along the river.

"What is there to laugh about?" Ellen asked sternly.

"No-one notices it!" the stranger giggled. "The plague has come, but no-one notices it. They've lived without noticing it, and now they're dying without noticing it. Their boots are the biers which carry them outside the city. Their rifles are the bearers which throw them into the pits. Plague sores, plague

60

sores, nothing but plague sores!" The stranger opened his mouth wide, swayed and rolled under the seat.

"Who are you?"

"I've fallen into the plague pit."

"Who are you?"

"I've sung a song."

"Who are you?"

"Oh, by Jolly Augustine, that's hard to explain!"

The carriage was still chasing the river. Telegraph wires glinted above black coal dumps, gulls swooped like diving aeroplanes towards the ice-grey water, and on the other bank a crane stretched its arms into the cold sky as if asking for loads to lift. Evening was approaching, and the autumn day was moving mysteriously, without noise or resistance, towards its end.

Not far from the abandoned shipyard, the man with the globe climbed aboard. He had been waiting on the wreck of a ship which hadn't been removed yet.

"Columbus!" he said, laughing politely and doffing his hat. "Everything is still there to be discovered! Every pond, every pain and every stone on the bank."

"In the end, America wasn't named for you after all!"

"No!" Columbus shouted forcefully. "But what's unnamed is named for me. Everything which is still there to be discovered." He sank back comfortably into the grubby upholstery and stretched out his legs.

"Does discovering things make you tired?"

"Wonderfully tired! You earn the night."

"Are there dreams which stand watch?"

"Oh, dreams are more watchful than actions and events, dreams protect the world from its end, dreams, nothing but dreams!"

"The plague has come, but no-one notices it," Jolly Augustine said, giggling from under his seat, "they haven't noticed that they were created, and they won't notice that they're already damned."

Now they were moving along the embankment which ran beside the great river, while the river ran beside the embankment. It didn't occur to either one to separate itself from the other. Quietly and fraternally, they ran on into endlessness. The coach passed through a village. The sky hung grey and deep above the low walls of the gardens. Reddish trees swayed in the dark, and little children were playing outside the yellow houses. They were drawing lines with their feet in the river sand and furrowing their brows. They were growing silently, sometimes screeching into the twilight and throwing stones at sparrows. They clung to the locked garden gates with claw-like fingers, bit down on iron and laughed as they tore the ears off an old, ugly dog. Then a boy jumped across the walls from the inside. He was wearing a short, light-coloured tunic and carrying a sling-shot in his right hand. His face glowed with anger and he killed the sick, whining dog with a single stone. Then he lit a fire in the middle of the street and threw the dog in. And he sang:

"We shall make God a burnt offering of all your sins. Come and give Him your sins, because you have nothing else."

And he played on the lyre as he sang. His song was tormenting, strange and insistent, and his fire spread the smell of burning over the abandoned street. He climbed onto a wall and began to preach, and after every sentence he fired a stone from his slingshot, shattering people's windows so that they had to look whether they wanted to or not. Angrily, sleepily, they put their heavy heads out through the jagged holes and called their children inside. But their children didn't come, instead they stood and listened to the strange, small preacher and opened their red greedy mouths wide, as if they wanted to swallow him whole.

"Stones, stones through your windows are the bread that you need, and the bread on your plates is the stone that burdens you. Everything which brings a benefit to you is raised by you onto the throne. Pain always brings a benefit, pain is the final benefit!" He became exalted and began making indistinct sounds of rejoicing when no more words occurred to him. The children from the village rejoiced with him, until suddenly one of them shouted: "Your hair is black and curly, you're a stranger!"

"Am I a stranger, because my hair is black and curly, or are you strangers because your hands are cold and hard? Who is more a stranger, you or me? The one who hates is more a stranger than the one who is hated, and the ones who are most strangers are the ones who feel most at home!"

But the children from the village weren't listening to him anymore. They jumped onto the wall and dragged him down among them. They screamed and howled and stopped growing. And the adults, who had stopped growing too, rushed out of their houses and threw themselves onto the boy who was a stranger. They rolled his body back and forth in the last glow of his dying fire, but while they thought that they were burning him they were only fitting the crown more securely onto his head. And while they thought that they were killing him, he eluded them, but they didn't know this. He jumped onto the black carriage, laid his head in the lap of the great Columbus, and cried a little as Jolly Augustine stroked his burnt feet. Later they played a duet on lyre and bagpipes, it was only after they had travelled more than a mile that the boy who was a stranger thought to introduce himself.

"David, King David," he said in an embarrassed murmur, "on the way to the holy land."

The carriage was travelling through the meadows, damp branches were whipping its roof.

"We're all on the way to the holy land!"

"We're on the way to the holy land too!"

"Who are you all, and what do you want in the holy land?"

"That's Ellen and I'm Georg, and we want to establish our identity, and be saved. Why didn't any of you vouch for us? Why did you abandon us? Don't you vouch for everyone? But they chase us away, they take everything from us, they jeer at us: You don't have identities! Go to the holy land, search for them there, your ancestors, and tell them: It's your fault that we're alive, do something, make it right! Make it right, so that we don't lose our homes, make it right, so that we're not persecuted, make it right, so there's no hatred in their hearts! Because it's your fault, it's your fault, it's your fault that we exist!"

"Why did you get into the black carriage?"

"We want to get across the border, we're searching for the people who have been."

The fog and the river were flowing into each other in waves. The line between the sky and the earth was dissolving.

Columbus played uneasily with the globe. When he began to speak, his voice was darker and more distant than before: "There are no people who have been. There are the people who are, and the people who are not, the ones who have become and the ones who haven't become – the game of Heaven and Hell, it's up to you! But the people who are always are, and the people who are not never are. But the people who are are everywhere, and the people who are not are nowhere. Stay and listen, love and create light! Let yourselves be despised and bathe in tears, tears make your eyes bright. Penetrate the fog and discover the world! To be – that's the passport for eternity."

"Don't believe it's as easy as that," David called out. "The people who believe that they are, are not. Only the people who doubt themselves are allowed to make landfall, only the ones who have suffered. For the coasts of God are flames above the dark ocean, and whoever makes landfall is burned. And the coasts of God are growing larger, for the people who are burning create light, and the coasts of God grow smaller, for the corpses of the people who do not understand drift out of the darkness!"

"The plague has come, but no-one notices it," Jolly Augustine giggled, "you should all sing the song in the plague pit, sing the song, sing the song! We can't establish your identities. Only the song which you sing establishes your identities."

"Strike dead the Goliath in your hearts!"

"Discover the world anew, discover the Holy Land!"

"Let yourselves be despised and bathe in tears, tears make your eyes bright!"

The carriage was racing now, leaping over stones. The children cried out. They clung onto David's woollen belt and hid their heads in Columbus's wide sleeves. "We want to stay, we want to stay!"

"Stay in order to go, and go in order to stay."

"Bend to the storm like the bushes on the bank!"

"Then you will be protected in the shaking of the black carriage. Then what has been moved will be still, and what is still will be moved."

"Then you will grasp what is fleeting, then it will be revealed to you!"

"And your pain will compensate you for what is lacking."

The river gleamed in the dark light of the night, grey and knowing. The gravel shimmered serenely.

"The border, where's the border? Where's the holy land?"

"It's everywhere that shepherds watch their sheep and leave everything when the angel summons them."

"The sheep cry out when they're abandoned!"

"The sheep cry out because they can't sing, the sheep cry out to praise God."

King David began playing on the lyre again, and Jolly Augustine joined in with the bagpipes, while Columbus sang a sailor's song in his deep voice, something about white stars and the longing for land. They paid no heed to each other, but in a curious way everything achieved harmony: David's psalms, Columbus's sea shanty and Jolly Augustine's comic ditties.

Evidently they were singing to honour God, and everything that is done to honour God achieves harmony.

The carriage was moving faster, ever faster, faster than fast, but this fast pace dissipated, became serene and imperceptible like that of the river and the roadway. A slow rushing on the edge of the eternal, where everything is already touching everything else. The line between the sky and the earth had disappeared. Nothing remained but a white wavy motion in the darkness, a customs house beside the roadway and the voices above the river.

"We're at the border!"

The three old men jumped down and blocked the road. The horses reared. The black carriage stopped.

"Are you ready to sing the song in the plague pit?"

"We're ready."

"Are you ready to strike dead the Goliath in your hearts?"

"We're ready."

"And are you ready to discover the holy land anew?"

"We're ready."

"Then cross the border, establish your identities, enter the holy land!"

"Leave the black carriage, leave the mourning coach, jump down!"

"Jump down!" the coachman shouted angrily, shaking the sleeping children. "Jump down, jump down! There are guards everywhere, we travelled in a circle. See that you get away from here!"

The children opened their eyes and lifted their heads dazedly.

"Time for you all to wake up!" the coachman shouted. "It was all in vain. Everything is lost, we won't get across the border anymore!"

"We're already across," the children called out. They jumped down and ran into the dark again without once looking back.

In the Service of a Foreign Power

The clouds are riding out on manoeuvres, in the middle of the war they're riding out on manoeuvres, daring and dancing and down deep above the roofs of the world, down above this no-man's-land between treachery and prophecy, deep above the depths. The clouds are riding faster than the blue dragoons in the song, they're wearing no uniform, changing their form constantly but still recognising themselves. The clouds are riding straight across wheatfields and battlefields and across the scattered bricks from a child's construction set which are called cities. The clouds are riding out on manoeuvres, in the middle of the war they're riding out on manoeuvres, and their secret ease makes them suspicious.

Riders in foreign service. Company halt, dismount!

In the middle of the street, a school exercise book was lying open on the grey roadway, an English vocabulary book. A child must have lost it, the wind from the approaching storm was turning the pages. When the first raindrop fell, it fell on the red line. And the red line in the middle of the page overflowed the banks. Horrified, the meaning fled from the words to both sides and called out for a ferryman: Transl... Transport me!

But the red line swelled and swelled and it became clear that it was the colour of blood. The meaning had always been in danger, but now it was threatened with drowning, and the words remained like little abandoned houses standing straight and stiff and meaningless on both sides of the red river. The rain fell in streams, but still the meaning wandered on the banks, calling out, and already the flood had risen to half its height. Transl... Transport me!

But the exercise book was lost. Herbert had lost it on the way to his English lesson, his bag had a hole. And the child without a uniform was being followed by someone in uniform. He saw the book, picked it up and took possession of it greedily. He stood still, leafed through it, trying to say the words aloud, but it was raining too heavily. The rain extinguished the last lights in the words. Again the meaning called out: Transl... Transport me! But the one in uniform pretended not to hear. The line was the colour of blood. We'll let the meaning drown sooner than betray the blood! He closed the book, put it in his pocket and ran to start his duties, following the child without a uniform.

Each entered the same building. The one without a uniform climbed five flights of stairs to get to the attic in which the old man held the lessons. The boy in uniform didn't climb any stairs, because the home with the light-coloured wooden benches and the dark picture on the peach-coloured wall was more conveniently situated.

"I've found something!" he called out.

"What have you found?"

"A vocab book."

The Song of the Blue Dragoons broke off. Silence swung itself over the firewall. This silence held the stamping of their horses, the rattling of their sabres and the fluttering of their coats. This silence held the shadow cast by their hanging reins, and the shadow crept across the children's faces, darkening the gleam of their uniform straps and concealing for some seconds the knives on their belts. The Song of the Blue Dragoons broke off. The blue dragoons halted. They had ridden into a sunken city. The jingling playing on harnesses and swords ceased. Or had they only just noticed that their drums and trumpets were making no sound?

"What have you found?" the leader repeated sharply.

Wet and lonely, the vocab book lay in the middle of the table. Unbelievably, meaninglessly lonely. It was open, at a page showing words which were blurred as if by tears:

"I shall stand – you shall stand – he shall stand – I shall go – you shall go – he shall go – I shall lie – you shall lie – he shall lie –" With the translation beside it. The children's cheeks shimmered palely.

Who shall lie?

Us perhaps, all of us? Stiff and cold and haggard, with spots, and a smile that we didn't want?

No, not us. Not one of us.

And on the battlefields?

You're torn to shreds, the ones who come on leave say.

"We shall lie – you shall lie –" Lie? No. The others shall lie dead, the ones without uniforms. The ones with the darker socks and the lighter faces. They shall lie dead, stiff and silent and haggard, with spots, and with the smile that we didn't want. It suits them better.

"Who does the book belong to?"

"The ones up there who aren't allowed to wear uniforms. The others!"

"An English vocab book?"

"What are they learning English for?"

"The borders are closed!"

The clouds are riding out on manoeuvres, in the middle of the war they're riding out on manoeuvres. And the children up there, the ones without uniforms? In the middle of the war they're learning English.

Haven't they realised it yet?

Not one of them will emigrate. They'll lie dead, so that we don't have to die. Haven't they realised it yet? What does someone learn English for, if they have to die?

Again suspicion fell like the shadow of hanging reins over their bright uniform straps. The blue-clad dragoons, they are riding – –

"Why don't you keep singing?"

The blue dragoons in the song seemed to be thinking things over too.

"Onward to the bright dunes…," it says in the first verse.

The dunes are moving. While we pause for breath, the dunes are moving. As quickly as a millennium, unstoppably. We mustn't pause for breath, or the wind will scatter us. Or we'll have to start thinking, or we'll become distracted, or we'll be deported like the children in the attic. We mustn't pause for

69

breath, or we'll be lost. The last verse ends: "And tomorrow, I'll be alone!"

No, not us.

That's what we're wearing the uniform for, so we won't be alone. So we'll never seem ridiculous to ourselves, so we'll never seem helpless in our own eyes. Ridiculous, helpless, alone, that's the others. The ones on the top floor, the ones without uniforms.

Don't think that we're poorly informed! Anyone who doesn't wear a uniform is alone, anyone who's alone starts thinking, and anyone who starts thinking, dies. Forget all that, is what we've learned. Where would we end up if everyone had their own idea about what's right? Everything has to fit in, one line of the song with the next and one person with the next. That's what we've learned: Because we have to live. But what does someone learn English for? Not one of them will get across the border. What does someone learn English for if they have to die?

"We'll ask them!"

"They'll have to give answers."

"We're in uniform, and there are still more of us!"

"As you were! As you were, I've got it."

"Got what?"

"A suspicion, the worst suspicion, the surest suspicion. What does someone learn English for? In the middle of the war?"

"What do you mean?"

"Haven't you realised it yet?"

The clouds are riding out on manoeuvres, in the middle of the war they're riding out on manoeuvres. But don't let the clouds triumph!

"There are spies on the top floor!"

"And we're down here."

"No-one should confuse us with them!"

Children without uniforms, obviously suspicious. Shadows in the attic, stamped without a stamp. Now the ring is closing.

"A vocab book, is that enough proof for you?"

"We can do better than that, we'll eavesdrop on them!"
"There's a storage loft next to the attic."
"And the key to the loft?"
"In the caretaker's apartment."
"His daughter is home alone."
"Then get a move on!"

'Knock harder!"
"Why are you frightened of us?"
"I'm not frightened. Each of you has a knife to protect me with."
"Hand over the key to the storage loft!"
"I don't have a key."
"You're lying!"
"How could I lie to you?"
"You could if you wanted to!"
"I'd want to if I could."
"Hand over the key!"
"There! Take it, it's old and rusty. And leave me in peace."
"What peace do you mean?"
"Just my own."
"Then you're no problem, then you're not dangerous!"
"Take yourselves off!"
"Hey, you! Do you know anything about the old man up there and about the ones without uniforms?"
"They want to be left in peace too."
"Just their own?"
"Maybe a different one."
"Exactly, that's what we think too!"
The glass roof has a hole. Above the hole is the sky. And the sky sucks you all up the flights of stairs whether you want to go up or not. Right to the top. And the sky softens your steps.
"Does the key fit?"
"Are you all here?"
"Go in fast. Number off quickly. Is anyone missing?"
"Do you know how many stars are in the sky?"

71

"Silence!'

You can still be counted like the blue dragoons. But the dunes are moving. And the last verse ends: And tomorrow, I'll be alone.

"How dark it is here."

"Careful, cobwebs!"

"There's a storm coming."

The door of the loft creaked. The pillar in the middle which bore the weight of the beams groaned in despair. The wind from the approaching storm ripped open the skylight. And the skylight stared blackly and vengefully in the wake of the galloping clouds. The clouds galloped faster.

Oh, they feared this blackness welling from the houses of men, these gaping dragons' maws, these endless fearful questions. Deep down and filled with fear, they floated away. Away from these blasphemous people, from these obsessive people who put their hands in all the wounds, these mistrustful eavesdroppers at the walls of their own hearts.

Angrily, the open hatch danced in the draft. Away from the narrow frame, in the wake of the clouds! Away from these mad people who raise weight to the status of law, away from the suspicions of these suspect people.

A flagpole rolled noisily against the open skylight, trying to stop the sky. And the sky caught on it, hanging like a tattered canopy over profaned relics. Blue, long-desecrated silk shone through and concealed itself again. Dust wove itself tightly into the sticky heat under the sloping ceiling.

The ones in uniform locked the door behind them silently, removed their shoes from their feet, lowered their heads and moved towards the wall at which they wanted to listen. Damp socks which were hanging out to dry over long lines moved warningly over their foreheads, mouths and eyes like a mother's hand. Annoyed, they moved aside. The floor made a cracking sound. In that instant they realised that there were too many of them. Too many. Their pride, their strength in outnumbering the others was reversed like an old glove and turned into a weakness; but no-one wanted to go back. The ones at the front had found the wall, and in the wall they found a small iron door which connected the loft with the old man's hovel. The ones at the back pushed forward. The door trembled. Am I not here to be opened? Am I not a great contradiction between what was thought and what became, between the ones in the universe and the ones in uniform? Tear me open, imagine I'm not here, take me off my hinges!

Enraged, the ones in uniform tried to silence the door. This impotent rattling had the power to betray them. Forcefully, they pressed their warm, wild bodies against the rusty dark.

Then they heard Herbert's voice. And the voice said: "There's someone next door." It said this as clearly and as artlessly as if it meant: My best friend.

"Do you all hear?"

"A cat," Ruth said.

"Birds."

"Wet socks."

"The wind."

"There's a storm coming."

"Is there a lightning rod here?"

"You're nervous today!"

"My vocab book has disappeared."

"No wonder, Herbert, your bag has a hole!"

"No wonder, that's it. No wonder there's a war on. No wonder we're hungry. No wonder an exercise book disappears. But there must be a wonder somewhere!"

"Speak more quietly, Ellen!"

"It'd make more sense to help him look for his book!"

"Come on, everyone, maybe it's on the stairs!"

"We'll be right back!"

"You can never say that. Don't go around the corner alone, all of a sudden you'll have disappeared."

"Disappeared?"

"The schoolbag has a hole, and the hole keeps getting bigger. My grandmother said –"

"Leave it, come back!"

"How dark it's turning outside."

73

"Don't cry, little one!"

"Have you got it now?"

"We found it on the stairs, but it's not an exercise book!"

"A knife!"

"A short dagger, like the ones they carry on their belts."

"Who?"

"The others, the ones down there, the ones in uniform."

"Mice in the trap, that's what we are!"

"The borders are closed."

"They're playing cat and mouse with us!"

"Not one of us will emigrate."

"What are we learning English for, if it's in vain?"

"Give it up, my father has been arrested, we're all lost. The people are saying –"

"Didn't we want to forget our German?"

"But it's taking too long!"

"Didn't we want to shrug our shoulders when people abuse us, because we can't understand them anymore?"

"We've already had twelve lessons. And we haven't forgotten a single word."

An armchair was knocked over, a loudspeaker roared from the depths. The announcer had just finished his report. At the end he said: "Anyone who listens to foreign stations is a traitor, anyone who listens to foreign stations will pay with his life." You could hear him right up to the very top floor, he could be understood clearly. Music began to play immediately afterwards, quick and cheerful, as if there was nothing more amusing on earth: Anyone who listens to foreign stations will pay with his life. A marvellous idea, to make death something you can pay for, death the most foreign of all the foreign stations, the one you can't switch off. The music broke off suddenly. The silence was picked up by a new voice. This voice was gentle and imperturbable. It seemed to come from high up.

"Who could pay for death?" the old man said. "Who pays for life?"

The children in uniform braced their heads more firmly against the iron door. This voice tore the braid from their chests and deprived them of their rank. This voice swathed long, light-coloured shirts around their uniforms, calmed them against their will and took the fear from their courage.

"Who among you is not a foreigner? Jews, Germans, Americans, we're all foreigners here. We can say 'Guten Morgen' or 'Es wird hell,' 'Wie geht es Ihnen?', 'Ein Gewitter kommt,' and that's all we can say, almost all. We only speak our language brokenly. And you want to forget your German? I won't help you do that. But I'll help you to learn it anew, the way a foreigner learns a foreign language, carefully, cautiously, the way you make a light in a dark house and keep walking."

The ones in uniform were angry with themselves. Their situation forced them into the silence of mocked contemplativeness, into the obedience of an old order.

"Transl... Transport yourselves, across a wild, deep river, and at that moment you won't see the banks. Transl... Transport yourselves, the others, the world nevertheless. The rejected meaning is wandering along all the banks: Transl... Transport me, transport me! Help the meaning, take it across! What do you learn English for? Why didn't you ask before?"

The children in the loft reached for their knives. They were like lost sentries beyond the front lines.

"What are you learning to read for, what are you learning to do arithmetic for, what are you learning to write for, if you have to die? Go on, run down into the street, ask them, ask all of them! No-one will give you an answer. Why are you only asking now?"

"Do you see the old man?"

"He's made a light."

"Let me go in!"

"Me!"

"Silence, they'll hear us!"

"I've got to laugh!"

"Ssst, don't give yourselves away! Go back now, back down!"

"Quiet!"

"Didn't you understand what I said?"

"The door to the hallway is locked."

"Which of you has the key?"

The caretaker's daughter with the black braids ran down the stairs, ringing at various doors before she hid herself behind the pillars. She had also opened all the windows without fastening them in place. Wind raged through the building. She disappeared like a shadow into the basement flat. In her hand she carried a great, rusted key.

The sky was turning darker and darker. The clouds had thrown black coats around themselves and were rushing towards unknown hurdles. Lightning flashed like foreign signals. Put your heads on! the thunder roared. For there is an old legend in which the dead riders carry their heads in their hands. You go to bed knowing, you wake up not knowing. Yield to resistance.

Put your heads on!

The children in uniform lifted their faces fearfully towards the open hatch. What had prompted them to leave the home with its light-coloured wooden benches? Who had ordered them to break off the Song of the Blue Dragoons before the first verse had been sung to the end, and who had ordered the blue dragoons to throw away their trumpets and to disperse like the clouds in the sky?

What had inveigled them to follow their suspicion up five flights of stairs like the Pied Piper's call? This foreign suspicion, this fearful suspicion: What do you learn English for, if you have to die?

They had played the messenger game, and what had come out at the end was: What are you crying for, what are you laughing for, what are you wearing your shirt for? Do you light a fire only to let it go out again? And do you let it go out only to light it again? Suddenly they had been drawn into the fate of those who were threatened, caught up in their own suspicion, locked into the storage loft. And the way out was the door to the others. What had inveigled them to give themselves up to those who were doomed?

Didn't they have the right to call them to account, to box their ears, and weren't they carrying knives with which they could ward off all suspicion?

Uneasily, the socks fluttered on the light-coloured lines. An aroma of dust and decay spread warmly in the darkness, pursued by sharp gusts of wind. Like blind bats, tobacco leaves rustled under the ceiling.

The manoeuvres in the sky seemed to have reached their climax, the skylight's threats were transformed into helplessness, and its blackness paled against the blackness of the sky. The wind from the approaching storm threw the flagpole inside. It fell onto the eavesdroppers.

The ones in uniform felt like they had been pushed behind the world's stages, behind everything which hitherto had only been shown to them from the front, and they saw that above the brightly-lit rooms there were hollow, high roofs which directed the players with invisible wires. And they were afraid.

Shaking with anger, they lay next to the iron door.

"It's your fault, you're the one who said –"

"And you bear the responsibility!"

"No, you all do!"

"You're making yourselves ridiculous!"

"Silence, or they'll find us!"

"Don't laugh, what are you laughing for?"

"We were going to arrest them. Now they'll arrest us."

"Don't laugh! And I'm telling you: Don't move, they'll hear us! Stop it! That's not fair, that's against the rules, don't laugh, you're making everyone laugh, ow – my sides, what are you all laughing for? It's your fault, and I'm ordering you all: Stop laughing!"

They held onto each other, half-suppressing their snorting, pressed their lips into their thick jackets, groaned and hid their heads in their sleeves, but things had gone too far.

"But you're laughing yourself!"

The damp socks trembled, the pillar creaked and the hatch rattled in inexplicable amusement.

What are you laughing for, what are you crying for, what are you learning English for? The iron door flew open.

"Let us laugh with you!" the old man said.

Herbert was clinging fearfully to his arm, the others didn't move.

The ones in uniform rolled almost as far as their feet, separated and jumped up. A fierce solemnity jumped like a cat into their faces.

"There's nothing to laugh about!" the leader shouted.

"Yes and No," the old man said.

The storm made the light flicker. The rocking-chair stood still and the cat jumped to the floor.

"We're conducting a search!" the leader announced.

"What do you think you'll find here?"

"Maybe a foreign station!"

The old man extended his arms in invitation. "Be my guests!"

They hesitated for a second and assessed the others. Then they set to work with a will.

Drawers flew open, boxes were pushed over, ripped-up vocab books covered the floor. A plate shattered. The dictionary fell noisily and remained open under their feet.

"Can I help you?" the old man said. They pushed him in the chest. The same storm that was darkening their foreheads and pushing their hair forward pushed the others' hair out of their faces, casting more light on them.

"Where did you get the knife?"

"Found it."

"That's what they all say. Do you know what that will cost you all?"

Windowpanes rattled, light green wallpaper hung down in tatters.

"Is there something behind it, Yes or No?"

"Where's your foreign station?"

The ones in uniform paused, exhausted. Their leader reached for his knife. The others knew what that meant. Without waiting for a further signal, they rushed forward. The washstand fell over, heads rammed into ribs, legs and arms became entangled. Hard soles slammed into faces. The cat jumped into the middle, yowled and flew towards the ceiling. The Flood engulfed the chaos. The rejected meaning wanders along all the banks.

"Leave him alone, leave Herbert alone, he's got a stiff foot!"

"Where are your rules written down?"

The window shattered. Black and blessed, the clouds danced, and the foreign signals continued at short intervals.

Noah himself stared silently over the confusion, holding the injured cat.

"Have you got it now, our foreign station?"

At a sign from their leader, the ones in uniform had drawn their knives. The old man threw himself in front of them. For the sake of the children, Noah left the Ark. Fists tugged at his beard, arms and legs were caught up in his long, green night-shirt. For a second the old man saw the leader's knife hovering above him, that lost, lent, long-forfeited knife. Again the red line overflowed the banks.

When they saw the blood, they retreated. They retreated step by step, and they retreated as one. Four walls stopped them. The magnitude of the suspicion made brothers of them.

For it could be that there is no foreign station.

Then what would we have eavesdropped for and what would we have learned for? What would we have laughed for and what would we have cried for? If there's no foreign station, we're nothing but a bad joke. If there's no foreign station, it was all in vain.

The storm receded slowly. Between his open bed and the overturned table, the old man lay. Flowing red seeped inexorably into the cracks in the boards. They pushed up his sleeve.

"Do you have bandages?"

"Down in the home," the leader stammered.

They all ran downstairs. They managed to bandage the wound after a fashion. They smoothed out the bed and lifted the old man onto it. They found schnapps somewhere.

"Put things in order!" the leader said morosely.

"By itself," Georg replied.

"By itself," the other repeated. It was a new expression.

They picked up the table and the chairs and dried the floor; then they pushed the drawers back into the chests, piled up the books into a kind of mountain and tried to put the vocab books back together again. Curious things came to light.

Sky blue, the sky was laughing. But they wouldn't let themselves be tricked again. That clear faithful blue, the blue of the sky, the blue of the gentians and the blue of the blue dragoons, reflected the blackness of the universe in the ball that was the sun, that endless, unfathomable blackness beyond the borders. If there's no foreign station, we're all lost.

"Wake up, wake up again!"

Desperate, they grabbed the old man and lifted him into the rocking-chair. His head hung heavily and composedly to one side. They pushed cushions behind his back and wrapped blankets around his feet. They forced schnapps into his mouth and rocked him gently back and forth. Sunlight played over their frightened faces like the track of someone who is fleeing.

"If you can't explain it," the leader began again, "if you can't explain why you're all here –"

"And you? Why are you all here? Because you can't explain anything to yourselves, you go to war! Because you seem ridiculous to yourselves, you slip into uniform. Protective colouring against yourselves. Because you don't want to get old and don't want to get sick and don't want to wear a top hat at every stranger's funeral!"

"Where is your foreign station?"

"If only we had it," Georg cried out in despair, "if only there was one!"

"There is one," the old man said, "don't worry, there is one."

He tried to lift himself onto his elbows, noticed the bandage and seemed to remember.

"Does it still hurt?"

"No. Are you all there?"

"Everyone," Georg said.

"Including the others?"

"Yes."

"Then come closer to me!"

They shuffled closer to the rocking-chair. Somewhere in the building a door slammed. On the next floor down, a child was practising the piano, it practised determinedly and constantly started afresh. Hand in hand, the triads flew across the gleaming roofs.

"What is it, our life?"

"Practice," the old man said, "practice, practice!"

"It sounds odd."

He nodded. "It sounds odd, can practising change that? We're practising on a silent piano."

"Secret language, still!" the leader said.

"Yes," the old man answered, "that's it, secret language. Chinese and Hebrew, what the poplars say and the fish don't say, German and English, living and dying, it's all secret."

"And the foreign station?"

"Every one of you hears it, if you're quiet enough," the old man said. "Tune in to the waves!"

It was already twilight.

Far down below at the intersection, the loudspeaker was shouting the evening news across the city. It was reporting something about ships sunk in the Norwegian Sea. The announcer's pleasant voice made it clear that he had no idea how green the waters were which had closed over the sailors on those ships. The children listened in silence. In the far distance the plains were disappearing in the twilight and dissolving gently into the unknown. The meadows lay like dark green upholstery in the bend of the river. And above them the sickle moon hovered in the hand of a foreign reaper who would not drop it. The night was near.

Holding the old man, the leader began his threats again: "What are you learning English for when it has no purpose anymore? There's a war on, the borders are closed, not one of you will emigrate."

"He's right," Leon said.

"What do I put a cloth on my table for," the old man said, "even when I'm all alone?" He put his finger placatingly to his lips and pushed off gently with his foot, rocking back and forth.

The children became uneasy and pushed closer together. Their faces were turned to him.

"It's true," the old man said calmly, "maybe you won't be able to flee anymore. The purpose has been removed. But the purpose is only a pretext to conceal the game, only a shadow of what's real. It's only for school that we learn, not for life. Not so that we can kill and not so that we can flee. Not for the sake of the things that are right in front of us."

They propped their heads on their hands and sighed. Across the street, a car drove up. Across the river, it was still raining.

"What do the thrushes whistle for, what do the clouds ride for, what do the stars shine for? What does someone learn English for, if it's in vain? All for the same purpose. And I'm asking you all, do you know the purpose? Do you know it now? What is your suspicion?"

"In the service of a foreign power!" the leader called out.

"That suspicion is correct," the old man said.

The Fear of Fear

The mirror was like a great dark coat of arms. In the middle stood the star. Ellen laughed happily. She stood up on her toes and folded her arms behind her head. This wonderful star. This star in the middle.

The star was darker than the sun and paler than the moon. The star had great, sharp points. In the twilight its radius became indefinable, like that of a stranger's hand. Ellen had taken it out of the sewing box in secret and pinned it onto her dress.

"Put that right out of your head," the grandmother had said, "be happy that it's not happening to you, that you don't have to wear the star like the others!" But Ellen knew better. Allowed to, that was the verb: Allowed to. She sighed deeply, with relief. If she moved, the star in the mirror moved too. If she jumped, the star jumped and she was allowed to make a wish. If she moved back, the star moved with her. She put her hands to her cheeks for pure happiness and closed her eyes. The star was still there. It had long been the most secret idea of the secret police. Ellen held the hem of her skirt between her fingers and turned in circles, she was dancing.

Damp darkness rose from the cracks in the boards. The grandmother had gone out. She had gone around the corner like a rolling ship. For as long as you could still see her, her umbrella stood out like a black sail against the wet wind. Vague rumours wafted shivering through the streets of the Island. The grandmother had gone out in search of something more definite.

Something more definite?

Ellen smiled thoughtfully at the star in the mirror. The grandmother wanted certainty. Between two mirrors. How uncertain all certainty was. What was certain was the uncertain, and it had been becoming ever more certain since the world was created.

On the next floor up, Aunt Sonja gave piano lessons. She gave them in secret. In the room to the left, the two boys were arguing. You could hear their bitter, high voices clearly. In the room to the right, the old deaf man was shouting at his bulldog: "Do you have any idea what's going to happen, Peggy? They don't tell me anything, no-one tells me anything!"

Ellen took two saucepan lids from the cupboard and banged them together angrily. She could hear the caretaker's wife shouting in the courtyard. It sounded like: Pack of – pack your bags – you'll be packed off!

For a moment Ellen stared at the empty, grey walls which appeared in the mirror behind her and the star. She was home alone. Strangers were living in the rooms to the left and the right. She was alone in this room. And this room was home. She took her coat from the hook on the door. The grandmother could come home again soon, she had to hurry. The mirror was like a great, dark coat of arms.

She tore the star from her dress, her hands were trembling. You had to shine a light when it was so dark, and how should you shine a light if not with the star? She wouldn't let anyone forbid her, not her grandmother and not the secret police. Quickly, with great, clumsy stitches she sewed it onto the left side of her coat. She sat on the table, bending her head close over the coat before she slipped into it, closed the door behind her and ran down the stairs.

Exhaling, she stood for a second at the entrance to the street. Fog hung in the air. She threw herself against the late autumn. That was the reason she loved it, without realising, because it gave everything something deeper, something dark, from which miracles seemed to arise, because it gave their secret back to those without secrets, gave them back an inkling of the incomprehensible. Because the late autumn didn't put on a dazzling show like the spring – look, everyone, I'm coming – but because it held back like someone who knew more: Come to me, everyone!

Ellen came. She ran through the old, foggy streets, past indifferent people and smooth people, and she threw herself into its hidden arms. The star on her coat gave her wings. Her soles clattered loudly on the hard pavement. She ran through the streets of the Island.

It was only the cake in the half-lit window of the café which brought her to a stop. The cake was white and gleaming, and it had "Congratulations" lettered in pink on top. The cake was for Georg, it was peace itself. Reddish bunched curtains surrounded it on all sides like transparent hands. How often had they stood here, looking. Once it had been a yellow cake, and once a green one. But today's was the best one.

Ellen pushed open the glass door. With the attitude of a foreign conqueror, she entered the café and walked with long strides to the counter. "Good evening!" the shop assistant said absently, lifted her eyes from her fingernails and fell silent.

"Congratulations," Ellen said, "that's the cake I'd like." Long and damp, her hair hung over the old coat. The coat was much too short and two hand-spans of the tartan dress were visible below it. But those wouldn't have been enough. The star was what made all the difference. Calm and bright, it shone on the thin, dark blue fabric as if convinced that it was up in the sky.

Ellen had put the money on the counter in front of her, she had been saving for weeks. She knew the price.

All the customers stopped eating. The sales assistant propped her plump, red arms on the silver cash register. Her eyes were glued to the star. She saw nothing but the star. Behind Ellen, someone stood up. A chair was pushed against the wall.

"The cake, please," Ellen said again, using two fingers to push the money closer to the cash register. She could find no explanation for this delay. "If it costs more," she murmured uncertainly, "if maybe it costs more now, then I'll get the rest, I've still got some money at home. And I can hurry –" She lifted her head and looked into the sales assistant's face. What she saw was hatred.

"If you'll be open until then!" Ellen stammered.

"See that you take yourself off!"

85

"Please," Ellen said anxiously, "you're making a mistake. You must be making a mistake. I don't want the cake as a gift, I want to buy it! And if it costs more, then I'm prepared, I'm prepared –"

"No-one's asking you," the sales assistant said icily, "get out! Get out now, or I'll have you arrested!"

She took her arms off the cash register and moved slowly around the counter. She walked up to Ellen.

Ellen stood quite still and looked into her face. She wasn't even sure that she was actually awake. She passed her hand over her eyes. The sales assistant was standing right in front of her.

"Get out! Aren't you listening to me? Be happy if I let you go!" She was shouting. The customers didn't move. Ellen turned to them, looking for help. When she did so, they all saw the star on her coat. A few laughed mockingly. The others smiled sympathetically. No-one helped her.

"If it costs more," Ellen began for the third time. Her lips were trembling.

"It costs more," one of the customers said.

Ellen looked down at herself. Suddenly she knew the price of the cake. She had forgotten it. She had forgotten that the people with the star weren't allowed to go into shops, still less a café. The price of the cake was the star.

"No," Ellen said, "no, thank you!"

The sales assistant grabbed her by the collar. Someone pushed open the glass door. The cake stood in the half-lit display. It was peace itself.

The star was burning like fire. It slashed through the blue sailor's coat and drove the blood into Ellen's temples. So you had to choose. You had to choose between your star and all the other things.

Ellen had envied the children with the star, Herbert, Kurt and Leon, all her friends, she hadn't understood their fear, but now the sales assistant's grip on the back of her neck was making her shiver. Since the regulation had come into force, she had fought for the star, but now it was burning like glowing metal through her dress and her coat onto her skin.

And what should she tell Georg?

It was Georg's birthday today. The table-top had been pulled out on both sides and covered with a great light-coloured cloth. The cloth was the colour of apple blossom. The lady who lived in the little room next to the kitchen had lent it to Georg for his birthday.

Georg found it odd to be lent something for his birthday. Lent. He couldn't get the thought out of his head. Stiff and lonely, he sat in the place of honour waiting for his guests, he was freezing.

His and his father's beds were pushed close to the wall, to make room. But they still wouldn't be able to dance, as Bibi wanted. Georg drew his brows together and put his hands on the table in front of him. It was sad that he wasn't able to offer his guests everything they wanted. Awkwardly, the great black cake stood in the middle of the cups, as if they had proclaimed it king against its will. They were making a mistake, it wasn't chocolate. It was just black. Georg sat still. He had been deliriously happy looking forward to this day. He had been just as deliriously happy as his parents had been fifteen years ago when they left the light-filled hospital and carried him in their arms down the street into the approaching dark. Georg was happy to have been born. But his pleasure had never been as great as in this year.

They had been talking about the birthday party for weeks; they had been planning and discussing everything with each other for weeks.

To heighten the sense of occasion, his father had let him borrow a dark grey suit. A narrow leather belt was holding up the trousers. The jacket was roomy and double-breasted, the father's shoulders were falling casually from Georg's shoulders. If only the star hadn't been there, the great yellow star on the nice jacket!

It spoiled all Georg's pleasure.

The star was the colour of the sun. It was exposed, the be-loved sun, this shining star of childhood! If you narrowed your eyes, it took on black edges which zig-zagged in and out adroitly, and in the middle stood "*Jude*."

Despairingly, Georg put his hand over the star and removed it again. Veils sank out of the silent courtyard through the flat windowpanes and tried to obscure the star. The secret police had forbidden any obscuring of the star. The twilight was committing a crime, just as the moon was committing a crime every time it cast its mocking light over the blacked-out city.

Georg sighed. His guests were already ringing the doorbell. He jumped up and ran around the table.

"Are you all here?"

"Ellen's missing."

"Maybe she's not coming anymore!"

"Maybe she doesn't want to come."

"Maybe it's not a good idea to associate with us."

"I don't believe that," Georg said thoughtfully. The veils were still sinking through the windowpanes. And the cake was still standing, black and unhappy, in the middle of the table.

"Just wait," Georg said, looking at the cake, "your bride is coming soon. Your bride is from the shop, with white icing and pink lettering. Congratulations! Soon you won't look so abandoned, my friend!"

The cake was silent.

"Ellen is bringing her," Georg insisted. "Ellen's bringing her for sure. Ellen doesn't have to wear the star, you know! She pushes open the glass door and puts the money on the counter. She says: 'The cake, please!' and she gets it. It's true. It's true, I tell you. You can get everything if you're not wearing the star!"

Bibi laughed, but it didn't sound as if she was really laughing. The others were sitting around and trying in vain to make conversation in the quiet and detached tone which the adults used. As if they couldn't hear the crying in the next room and as if they felt no fear. In the next room someone was crying, it had to be the young man who had been quartered here recently.

Georg stood up, drew his belt tighter and placed the flats of his hands uneasily on the tablecloth. He coughed and drank some water. He wanted to make a speech and he wanted to do things ceremoniously. He wanted to say: Thank you all very much for coming, and it's a pleasure to see you here today. I'd like to thank Bibi and Hanna and Ruth for the three silk handkerchiefs, I'll make good use of them. And I'd like to thank Kurt and Leon for the leather tobacco pouch, which is just what I needed. When the war is over I'll take it out of my pocket suddenly, and then we'll smoke the pipe of peace. I'd like to thank Herbert for the red ball, it belongs to all of us now. Next summer we'll play dodge-ball again.

Georg wanted to say all of that. That's why he had stood up and put both hands on the tablecloth. That's why he was drumming his fingers incessantly on the edge of the table. He wanted to get silence so that he could speak.

The children had been silent for a long time, but the young stranger in the next room could still be heard. His crying extinguished the words in Georg's mouth, like a draft extinguishes one match after another.

Georg had wanted to make a great speech. He had wanted to say everything, but now he said simply: "Someone's crying!" and sat down again. "Then someone's crying," Kurt repeated morosely. A spoon fell to the floor. Bibi slipped under the table and picked it up again. "Isn't it ridiculous," Herbert said, "to cry like that? For no reason, no reason at all!"

"No reason, no reason at all," Leon said despairingly, "that's what bothers me. That's what bothers me, I'm telling you!"

"Take some cake!" Georg called out. That was supposed to sound encouraging, but it sounded frightening. They all took some cake. Georg watched them anxiously. They ate quickly and with an effort, the cake was too dry. They choked. "But Ellen will be here soon with the other cake," Georg said. "And it's always good if you save the best –"

"Ellen's not coming," Kurt interrupted, "she doesn't want anything to do with us anymore!"

"Anything to do with the star."

"She's forgotten us."

Ruth stood up and poured the tea, silently and quickly and without spilling a drop. The children's lost eyes gleamed over the white cups. Herbert pretended that something had gone down the wrong way, and began to cough.

Georg moved slowly from one to the next, patting each on the shoulder in passing, calling out "Old boy!" and things like that, and laughing as he went. The others laughed with him. The instant they stopped, they heard the crying from the next room again quite clearly. Kurt tried to tell a funny story, and knocked over a cup with his arm. "It doesn't matter," Georg called out, "it doesn't matter at all!" Bibi jumped up and put her serviette under the wet spot.

The veils which were falling through the windowpanes changed from grey to black. Light from the empty preserving jars gleamed down purposelessly from the dresser.

Bibi whispered something to Kurt.

"There are no secrets on my birthday!" Georg grumbled, offended.

"Be happy that you don't know it!" Bibi called across the table in her high, rather loud voice. "Be happy, Georg, it's nothing about your birthday!" Bibi was pleased when she could have secrets. She never thought about what else something meant. If it was a secret, then that was enough for her.

The crying in the next room gave no sign of stopping. Hanna jumped up suddenly. "I'll ask him now," she called out indignantly, "I'll ask him right away!"

Georg blocked the doorway. He spread out his arms and pressed his head against the wood, a living barricade against the crying which is in all the next rooms if you're prepared to hear it. Hanna had grabbed his shoulders and was trying to pull him away. "I want to know, do you hear?"

"It's none of our business! It's bad enough that we have to live packed together with strangers. What they're laughing for and what they're crying for is none of our business!"

"It is our business!" Hanna shouted, beside herself, "it always has been our business, we were much too tactful. But now it's very definitely our business!" She turned to the others. "Help me, please help me! We have to get certainty!"

90

"You mustn't demand certainty," Georg said quietly, "that's what the grown-ups do, that's what almost all of them do, but that's why you die. Because you demand certainty. However much you ask, it will always remain uncertain, always, do you all hear me? For as long as you live." He clung onto the doorframe with fingers clenched. His arms were going slack gradually and threatening to drop.

"You're ill," Hanna said, "you're ill, Georg."

The others stood in a circle without speaking.

Herbert pushed himself forward.

"Do you all want to know what Bibi said before? I know! I heard. Should I say it? Yes? Should I say it?"

"Say it!"

"Don't say it!"

"You'll be in trouble, Herbert!"

"Bibi said, she said –"

"I don't want to know!" Georg shouted. "Today's my birthday and I don't want to know!" His arms dropped for good. "Today's my birthday," he repeated, exhausted, "and you've wished me all the best. Every one of you."

"He's right," Leon said, "today's his birthday and that's all. Let's play something!"

"Yes," Georg said, "please!" His eyes began to gleam again. "I've got bingo all ready."

"And what are we playing for?"

"For the honour and the glory."

"For honour?" Kurt's voice was mocking and bitter. "For what honour? The big prize should be the star!"

"Now you're all starting again," Georg said stiffly.

"And now," Herbert stammered, "now I'll tell you what Bibi said, too! She said –" and before she could manage to put her hand over his mouth – "Bibi said: The star means death!"

"That's not true!" Ruth said.

"I'm afraid," Hanna said, "because I'd still like to have seven children and the house on the Swedish coast. But sometimes, recently, my father keeps stroking my hair, and before I can turn around he starts whistling –"

"The adults," Herbert called out excitedly, "the adults at our place speak in foreign languages!"

"They always do that," Leon said, "they've been doing that for ages." His voice shifted. "Everything is becoming more clear."

"Less clear," Ruth said, confused.

"It turns out the same," Leon explained. But it seemed to him as if he was revealing a secret which he would have done better to conceal. Yield to the uncertain, so that you become certain.

The others turned away. "Are we allowed to, Georg? The air is getting stuffy here." They tore open the window and leaned out. It was dark and deep like an ocean. You couldn't make out the courtyard.

"If we jumped now," Kurt said hoarsely, "one after the other! Only a moment, then we wouldn't feel fear anymore. No fear. Just imagine!"

The children closed their eyes, they could see themselves clearly, one after the other. Black and quick and straight, as if they were jumping into water.

"Isn't it good?" Kurt said. "When they find us then, long and motionless. There are those who say: The dead people laugh. So we'll laugh at them!"

"No," Herbert shouted, "no, we're not allowed to!"

"Mama won't let us!" Kurt mocked.

"Everyone should know it," Ruth said calmly from the dark of the room. "What you're given on your birthday isn't to be thrown away."

"And today's my birthday," Georg repeated, "you're all being rude." He tried everything to lure the others away from the window. "Who knows if we'll still be together next year. Maybe this is our last party!"

"Next year!" Kurt jeered. Again despair took possession of the children. "Please take some cake!" Georg shouted, beside himself. If only Ellen had been here. Ellen might have helped him. Ellen would have convinced them and got them away from the window. But she wasn't here.

"If we did it," Kurt repeated urgently, "if we did it now! We've got nothing to lose."

"Nothing but the star!"

Ellen was frightened.

The fogs dispersed suddenly. The sky was like a high curved mirror. It wasn't reflecting any figure anymore, any silhouette nor anything with borders, any question nor any fear. The only thing it was still reflecting was the star. Flickering, calm and imperturbable.

The star led Ellen through damp, dark streets, away from Georg, away from her friends, away from everything that she wished for, in a direction which opposed itself to all other directions by uniting them. The star led Ellen towards herself. Staggering, with arms extended, she was stumbling after the star. She jumped and grabbed, but there was nothing there to grab. There was no wire hanging down.

Hadn't the grandmother been right with all her warnings?

"Woe betide you if you take the star, be happy if it doesn't apply to you! No-one knows what the star means! And no-one knows what it leads to."

No, of course you couldn't know that, and you weren't allowed to know that, you just had to follow it, and this regulation applied to everyone.

So what was there left to be afraid of? And why should you listen to people who predicted the future if you knew about the star? Didn't it alone have the power to dissolve time into something else and to break through the fear?

Ellen stood still suddenly. She seemed to have reached her destination. Her eyes detached themselves slowly from the star and moved down the sky as far as the roofs. From the roofs it wasn't much further to numbers and names. Everything was the same, they were hiding themselves from the star.

Ellen stood in front of the building where Julia lived. Julia, whom people didn't talk about and whom they had excluded after she had excluded herself. She didn't want to belong with them at all, the fear was obvious in their faces. They were bound to meet with misfortune. As long ago as at the quay, Julia hadn't wanted to play with them anymore. She would have had to wear the star, but she didn't wear it. Since the regulation about the star had been in force she had never set foot in the street.

Julia no longer counted herself as one of the children with the star. "I'll only leave the building to go to America!"

"You won't get the visa, I didn't get it either!"

"You didn't, Ellen. But I'll get it. I'll leave on the last train, on the very last train!"

Since then Ellen hadn't seen Julia again. Julia, that was the name of permanent incomprehensible success, beside which Ellen was the name of permanent failure. And among the children, visiting her was considered a betrayal. What had the grandmother said the other day: "Julia is going to America. You should say goodbye to her."

Say goodbye? On top of everything else? Like be friendly and wish her all the best for the journey?

Ellen groaned and turned up the collar of her coat.

Some seconds later she was embraced and understood amidst many rapid tender kisses that Julia had received the American visa a few hours before. Julia, who was sixteen years old, wore long silk trousers and was occupied in sorting handkerchiefs by colour.

Now Ellen was sitting, pale and stiff, on the light green stool, trying to choke back her tears and pulling back her feet so as not to dirty all the clothes which were strewn around. A shipping trunk stood beside the window. "I used to play at packing quite a lot too," Ellen said with an effort.

"Play!" Julia exclaimed.

"But not for a long time now," Ellen said.

"What are you crying for?" the older girl asked in astonishment. Ellen gave no answer. "Green ones with white rims!" she said instead admiringly, picking up a pair of sunglasses from the floor. "Will you take a prayer book with you?"

"A prayer book? You think of some odd things, Ellen! It's because you're developing, I think."

"Most thoughts are because people are developing," Ellen murmured.

"But what would I need a prayer book for?"

"Maybe –" Ellen said, "you see, I was thinking, in case the ship sinks. Then it would be quite good –" Julia dropped the handkerchiefs and stared at her in shock. "Why should the ship sink?"

"Aren't you afraid?"

"No," the older girl shouted angrily, "no, I'm not afraid! What do you think I should be afraid of?"

"It's quite possible," Ellen said more calmly, sticking to her point, "it's quite possible for a ship to sink."

"Maybe you wish that will happen to me?"

They were both breathing heavily. And before either of them realised what was happening, they had grabbed each other and dragged each other to the floor. "Take that back!"

They rolled half-way under the piano. "You envy me. I'm having the greater adventure!"

"It's me who'll have the greater adventure!"

Anguish lent Ellen strength. While Julia's arms clasped round her frantically, she butted her head at Julia's chin. But because the older girl was bigger and much quicker, she managed to defend herself quite well. As the struggle continued she whispered cruelly: "The ocean is blue-green. They'll be waiting for me on the pier. And there are palms in the west."

"Stop it!" Ellen panted, holding Julia's mouth closed, but she kept rattling on about college and golf, right through Ellen's fingers, and when the smaller girl let go for a moment Julia said clearly: "Three people have vouched for me."

"Yes," Ellen shouted bitterly, "and no-one is vouching for me!"

"No-one can vouch for you."

'Thank God for that," Ellen said.

Exhausted, they both lay still.

"You envy me," Julia said, "you've always envied me."

"Yes," Ellen replied, "that's true, I've always envied you. From back when you could walk and I couldn't yet, because you have a bike and I don't. And now? Now you're going across the sea and I'm not. Now you'll see the Statue of Liberty and I won't –"

"Now I'm having the greater adventure!" Julia repeated triumphantly.

"No," Ellen said quietly, letting go of her completely, "maybe the greater adventure is not having all that."

Julia grabbed the smaller girl again, pressed her shoulders against the wall and looked at her, filled with fear: "Do you wish that my ship will sink? Yes or No?"

"No," Ellen called out impatiently, "no, no, no! Because then you would have the greater adventure and as well as that –"

"As well as that?"

"You couldn't take a message to my mother for me either."

They fell silent in shock, the last stage of the struggle proceeded without a sound.

Anna opened the door and stood against the dark. She was wearing a light-coloured scarf and laughing. "Like drunken sailors!" she said casually. She lived in the same building and came up now and then. But she was older than Julia.

Ellen jumped up, bumping her forehead on a piece of furniture, and called out: "I think your star is shining."

"I washed it again yesterday," Anna answered. "If I have to wear it, then I'll make sure it shines." She leaned her head on the doorpost. "Everyone should have to wear stars!"

"Not me," Ellen said bitterly, "I'm not allowed to wear it. I'm short two grandparents of the wrong kind. And they say I don't belong with them!"

"Oh," Anna said, laughing again, "maybe it doesn't matter whether you wear it on your coat or show it in your face."

Julia stood up slowly, groaning. "You've definitely got it twice, on your coat and in your face. Do you always have a reason to look pleased?"

"Yes," Anna answered, "don't you?"

"No," Julia said hesitantly, "although I'm going to America next week. But Ellen envies me."

"Envies you what?"

"Isn't that obvious?" Ellen murmured.

"Quite obvious," Anna said, "America. I just wanted it more exactly."

"The sea," Ellen stammered in confusion, "and the freedom!"

"That's less exact," Anna replied calmly.

"How do you do it, Anna," Ellen said, "I mean: do you have a particular reason for it?"

"For what? What do you mean?"

"What Julia said before. Shining!"

"I don't have a particular reason for it," Anna said slowly.

"Yes you do!" Julia insisted. "What did you come here for?"

"I came to say goodbye to you."

"But I only got the visa today and you can't possibly have known yet –"

"No," Anna said with an effort, "and I didn't know. But I still came to say goodbye to you."

"I don't understand!"

"I'm going away too."

"Where to?"

Anna gave no answer.

Ellen had jumped up again. "Where are you going to?"

Julia's face reddened with joy. "We're going together!"

"Where are you going to?" Ellen repeated. Anna turned her eyes towards her and looked calmly into her anguished and very pale face.

"Do you envy me, Ellen?"

Ellen turned her head aside, but felt compelled to look at Anna.

"Yes or No?"

"Yes," Ellen said softly, and it seemed to her as if her words remained quietly in the room, despairing, "yes, I envy you."

"Be careful!" Julia said mockingly. "She'll throw herself onto you next!"

"Leave her alone!" Anna said.

"She's right," Ellen murmured tiredly, "but my mother is over there. And freedom."

97

"Freedom, Ellen, freedom is the place where your star is."
She drew Ellen to her. "Is it really true, do you envy me?"

Ellen tried to tear herself away, bit down on her lips and
couldn't get free. Again she turned away and again she felt
compelled to glance at that face again. And she saw just for a
second how the shining light shattered. And she saw fear in
Anna's face, deadly fear and a distorted mouth.

"No," Ellen stammered in horror, "no, I don't envy you.
Where are you going to?"

"What's wrong with you two?" Julia said impatiently.

Anna stood up, she pushed Ellen away from her. "I've come
to say goodbye."

"Aren't we going together?"

"No," Anna said. "We're going in different directions." She
leaned lightly against the wall, searching for words.

"I – I've got the order for Poland."

That was what they didn't dare to say aloud – the grandmother, Aunt Sonja, all of them, all of them. That was what
made them tremble. Now Ellen heard it spoken for the first
time. For her, it encompassed all the fear in the world. "What
will you do?" Julia asked, frozen.

"I'll go," Anna said.

"No, that's not what I mean. I mean – what do you hope to
gain?"

"Everything," Anna said. And the radiant gleam of a greater
hope extinguished the fear in her face again.

"Everything?" Ellen said softly. "Everything – did you say?"

"Everything," Anna repeated calmly. "I've always hoped to
gain everything. What would I give it up for, now of all times?"

"That –" Ellen stammered, "that's what I meant. That's
what the star means: everything!"

Julia looked from one to the other in confusion.

"Wait!" Ellen called out. "It won't take long, I'll just fetch
the others."

And before anyone could stop her, she had closed the door
behind her.

Frightened, they moved back from the window.

"Come with me!"

"Where to?"

"If you want to know what the star means –"

They were so weakened by fear that they asked no more questions. They were happy to be fetched away from the encroaching depths. Silently, they ran along behind Ellen. They no longer saw the small, heavily laden carts in the dark at the side of the road, nor the tear-stained faces, nor even the laughter of the indifferent people. Like Ellen, the only thing they still saw was the star.

They recoiled from the entrance to the unfamiliar building.

"We're not going to Julia!"

"No," Ellen said and pushed open the door.

Julia had tidied away the mess of handkerchiefs. In greeting the children, she didn't mention her visa and she didn't look into their eyes.

"We'd never have come to you again," Bibi said in her high voice, "it's Ellen's fault!"

"Never!" the others repeated.

"We could easily have done without it," Kurt said.

Their heavy shoes left marks on the light-coloured floor.

"Anna's here," Ellen said.

Anna, that was like a breath. Like accepting and yielding at the same time.

Anna was sitting on the shipping trunk and laughing at them. They lost their self-consciousness. "Don't you want to sit down?"

They sat down in a circle on the floor. 'Tween deck. It seemed suddenly as if they had been sailing for a long time.

"And what do you want to know?"

"We want to know what the star means!"

Anna looked calmly from one to the next. "What do you want to know that for?"

"Because we're afraid." Their faces were flickering.

"And what are you afraid of?"

"Of the secret police!" They were all speaking at once.

Anna lifted her head and looked at them all. "But why? Why do you fear the secret police, of all things?" The children were startled into silence.

"They forbid us to breathe," Kurt said, turning red with anger, "they spit at us, they're after us!"

"Curious," Anna said, "what do they do that for?"

"They hate us."

"Did you do something to them?"

"Nothing," Herbert said.

"You're in the minority. You're smaller and weaker compared with them. You don't have any weapons. But it still makes them uneasy."

"We want to know what the star means!" Kurt called out. "What's going to happen to us?"

"When it gets dark," Anna said, "when it gets very dark, what happens then?"

"You're afraid."

"And what do you do?"

"You defend yourself."

"You wave your fists around, don't you?" Anna said. "You realise that doesn't help. It gets even darker. What do you do then?"

"You look for a light," Ellen called out.

"For a star," Anna said. "There's a thick darkness surrounding the secret police."

"You believe – – do you really believe that?" The children were becoming uneasy. Their faces shone with a white, wild light.

"I know!" Georg jumped up. "I know now, I know!"

"What do you know?"

"The secret police feel fear."

"It's obvious," Anna said. The secret police *are* fear, living fear – and nothing more." The radiant gleam on her face intensified.

"The secret police feel fear!"

"And we're afraid of them!"

"Fear of fear, that cancels itself out!"

"Fear of fear, fear of fear!" Bibi called out, laughing. They grabbed each other's hands and leapt around the big trunk.

"The secret police have lost their star."

"The secret police are following a foreign star."

"But the one they've lost and the one we're wearing are one and the same!"

"But what if we're enjoying this too soon," Bibi said, and stood still. "What if it's true after all, what I heard?"

"What did you hear?"

"The star means death."

"How do you know that, Bibi?"

"Because my parents thought I'd already fallen asleep."

"Maybe you misunderstood," Ellen murmured, "maybe they were saying that death means the star?"

"Don't let yourselves be led astray," Anna said calmly, "that's all the advice I can give you: Follow the star! Don't ask the adults, they'll deceive you, as Herod tried to deceive the three kings. Ask yourselves, ask your angels."

"The star," Ellen called out, and her cheeks were glowing, "the wise men's star, I knew it!"

"You should feel sorry for the secret police," Anna said. "They fear the king of the Jews again."

Julia stood up, shivering, and closed the curtains. "How dark it's got!"

"All the better," Anna said.

The Great Play

Mary dropped the bundle and Joseph prodded the angel gently in the side. The angel turned his head and smiled helplessly at the three holy kings, who were disguised as tramps and sitting next to each other on the big packing case. The three holy kings lifted their legs a little and stared at the door with a burning intensity, their faces pale and sombre. The doorbell had rung.

The angel lost all his superiority. The same angel who with a slight whoop in his boy's breaking voice had just commanded them: "Cast off your coats!" as proof that they were searchers, that they came from afar, that they bore gifts and had wound strands of silver Christmas tinsel around their bodies beneath their dirty rags, that – that –

But there was no time left. The doorbell had rung.

And they were forced, in the half-twilight, their hands wrapped around their knees, embittered and motionless, to keep enduring the old uncertainty about whether we're nothing, or kings. And they weren't allowed to cast off their coats, because they felt fear, they still felt fear. Even the smallest movement could betray them. Their guilt was having been born, their fear was of being killed and their hope was of being loved: the hope of being kings. Perhaps it is because of this hope that people are persecuted.

Joseph was afraid of his own fear and looked away. Mary bent down and picked up the bundle again with a noiseless movement. Nothing will stop a mother. She nestled against Joseph, who was looking away, as the king in her arms would nestle against the cross to which he was nailed. While the children felt fear, they had an inkling of his teaching about how you should nestle against the thing you're being nailed to, and they feared this inkling more than the shrill swift ringing which could be heard outside the door.

But perhaps this inkling itself had begun to be heard.

Silently, they waited in the darkness. Using a rusty safety pin, the angel fastened the sheet more securely around his shoulders. "It'll be nothing," he stammered, "really it only sounds as if –" he broke off.

"Be quiet," the biggest tramp said mockingly, "stay in your role!"

And the doorbell rang. It rang: four short and three long. But the agreed signal was different.

"Someone's making a mistake," the tramp with the stiff foot whispered, the littlest of them all. "Someone doesn't know whether he belongs with us or with the secret police. Whether he's a friend or a murderer."

But does anyone know that about themselves?

The little black dog under the table began to bark.

"Hold his mouth closed," Joseph said angrily, "he's no more use to us."

"I said from the start that we shouldn't keep him," Mary said, "we don't have any food for him, and he might betray us. And anyway, that passage only says something about a donkey. Something that carries things," she sighed then, "something silent that carries things."

"Jews aren't allowed to keep pets," the angel whispered, "and a sealed railway waggon carries things too. The only question is, where does it carry them to."

"There's fighting off the coast of Egypt!"

"Then it'll carry them to Poland."

"And the king of the Jews?"

"Will go with them."

The ringing at the door began again, it sounded like it was pleading now.

"We'll start the play, we won't open the door!"

"Then quick, hurry up! Ready – set –"

"Go!"

The three tramps jumped up. They held up their lanterns so that they were reflected in the glass panels of the old chest of drawers.

"Have you seen peace?" the littlest tramp called out.

"But you're holding your lantern all crooked!" The angel interrupted him. "Herbert, it almost looks like your hand is trembling. Are you afraid? That doesn't belong with your role. Have you seen peace? Ask like a man, little one, reach over their shoulders so that they start searching, in their ammunition pouches and under their pillows –"

"Have you seen peace?"

The ringing fell silent, and seemed to be waiting for an answer too. The children shivered and moved closer together. A yawning, bottomless emptiness opened up in front of them and ordered: fill me, fulfil! Then they got the second tramp to say:

"There is no-one here."

"No-one, do you hear, Georg? No-one, a dreadful word. Everyone, but still no-one, millions of people, but still no-one. No-one, everyone who hates, and everyone who looks away, do you all hear: No-one hates us, no-one is persecuting us – no-one! Why are you afraid? No-one, say it again, Georg! It should start singing, your sadness, and they should hear it at their mass meetings: No-one, no-one, no-one is here!"

Boldly, the three tramps' lanterns sent their flickering light into the dark room.

"Our search has been too long in vain!"

"And now our strength is waning."

"We will not find peace anywhere."

"And now our light burns low."

"Yes, if we knew –"

"Just what peace is!"

"But here we cannot know."

Discouraged, they dropped onto the dirty carpet.

"It can't be found upon this earth."

"Though every one of us has searched –"

"We've shouted –"

"Threatened!"

"Pleaded!"

"Cursed!"

The ringing began again. The children all spoke in a rush. For several seconds their voices managed to drown out the bell.

"We shone our lights in every house."

"And everywhere they cast us out."

"Your light is much too weak!"

the angel said, as the humans paused for breath.

"What did you say?"

"I didn't speak."

"I heard you say –"

"It wasn't me!"

Undeterred, the tramps continued their argument, pulling apart the angel's voice and dissolving it into uneasiness.

"Oh yes! You said –"

"No, you!"

"And you!"

"Oh woe, you lie –"

"It came from you!"

"Don't push me, now!"

"My fault, I slipped."

"Your fault, you slipped?

Or so you say,

Make sure you stay out of my way!"

"You're all so scared,

But I am brave!"

"You're searching for peace!" the angel called out, lifting himself onto the top of the cupboard. "For peace!" he sighed, but the ringing was still there, like a steel frame around a dark picture.

"Though every one of us has searched."

"Through every street, we searched them well,"

"And we have left no stone unturned."

"Plundered, murdered and burned up,"

"We even went down into Hell!"

"And found nothing –"

The tramps lay on the earth, entangled in each other and cursing. The angel's voice seared ever more swiftly and urgently across their scuffling. The cowls swayed and the bell in the hallway sounded shrilly above the angel's voice. Like icy rain, this ringing was dashed into the children's averted, concealed faces. Open up, open up!

This dark room had become simply a single, swaying cowl which didn't close properly.

And the doorbell rang. Four short and three long. The tormenting insistence of the wrong password.

The three tramps lowered their knees and fists onto the old carpet, crouching expectantly. The youngest lifted his index finger.

"And then we saw
A pale light shining through the door."
"There's no-one here –"
"We don't know what to do."

The voice of the littlest one was trembling. The others pushed him aside. Each of the three tramps wanted to be the first to speak:

"Who'll tell us now just where peace is?"
"And tell who finds it?"
"And who describes it?"
"Yes, if we knew –"
"Just what peace is!"

Exhausted, they let their heads drop.

"Our clothes are rags and thread,"
"Our shoes are shreds and dust!"
"There'll be no rest for us
Even after we're dead!"

Again the littlest one lifted his index finger.

"Now you should all try it,
Try to be very quiet."
"It's Christmas time,"

the angel sighed, over at the curtained window.

"Christmas time?"

The three tramps straightened up hurriedly. It went together with gifts, with cakes and sprigs of mistletoe and the adults' uncomprehending, excited faces. But how did it go together with the shrill ringing of the bell, which now continued relentlessly?

"Hurry up!" the war urged, leaning on the door to the little entry room with a huge, stolen air-raid helmet pulled well over half-way down his face. "They're battering our door in, and we don't want them to load us up before we've finished."

"All the better," Joseph grumbled, "January is so grey. All the silver cords have been cut up by then, and you have a stomach-ache."

"By the time May comes, we'll already be cherry trees," the war said mockingly.

"Be quiet," Mary called out, holding the bundle pressed tightly to her, "stop it, I don't want to be a cherry tree! Or any other kind of tree!"

"Keep the play going!" the angel called out.

"What do you think?

Maybe we should sing!"

"Come, let's sing the Christmas song!"

The three tramps were moving their lips, but they couldn't sing, in the eternity of the last quarter-hour they had forgotten how. The pleasure in pleasure had abandoned them, some strange thing had sealed their lips.

"Now I'm too weary,

I'm much too weary!"

"And your flute has a hollow sound,

The notes are all confused and soft!"

"Listen –"

"Look, peace is running off!"

"Let me go! I'll –"

"No, I'll –"

"Oh no!"

"Where is the light?"

"It's dark as night –"

The children jumped up. The ringing outside had broken off suddenly. Suddenly and, it seemed to all of them, conclusively. Everything had stopped moving.

"Open up," the angel said softly, "it's better to open up!"

The sheet still hung around him, preventing him from jumping off the cupboard. The war pushed open the door to the little entry room. The three tramps rushed out.

Open up, open up to everyone who wants you! Anyone who doesn't open up doesn't connect with who they are.

The children tore open the door to the hallway resolutely, and recoiled in disappointment.

"You? And no-one else?"

Exhausted and crying, Ellen was leaning on the icy, grey-black banisters.

"Why didn't you open the door?"

"You didn't know the signal!"

"You didn't tell me it."

"Because you don't belong with us!"

"Let me play with you!"

"You don't belong with us!"

"And why not?"

"You won't be taken away."

"I promise you," Ellen said, "that I'll be taken away."

"How can you promise such things?" Georg called out angrily.

"Some people know it," Ellen said softly, "and some people don't know it. And everyone is taken away."

She pushed the others aside and ran ahead of them all into the darkness. And she almost dragged the angel off the cupboard by his white sheet and begged: "Let me play with you, go on, please, please let me play with you!"

"Your grandmother has forbidden you to play with us," Leon said, the angel on the cupboard.

"Because my grandmother still believes that people who stay behind are fortunate."

"Do you believe that?"

"Not for a long time," Ellen said, closing the glass door behind her. Once more the room closed around the children like a black cowl.

"We don't have a role left for you."

"Let me play the world!"

"A dangerous thing to play," Leon said.

"I know," Ellen called out impatiently.

"Hanna's playing the world," Kurt said morosely.

"No," Ellen said softly, "no! Taken away during the night."

The children moved away, forming a circle around her.

"Go on!" Leon called out feverishly. "We have to keep the play going!"

"Leon, who gave us such terrible roles?"

"Difficult roles, and aren't the most difficult roles the best ones?"

"But what a dreadful audience we have, a dark maw which devours us, people without faces!"

"If you had more experience, Ruth, you'd know that in front of every stage there's a sighing blackness which wants to be comforted."

"We're supposed to give comfort? Who's going to comfort us?"

"Who'll help us onto the truck, if it's too high?"

"Fear not!" Leon called out, his head flickering like a narrow, dark flame from out of the white sheets. "For behold, I bring you tidings of great joy!"

"You're allowed to die, that's all it is," Kurt interrupted him.

The angel fell silent before the mistrust in the night-covered fields, before the pale faces of the doomed. He didn't know what to do next.

"That's not all by a long way," one of the children said, coming to his aid out of the darkness, "for unto you this day is —"

Down below, a heavy truck was driving through the narrow street. The windows trembled, and the sky outside the windows began to tremble as well. The children started in fear, were tempted to rush to the window, but didn't move. The truck roared, became quieter, drove past the building and moved into the distance. Every roar eventually falls dumb before silence, every sound is in vain unless it is filled and fulfilled by silence.

"Go on, keep the play going!"

To play. It was the only possibility remaining to them, composure before the incomprehensible, grace before the secret. This most unutterable commandment:

Thou shalt play in my presence!

Inundated by torment, they had divined it. Like the pearl in the oyster, love lay in their play.

"This wrangling now must cease!"

"See how our light burns low,
Fades as the tempest blows,
And now our strength is waning."

"'Tis time for us to sleep."

Silence ensued, the cue for the angels. Leon roused himself and jumped off the cupboard into the dim circle of the lanterns. He jumped into the middle in order to remain above. And he returned their question:

"Have you seen peace?"

"We did not see it."

The tramps sank down, pulling their cowls deeply and conclusively over their confused faces.

"If you could all see how I see you!" the angel stammered, trying to return to his role. "How quietly you're lying there, and with what inhuman courage in this dark room."

He let his arms hang down. Here too the pleasure of watching, and the responsibility of maintaining the picture, overwhelmed him. If you could all see how I see you. But the light was fading.

"What a pity, Leon, that you'll never be a theatre director!"

"Oh yes I will be. On the truck and in the railway waggon, it'll be a good piece, you can all believe me! No happy ending and no applause, they'll be walking home in silence, with pale faces which shine a light in the darkness –"

"Be quiet, Leon! Don't you see how red their faces are and how bright their eyes? And don't you hear how they're already laughing, how they'll laugh when we're being led across the bridges?"

"Leon, which currency will you be paid in, and which company have you signed a contract with?"

"The company of all mankind, pays in fire and tears."

"Keep being an angel, Leon!"

Leon hesitated. He extended his arms over the sleeping tramps. "Sleep deeply," he breathed in, was silent for a moment and then continued speaking:

"Perhaps in a dream
God will give you
What you set out to find
On an ill-chosen path.
Snuff your lights' glow,
For they won't lead you home,
Only the light of love will shine
Across the dangerous depths!"

The angel bent down and blew out the lanterns. Like the last lonely candle in a dark window, he remained in the blackness.

"Cast from you all your pride,
It is no cloak against your cares,
For love comes in another guise.
Now you must tell me: where
You're going on your search for peace.
Your wrangling here brings no release,
For peace lies in you, deep inside,
You should have realised."

The angel extended his arms as widely over the sleeping tramps as if he wanted to embrace all the sleepers along with them, and the secret police too, who thought that they were the most alert and awake, and were sleeping the most deeply.

"Sleep deeply,
Perhaps in a dream
God will give you
What you set out to find
Struggling through fire and death.
Snuff your lights' glow,
For they won't lead you home,
The light of love alone will guide
From one land to the next."

111

The angel stepped back. The tramps moved uneasily in their sleep. In the darkness you could hear Joseph talking animatedly to Mary. "Come on, it's our turn now!" But she didn't move.

"Come on!" the angel called out.

Mary gripped the bundle more tightly. "I don't have a veil," she said, "and I won't play my part without a veil."

"What's that supposed to mean?" Leon asked. "And why are you telling us now?"

The three tramps jumped up and urged her on loudly. "Play your part, do you hear, play your part!" And even the war, his helmet in his hand, asked her: "Keep the play going, do keep the play going!" Their shouting could be heard in the hallway.

"Did you want to play Mary, Yes or No?"

"Yes," Bibi replied, "but not without a veil. You promised me a veil, and I won't join the play without a veil!" She pressed the bundle to her fearfully.

"If it's just that," Ellen said slowly, opening her bag briskly. A white cloth shone a light into the dark room. Bibi laid the bundle aside. The others climbed quickly from their packing cases and armchairs, came closer and reached for it with cold fingers. Bibi had already grabbed it and enveloped herself in it.

"How beautiful you are!" the children called out. They clapped their hands, made folds in the cloth, smoothed them out again and looked up, dazzled, like poor souls on the edge of the bonfire, on the border where the outermost peninsulas of Heaven and Hell meet. And they laughed happily. If you could all see how I see you, Leon said to himself. But while he thought he was losing sight of the scene, it remained under the sharp eyes of the God who had been laid aside.

"If it's just that," Ellen repeated angrily. Her face appeared threateningly behind Bibi. And before the other girl could move away from her astonished mirror-image, Ellen had torn the veil from her head, swirled it up and wrapped it around herself. Her eyes flashed out darkly from among the flowing gleam.

"Hey," Bibi called out, "you look just like a camel driver!"

"That's fine with me."

"Give back the veil!" Bibi said in an unclear voice. Silent and aggressive, they stood facing each other. The miracle had come upon the world, but the world wanted to be the miracle herelf. Mary had set conditions, the angel had forgotten to warn the three kings, and God had fallen into Herod's hands. "Give back the veil!" Bibi said again. She was trembling with anger. Like a gentle, unfamiliar weapon her hand flew out and grabbed the veil tightly. Ellen moved back. They tangled with each other, tugged and held on tight. Nothing else remained but the quiet rustling of the silk, the fear felt by all veils of being torn asunder. But before that could happen, the veil unfolded itself, brighter and ever brighter, floating like something very conciliatory, like the silence of prophecy, and then sank suddenly, beyond their grasp, serenely to the floor. The spark ignited, they had understood what they were fighting for.

"The curtain," Leon stammered, pushing out his arms defensively as he stood up.

"Hanna's curtain, that she was sewing recently."

"For the house on the Swedish coast."

"For the white room with the high windows where her seven children were supposed to sleep."

Her seven children, who are sleeping so deeply that no-one can wake them, her seven children, who are dreaming so sweetly that no god disturbs them. Her seven children, who aren't cursed to be born, branded and killed.

"When did you see her, Ellen?"

"Yesterday, late in the evening."

"Did she already know something?"

"Yes."

"And what was the last thing she did?"

"Sewed on coat buttons more securely."

"Seven buttons," Leon said. The ice on the dark pond was splintering again, and the risk of walking further was becoming greater and greater.

"She was wanting to write you all a letter," Ellen said, "but then she couldn't do it, and just gave me that. She said that if we could use it in the play, that would be fine with her."

"You shouldn't have taken it, Ellen, it was supposed to keep off flies and too much sun."

"Too much sun!"

"Because Hanna didn't want the sun. You remember, lately she kept saying it was a trickster who deceives people and makes them brutal."

"And that's why the curtain was supposed to flutter in the sea breeze. Flutter quite gently out of the window!"

"It'll flutter," Ellen said.

"A pall," Georg said softly. "When children die."

"Who do you mean?" Herbert was smiling anxiously.

"Not you, little one!"

"Yes you did, you did mean me!"

"Maybe I meant all of us," Georg murmured.

"Hanna should have kept the veil, maybe it would have protected her."

"You only keep what you give away."

Startled, the children lifted their heads. It was never determined who had said that. The bright voice of the angel in a dark dream. You only keep what you give away.

So give them what they take from you, for that will make them ever poorer. Give them your toys, your coats, your caps and your lives. Give away everything in order to keep it. Whoever takes, loses. Laugh when they tear the clothes from your bodies and the caps from your heads, because you only keep what you give away. Laugh at the satiated people, laugh at the placid people, who have lost hunger and uneasiness, the most precious gifts which are vouchsafed to human beings. Give away your last piece of bread to preserve hunger, give up the last inch of ground and remain uneasy. Cast the gleam on your faces into the darkness to protect that radiance.

"Keep the play going!" Leon said.

Joseph leaned on his knobbed stick. Mary had put her arm gently on his, and the little dog with the white spot above his left eye ran along beside, although he wasn't mentioned anywhere in what was written. Without asking, he played the unknown, the silence that carries things.

"We've travelled far from home,
And our names are unknown
Upon this earth."
"But see what we bring with us!
We're holding God's forgiveness,
As He us holds."
"And bearing His intention
To grant mankind's redemption
Through this child's birth."
"And bearing all the pain
God feels from man's disdain
Through dark and cold."

Joseph and Mary stood still in exhaustion, trying to look into each other's faces, but you couldn't see much anymore. The others' faces drained away too, like bright colours into the blackness of the shadows. As the light became less and less clear, they understood how unreachable one was for the other, how unreachable for himself and the rest of all the pursuers.

Mary started in fear.

"But we are not alone,
Look here at these three travellers!"

She grabbed Joseph's sleeve and pointed at the three sleeping tramps in front of the chest of drawers. One of them rolled onto his other side and moved his lips in his sleep:

"Our shoes are shreds and dust,
And we can find no rest!"
"He speaks in a dream."
"Wake up, poor man, and understand
How brightly God's love glows for you!
Wake up, for you must hear me!"
"Who summons me from sleep?
But I'm too weary, I'm much too weary."
"He sleeps so deeply,"

the angel said. Disappointed, Mary straightened up.

"Our clothes are rags and holes,
Our road is much too long,"

the second tramp whispered.

Mary bent over him again.

"Wake up, poor man, and understand –"

"He sleeps so deeply,"

Joseph interrupted her wearily. You could see that he would have liked to lie down beside her, if he hadn't been Joseph, Joseph, one of those who had been summoned, and who was afraid of being chosen.

"I'm freezing,

Who wakes me from my dream –"

For the third time, Mary started in fear. Someone had turned on a light in the little entry room, and the light was coming through the glass door. The glass door trembled without showing the contours of the children's bodies, which remained dark in the face of this cold brightness.

There was a knock, and someone opened the door immediately. It was the lady from the next room. She was carrying a small suitcase tied with leather straps in her right hand, a rolled-up umbrella in her left hand, and wearing a bright-coloured cap with a feather on her head.

"By all that's holy," the war said, without finishing the sentence, and took off his helmet. This wasn't part of the play.

"What are you all doing here in the darkness?" She groped for a switch.

Joseph put his arm protectively around Mary, as if he could defend her against the tricky light. The others didn't move. The lady from the next room repeated her question, but she didn't receive an answer.

"You're all ill," she said, shocked. She had noticed three tattered, motionless figures lying on the old carpet, and behind them the war and the angel sitting next to each other on a packing case and whispering, and the black dog between Joseph and Mary.

"Where are you going to?" Georg asked.

"Away!" she replied.

"Away," Leon said thoughtfully, "lots of people are going away. But maybe it's the wrong direction."

"You children should go away too, at all costs! This is a dangerous area."

"As time goes on, almost every area becomes dangerous," Leon said.

"We don't want to go away anymore."

"You'll regret it!"

"Regret is a great feeling," the war said, putting on his helmet again. Herbert had to laugh, and cleared his throat.

The lady from the next room shook her head helplessly. She couldn't cope with this kind of rebellion. "I'm going now, anyway, you'll be alone here in the apartment!"

"Goodbye," Leon said.

Joseph and Mary followed her and locked the door. The little dog ran after them excitedly. They turned out all the lights, keeping only the lantern and the bundle they carried.

"I place it in your care,
Put it into your hands –"
but before Mary could put the bundle down between the sleeping tramps, Ellen's shadow fell over her.

"I am the world,
And I must flee,
Oh, would I could find peace!"
The world was barefoot and had slung an old blanket around her head and shoulders, with a profusion of long hair showing underneath.

"The war hunts me from house to house,
He catches me and laughs aloud,
He drives me from myself and out
To fear and raging fires."

"Who is the object of your quest?"

"No-one! All that I seek is rest."

"Your hands in blood are mired!"
Shocked, Mary leaned on Joseph's stocky body. She could hear his heart beating beneath his hunter's coat, and that gave her courage.

"We're bearing God,
And we must flee.

117

The world hunts us from door to door,
And has no lodging for us.
That's why we're seeking shelter here,
You know we fled from you."
"From you!"
"And now you have come to us."
The black little dog pricked up his ears and snuffled. The surprise felt by the holy family was taking possession of him too. It penetrated the coolness of the forgotten room and overwhelmed them: Will you be coming after us again and again? Do you only crucify what you don't understand, and will you finally find refuge under your own crosses? Scourge us, kill us, trample us down, you can only catch up to us at the place where you want to love or be loved. Where you stay on the tracks of those who are fleeing so that you can find refuge among them. When you throw away your weapons, you'll have reached them.
"Won't you all conceal me
In your bright-coloured veil?"
The war was pushing against the edge of the packing case with trodden-down heels to signal his coming. Filled with dread, the world stared all around.
"That's him,
Do you hear?"
The war had jumped off the packing case. The darkness rustled silkily.
"Oh, let me in,
If you would just trust me!"
"We too are strangers here
And forced to flee –"
Mary dried up. The war, ready to grab her, recoiled from himself. Because the doorbell had rung, and it was still ringing. It was ringing for the second time.
But in this play there was no prompter, no-one who relieved the seriousness and undermined the audacity of all kinds of play in a whisper, no-one who gave the cues without taking any cues himself. In the end, the two things came together. Anyone who misses his entrance is at fault, and anyone who misses his exit is

doubly at fault. How difficult it was to come and to go at the right time like morning and evening. Timing was everything. But the children didn't know what to do next, because the doorbell was ringing like an alarm.

"The Christ child," Herbert whispered, but no-one laughed.

"The postman," Ruth said rapidly, without believing it.

"The lady from the next room, maybe she's forgotten something."

"Herself is what she's forgotten."

"Be quiet!"

"But she has keys!"

"Keep the play going!"

"Which play do you mean?"

"The play that we're performing or the one that's being performed with us?"

The children hesitated. The ringing stopped and started again, driving like the bloodied head of a bird of prey against the closed door.

"Keep the play going, do you hear!"

But transforming the play that's being performed with us into the one that we're performing causes pain. They were in the middle of the transformation, feeling clearly the odour of the rags around their bodies, at the same time sensing more strongly the hidden gleam of the Christmas tinsel around their hips and throats. Already the two plays were beginning to flow into each other, weaving themselves inextricably into a new play. The wings moved aside, the four narrow walls of what could be comprehended shattered, the incomprehensible broke forth victoriously like a waterfall. Thou shalt play in my presence!

"Keep the play going!"

Mary gripped the bundle more tightly. Mockingly, the war emerged from the shadows. He jumped out from the corner, and yet simultaneously from all the corners, and like the shrilling of the bell he seemed to break out from the ceiling and the floor through a multitude of trapdoors. His coat was too long and too grand, and he pulled it along behind him. Joseph tried to push him away. Outside the ringing continued without interruption.

Harried, the world swung around. Torches and arc lamps fell soundlessly into endless depths and were extinguished. The bundle seemed to be shining.

The war let out a piercing whistle. He grabbed the world and dropped her again, threw her into the air and pushed her away again.

"Be off, now – Shoo!
Stay with me, too,
I'll play my crazy game with you!"

The tramps were squinting through their fingers, while the angel propped himself on his left elbow and hung in the dark as if on the edge of a dome. The world hesitated.

"Stay, you!"
"Now leave the little child alone,
Be off now – Shoo!
Stay with me, too,
My own!"

The bell in the hallway was raging, demanding a decision. The tramps moved uneasily in their sleep. Mary held out the bundle clumsily into the cold twilight.

"Now make your choice,
Take me!"
"Take me!"

The world swayed on her feet. She threw the blanket around herself and shivered. The war bent forward and tried to look into her face. Her eyes were flashing into the blackness, seeking the greater risk. Again the angel raised his voice in warning. The bell in the hallway whimpered, it seemed to be out of breath. Which is the greatest risk?

The world stretched out her arms from the blanket towards the child.

"I have made my decision,
For you."

The war snatched his helmet from his head.

"I am so pleased,

For I am peace."

Exulting, he threw his soldier's overcoat back into the darkness. The tired woodpile caught alight. The bell shrilled.

"Open up, it's no use!"

"Quiet!"

"Keep the play going!"

The pangs of transformation took hold of the children. Deep in the dark, they stood facing each other. Joseph tore himself away from Mary, the knobbed stick fell clattering to the floor. The angel looked down at his hands as if they had been bound.

Georg groped his way along the wall, trying to find the door.

"Where are you going to?"

"I'll open up."

Horrified, the three tramps jumped up, wanting to hold him back. The door wasn't oiled, and sang a strange song.

"Who are you opening up to, Georg?"

It was the gentleman from across the way. The children exhaled with relief. The gentleman who wanted to help them. Leon knew him slightly from before. He visited him quite often and seemed not to be bothered by the star on the door; he also knew Leon's friends. He had, as he assured the children again and again, some understanding of what was going on. And he had also promised to warn them immediately if he heard anything.

They turned on the light and brought an armchair. The stranger asked for a glass of water. When he noticed the helmet under the piano, he enquired where they had got it from.

"Borrowed," Kurt murmured.

"What's up?" Leon asked impatiently.

The man didn't answer immediately. The children stood around him in silence. Ruth brought a glass of water. He drank slowly, and they watched him respectfully. None of them dared to ask any further question. He stretched out his legs and they moved back a little. When he drew in his legs again, they stayed where they were. He said: "Fear not!"

"But I am afraid," Ellen returned. The man threw her an annoyed glance. He wiped a drop from the corner of his mouth and coughed. Georg patted him on the shoulder, was shocked by his temerity and said: "Excuse me, please!"

The man smiled, nodded and looked thoughtfully along the line of their little stiff feet. If you ignored everything else, it looked like a row of shoes ready for cleaning. Ruth sighed. He lifted his head and looked at her attentively. Then he said suddenly: "It's all called off. The deportations to Poland have been discontinued."

The children didn't move. In the distance you could hear the siren on a fire truck, with the last note always a semi-tone too high.

"So we're saved?" Leon said. "Saved," Herbert repeated. It sounded as if they were saying: "Lost."

"I don't believe it!" Ellen called out. "Do you know for certain?"

"And how do you know it?"

The stranger began a forced, loud laughing, continuing until they crowded around him: "Is it true, is it really true?" and the black, little dog jumped growling at his throat.

"As true as I live!"

"But how truly do you live?" Ellen murmured.

He jumped up, shaking her off indignantly. "You should all be ashamed. What is it that you want?"

"To play," Georg said, "we were right in the middle of it!"

His face lowered from beneath the tattered cowl: Don't disturb us, don't deceive us, leave us alone! Saved, a strange word. Word without a meaning, doorway without a house. Is there a human being in the world who is saved?

The stranger was talking angrily to himself and looking for his hat.

"Stay," the children asked, "don't you have any certain information, then?"

"It's certain that you're all mad!" He dropped back into the armchair and began laughing again. "I'd like an explanation," he said, after he had calmed down again.

122

"It's not so important to us anymore," Georg replied.

"One day," Leon said, "when maybe it was all over, we'd walk past each other and not recognise each other."

"Underneath great umbrellas!" Ellen called out.

"It's true," Leon said thoughtfully, "we don't want to go back anymore."

"I do," Bibi interrupted him, "I do, I want to stay here and go dancing. I still want someone to kiss my hand!"

The stranger stood quite still. Then suddenly he bent over her and did it. "Thank you," Bibi said, embarrassed. Her breath hung fleetingly and brightly in the air. The storm could be heard around the building, it had turned colder.

"You can see the breath!" Herbert said.

Georg looked at the clock. The small hand moved as if it was being pushed, but then it seemed to notice that it always ended up in the same place, and stopped. It had been tricked. Since the children had interrupted the play, heavy pauses had been sinking between the seconds, the intervals were increasing.

"What was it you were playing?" the stranger said.

"Searching for peace," Herbert replied.

"So keep the play going!"

"First tell us more exactly what's supposed to happen to us!"

"I don't know anything more exact. Orders from above, the deportations have been discontinued. Quite unexpectedly."

"Right," Georg called out, "quite unexpectedly, but why was no-one waiting for it? Why do good things always happen unexpectedly?"

"Keep the play going now," the stranger said, "perform for me!" It sounded like an order.

"We play," Leon said, "but we don't perform for anyone."

"Join in the play with us!"

"Yes, join in with us!"

"But no!' the stranger said indignantly, shook his head, turned a little paler and pushed the children away. "A ridiculous company!"

"Why are you so angry?" Herbert asked in astonishment.

123

"I'm not angry. I have no interest."

"It's better if you're angry," Georg said fraternally.

"We'll do the play once more, for you. But you have to join in with us!"

"Is this the rehearsal or is it the performance?"

"We don't know that ourselves."

"And do you have a role for me?"

"You can play a tramp."

"Not something better?"

"At the end you'll cast off your rags and be a holy king!"

"Will I? And aren't there only three holy kings?"

The stranger joined in the play with them. He played in the name of every unholy king, a great non-speaking role. He walked around behind the children and eavesdropped on their all-consuming longing. He heard their despairing "There's no-one here!" and was shocked.

Over their heads, he stared at the door.

"Why are you playing in the dark?"

"We can see better like that!"

He avoided asking any more questions. Herbert had put his warm fingers in his great, damp hand and was cautiously show-ing him the way. Close behind the three tramps, the strange man walked with heavy clumsy steps.

"There's someone here!"

"Who can it be?"

"Perhaps it's all just in our minds."

"Alone are we,
We are too weary!"

"Then shut the door,
The light is fading,
The cold and dark are drawing nigh,
And all our hope is fleeing."

The stranger dropped hesitantly to the floor with the tramps and pretended to sleep. Big and silent, he lay among them. In the apartment above you could hear footsteps. Someone was walking up and down uneasily.

The stranger buried his head in his arms.

"Wake up, poor man, and understand
How brightly God's love glows for you!"
Wake up, for you must hear me!"
"Who summons me from sleep?
But I'm too weary, I'm much too weary!"
"He sleeps so deeply!"

Joseph wanted to entice Mary away, away from these shrouded figures who still didn't know if they were good or evil, away from this fourth silent tramp, but she hesitated.

"He's laughing!" she called out suddenly. "Look over here! He's laughing at us!"

"He's almost suffocating himself!"

"So what is there to laugh about?"

"Why are you laughing?"

Georg shook his shoulders angrily. They tore the scarf from his neck and tried to lift his head, but they couldn't manage it.

With all his strength, the stranger tried to hide his face. Like a quaking mountain he lay among them and let their hard, square fists beat on his coat. He seemed to be enjoying it. His temples had turned red. Herbert tugged at his collar.

"So what is there to laugh about? What are you laughing about?"

"Let go," Leon called out angrily, "let go right now!" But Herbert didn't hear. He believed in the stranger, he had held his hand. He tugged at the coat feverishly.

"Careful, or you'll tear my collar off," the man said, lifting his head.

"He's crying," Ellen said.

"Give him back his hat!"

"No," the stranger said, "no, that's not it."

For a moment, for the sake of another duty, he forgot the duty imposed by his authority. He forgot that he was a hunter, he forgot the secret police and the order to delay these children until the men came to take them away. None of them was allowed to leave the apartment until then.

125

Outside in the building, the lift was ascending. Gently and unstoppably, it made its way through the walls. The man wanted to jump up, wanted to warn the children: "Move, run away, your gatherings have been uncovered!" but he felt paralysed and, in a way he did not understand, under their spell. The lift went past.

"A gentlemen with crutches lives on the fourth floor," Ruth said.

"But no," the man said.

"Go on!" Leon interrupted.

"Now you must tell me: Where
You're going on your search for peace –"
The dreams began to glow.

The stranger felt the floor beginning to tremble under the world's fleeing steps. He heard the windows rattle and wished for nothing else but to remain lying here. In the light of the lantern he saw Mary give her child over to the world.

He heard the angel's warning, and when the bell rang for the third time he was the last to jump up. As in a dream, he brushed the dust from his coat and turned back the collar. He had to play the role of the unholy king to the end. For there are only three holy kings.

"Cast off your coats!"
Blessed, the silver cords blazed with light. None of the children paid any attention to him, they were rushing to the door.

Like a great, dancing flame, their play closed over their heads.

The Death of the Grandmother

The night jumped from the sky. Swift and curious like an enemy battalion which had been expected secretly again and again. Silently, the black parachutes opened. The night jumped from the sky. She's covering us, the people stammered, casting off their clothes and sighing, but their sighing was hypocrisy. She's covering us. The night shook with laughter, but she was laughing silently, and pressing both hands cautiously over her eyes and mouth. Because she had a different order: "Jump down and uncover!" And beneath her coat she carried the strongest lamp of her lord, the darkness. She shone through the walls, penetrated the concrete and surprised the entangled and the abandoned, the foolish and the wise, the simple and the ambiguous. She fell like the iron curtain at the end of a comedy and cut off the stage from the audience. She fell like a sword through man and separated the player from the spectator and cut him off from himself. She fell like a shower of ash from a fire-spitting mountain which no-one had taken seriously before, and she ordered everyone to maintain their position and await the verdict. And the crouched stayed crouched, and the screaming were incapable of closing their mouths.

The night jumped from the sky and she uncovered the world's mercilessness in the same place where her own mercy was to be found. She uncovered the new-born, despair in their tiny, wrinkled faces, fear of becoming embodied, pain for the lost radiance. And she uncovered the dying in their fear of the coming radiance.

Intermittently this March night felt like crying, but tears were not part of her duties. So she tried to be more cheerful and put nightcaps on the sleepers' heads. What do you look like, with your hair in curlers and your slack stockings, she thought, how many fastenings and ribbons you need to be safe. She stopped the dreamers, who were fleeing their consciousness in droves and, like a deceitful customs official, she let them fall into all the rivers on the borders. There they flailed despairingly with their arms and legs until the morning before climbing, exhausted and swollen, back into their consciousness and trying to interpret dreams which they hadn't had.

This night forced the great into the poverty of lowness and the small into the poverty of greatness, and she made them write reluctantly with trembling fingers and split pens in their diaries that one must first become nothing in order to be everything. She uncovered the new in the old and the old in the new, she made the falling stand and the standing fall. But all of that wasn't enough. Nothing was enough.

Trembling, the night struggled for the forgotten word, for her particular duty. Help me, she asked the wind, and he loved her and tore open doors and windows for her, threw the slates off the house-tops, uprooted the young trees and robbed them of their growing souls. In their fear they shattered the windows and lifted off the roofs, but they found nothing. God will punish me, the night groaned, I'll never turn into day again. And she fled from her beloved, the wind, across the silent bridges, leaving him hanging, and sliding down the stone pillars.

Across the bridges there was a smell of smoke. The night was feverish with excitement, her darkness grabbed through the many windows confusedly. I must turn into day, she groaned. You will turn into day, someone beside her whispered, but no night believes that she will turn into day. Harried, the night swung around. Who are you? She saw no-one, and no-one answered her. For the last time, she cast out her darkness and caught the stranger. This stranger was standing there, leaning motionless on the wall of the old church.

Who are you?

I am persecution.

The night was shocked. This one here was superior to her, and the greater uncoverer. This one's darkness was blacker, more penetrating and more impenetrable, and her silence was greater, because she no longer had a wind or a moon as her beloved. This one here found what she was seeking more quickly, because she knew how to efface herself and make herself small like the genie in the bottle. Her duty was to lose herself, and she had to pass on this duty to everyone that she drew to her, to her into the abyss which was blacker than any night.

What are you doing, the night asked curiously, what are you seeking, is there some news?

Too many questions at once, persecution said dismissively. A very young night, she thought, immature and like the humans with their unending questions: "Will we survive? Why should we die? Will we die of hunger, be choked by plagues or will they shoot us? And when and how and why?"

They didn't understand how to crystallise all the idols into one god, all the questions into one word, and then not utter it.

The night maintained her composure, as she realised the stranger's disapproval. Listen! persecution said. They were silent, listening intently into the silence. From a half-open window they heard the sobbing of a child who didn't want to go to sleep. They set off on their way.

The wind flew secretly along behind them, entangling himself in their garments and carrying their long trains carefully over the dust. The closer they came to the sobbing, the more they hurried, and the wind began to sing, accompanying it softly. In a narrow bleak street they stopped suddenly. The sobbing had fallen silent. The wind sank in upon himself and lay down like a little dog at the feet of the other two.

Quiet, it must have been here!

Badly blacked out, the night whispered, pointing triumphantly to a window high up. She turned back: persecution had disappeared. The night commanded the wind to give her a leg-up and climbed like a thief up the outside of the building. Fleetingly she greeted the weak light which was flowing from the window: Good morning. She noticed that the window was standing half-open and the black paper was swelling in an effort to tear itself to shreds. Help can be given you! And she ordered the wind to tear a little bit more.

What do you see? the wind whispered curiously.

But the night gave no answer. She had put her arms on the windowsill, her train was fluttering over the roofs and her eyes were pulsing into the little miserable room. Go away, you'll have other nights! she called out to the wind. And the wind took himself off, flying faithlessly towards the sun. The night remained alone with the child and the old woman, with the shipping trunk, the map, and the rosary with the cross swinging directly above Southwest Africa.

Ellen had buried her head in her arms, pretending to sleep as she observed her grandmother intently, while the grandmother sat on the side of the bed and looked intently across to Ellen.

"Are you asleep?"

"Yes," Ellen said softly, but the old woman didn't hear. She had pulled open the drawer of her night table and began rummaging. A bottle of eyewash appeared, a volume of old poems, string and a broken thermometer, but evidently she wasn't searching for the eyewash nor the thermometer, nor for the old poems; for its part, the string was too short. She laid bare the bottom sheet on her bed, shook the pillow, poked under the covers and between the mattresses, but she found nothing. She moved over to the wardrobe, opened it and felt with trembling hands in the pockets of her clothes and behind her underwear.

Searching, searching, searching, the night thought with compassion, have we really only been created to seek and to find nothing but the unsought? And Ellen thought: "How ugly the grandmother is, how white and sad, I'd rather die when I was forty!"

Immediately she despised herself for this thought. "You should do something to fight it, but how can you fight spat-out fruit pits, dead rats and furrows under the eyes? Dear God, how can you fight decay?" She groaned, turned around quickly and stretched her arms and legs between the bars on the bed which had become too short for her. Again the grandmother asked: "Are you asleep, Ellen?" moved over to her and shook her anxiously, but the child remained silent like a sad puppet, like a bag with ripening fruit. "Dear God, how can you fight decay? And why does the fox eat the cat and the cat the mouse?"

Now the grandmother had grabbed the wastepaper basket and was rummaging in it, she tore open the door of the oven, poked inside and fumbled with her hands between the glass panels, her movements becoming ever faster and greedier. Frightened, Ellen turned away and began to cry silently again.

What's she searching for, my God, what's she searching for, the night asked herself, and what am I commanded to do? The broom was overturned noisily, the underwear fell with a whoosh out of the wardrobe.

Tensely, the night bent over the windowsill. She had noticed long ago that Ellen wasn't asleep, but alert and expectant, secretly putting her hand beneath her pillow every so often. How little human beings know of each other, the night thought. And Ellen thought: "I mustn't fall asleep, or she'll find it, and she mustn't find it, I have to stay awake!"

In that instant, Ellen forgot her pain. She forgot that she was free against her will, that they had released her from the camp, back into the freedom of these cursed people, and she forgot the sad, mocking smiles of her friends: "We told you at the beginning that you don't belong with us!" She forgot the envy with which she envied her own grandmother: "You'll go with them, they won't release you, you'll see them all again, Herbert, Hanna and Ruth!" And she forgot the shoving and the astonished laughter of the hunters. "Let me go with them, please let me go with them!"

Because of these entreaties, Ellen had been released, shoved back into the prison of her own heart, from the ultimate into the penultimate, from the conclusive silence into the little tormenting questions. But she forgot all of that now, because the grandmother was bending over her again and shaking her shoulders. "Are you asleep, Ellen?"

The night climbed conclusively over the white windowsill and into the room. The light extinguished itself for no reason, outside it began to rain gently. The wind flew past, playfully driving clouds before him like a gaggle of quite young girls. The rain grew stronger, and wherever he could he painted gleaming puddles which reflected the feeling of abandonment. The abandonment of all beginnings, the abandonment of the seed grains which fall from warm hands into the cold, damp earth.

"Are you asleep?"

"No," Ellen replied. She sat up and clung onto the cold bedrail. White and horrified, the thrown-out underwear shone from the floor, and light began to flash from the cross above Southwest Africa.

"What are you searching for, grandmother?"

"You know what I'm searching for."

"But do you know what you're searching for?"

"What do you want from me?" the old woman said despairingly.

"Pin up your braid, grandmother," Ellen said, "and put on a dressing gown!" Looking through the darkness, she saw Georg, Herbert and Ruth squatting on one-third of a mattress, tormented and humiliated by lice and fear, but quiet, with arms folded, and through the hissing of the rain she heard Bibi's answer to the question put by the *Scharführer*: "Last occupation?" "Playing!" And last of all she felt Georg pressing her hand. "See you later!" That was all he'd said, just as if they were to meet again the next day, outside the lending library or outside an unfamiliar doorway.

"What do you want from me?" the grandmother repeated, as she pinned up her hair.

"Dignity," Ellen replied quietly, "no, more than that, I want you to want dignity from me."

"I want something else from you," the grandmother said, "you must have hidden it."

Despairingly, Ellen thought of all the people who could have helped her now and who were gone, and she searched for the word which would have conjured them up. It was the attempt to summon reinforcements – not only her grandfather from the last cemetery at the edge of the fields, her mother from an unfamiliar table in a foreign country, but also Aunt Sonja, who had gone out only recently to get her hat remodelled. But she hadn't come back. "Disappeared," the people said, and in fact Aunt Sonja had disappeared like a gleaming coin through a rusty sewer grate. The hat was not remodelled. Many of her acquaintances searched for explanations: She had hidden, or been arrested at a friend's place. But Ellen knew better. She knew of Aunt Sonja's wonderful ability to disguise herself and to imitate people, of her longing for a single direction, the east, of her love for the horizon and of her way of accepting blows like strokes of fortune and strokes of fortune like blows. She knew that Aunt Sonja was also capable of savouring death like a foreign country.

Ellen couldn't find the word to conjure them up. But she felt that Aunt Sonja was here now, just like her grandfather and her mother, that they had hurried here from all directions and were sitting with her on the white sheet in order to help her. She'd known for a long time that only the dead die, not the living. Ridiculous of them to believe that they could murder the incomprehensible before they had grasped it. Ellen saw Aunt Sonja quite often during the day too. She was moving towards the horizon and sometimes she turned around and said: "You'll see, I'll get there!"

She was walking like a blind woman, her hands extended in front of her, wearing her grey fox fur around her neck. When she reached the edge of the world, she waved back once more before she went down.

"Grandmother," Ellen said gently, "I'd like you to sit with me now and tell me a story. A quite new one, one I haven't heard before. Or it could be a fairytale."

"It's possible that I'll be taken away during the night," the grandmother said.

"That's nothing new," Ellen replied, "but maybe they'll let me go with you, and then walk behind you with your suitcases. Wherever you go!"

"Yes?" the grandmother said imploringly, clinging onto the bars of Ellen's bed. "But how many suitcases?"

"Two, I think," Ellen said, "that makes the carrying easier."

"Two," the grandmother repeated absently, looking beyond Ellen.

"Tell me a story now, grandmother!"

133

"But it might be that they don't come tonight."

"A story, grandmother, a new story!"

"And do you know if they put tarpaulin roofs over the trucks? Someone told me the other day that he'd seen –"

"But that's not a story."

"Well, I don't know any."

"That's not true, grandmother!"

The old woman started up, looked at Ellen fiercely and seemed in the next second to be looking straight through her again. She moved her lips angrily, but gave no answer.

"Once upon a time, grandmother, once upon a time! Something must have happened some time, something that no-one but you knows about yet, grandmother. Didn't you always know what the Turkish mocha cups are saying when it turns dark, and what the fat dog in the courtyard is telling the pigeons?"

"I made that up."

"Why?"

"Because you were still little."

"No, because you were still big, grandmother!"

"Back then we weren't in danger, no-one was allowed to take us away!"

"You always said that when it turns dark the thieves come."

"I was right about that, unfortunately."

"Keep being right, grandmother!" Ellen said.

The old woman didn't answer, but fumbled uneasily with her hands across the thin sheet. "You must have it, you've got it. You must have it!"

"Nothing," Ellen whispered angrily, threw herself back again and pressed her head onto her pillow, observing the bony, poor hands moving like those of a dying woman over the sheets and the bars. What's she searching for, the night thought, my God, what's she searching for? The night was cowering, crouched in the middle of the room, and had spread her train across the rough, dirty floor. But for the moment she too received no answer, all the questions remained open, sighing. And the rain rustled like someone leading a prayer whom no-one understands.

"Tell me a fairytale," Ellen stammered despairingly, because the grandmother had got to the pillow and was trying to push her off. Ellen drew up her knees and covered the pillow with her whole body, but fear made her dizzy and she was weakening. She clenched her fists to ward off her grandmother, but she couldn't manage it anymore. The pillow moved, Ellen was pushed to the foot of the bed, and a little glass vial fell over the side, rolled across the floor, made a rattling sound, opened up and kept on rolling. The night remained motionless, some white pills scattered themselves across her black train. Ellen jumped out of bed. She pushed the grandmother aside, ground down the glass of the vial with her bare feet, began to bleed, and tried with stiff fingers to pick up what had been scattered. The grandmother threw herself onto her again, but Ellen forced her off. Her long blue nightgown bunched and formed folds, like the robe of a wooden angel on an old, dark altar. Their heads banged together, but the struggle did not last long. Ellen had managed to gather up some of the poison, while the grandmother held the remainder in her clenched fist. And only what was in both fists could satisfy death, that arrogant black marketeer, who is only cheap where he's cursed, and becomes unaffordable where he is profoundly desired.

"You have no right at all to prevent me!" the grandmother said.

"Oh yes," Ellen replied, "I do," but in that instant she felt doubt and moved back. In trying to attack, the grandmother stepped into empty space and fell headlong into the darkness.

Ellen stood upright and disconcerted, heated by victory as by a heavy, old wine, pushed down her sleeves and groped forward one step. Some kind of rejoicing was within her, and the longing for sleep, the dangerous consequence of all victories. The groaning came from a strange planet, barely reaching her. At a loss, she lowered her arms, but then she knelt down beside the grandmother after all, opening the damp, strange hand and taking possession of the poison without much difficulty. She pushed her arms underneath the bony body and tried to lift it up. But this body was heavy with weariness and reluctance.

"Grandmother, get up! Do you hear, grandmother?" Ellen grabbed her by the shoulders and dragged her towards the bed, let her drop, lifted her up again and dragged her further. The groaning was unbearable. "Be quiet, grandmother!" And she threw herself down beside her on the hard floor. The grandmother fell silent. "Say something," Ellen begged, "you must say something!" And she tried to take her in her arms. "You're alive, grandmother, I know quite well that you're alive, you're just pretending to be dead like a beetle in the forest! I can't hold you anymore, get up!"

"I'm not getting up until you give me what's mine," the grandmother said calmly, directing her gaze at Ellen. "You've stolen from me. I pawned my fur and the prescription cost me enough too." Her words were changed suddenly, framed in the last bitter remnants of her forfeited authority.

"I won't give it to you," Ellen replied.

"Maybe because you need it for yourself?"

Ellen didn't move. Then she let go of the grandmother, got up and slowly put the poison on the table. "I'll give it to you, grandmother. But not until you've told me the story."

"Do you promise me that you'll give me everything then?"

"I promise you," Ellen said.

The old bed made an angry, cracking sound. Ellen shook the pillows straight, covered up the grandmother like a child, then wrapped herself in her own blanket and sat down on the side. The rejoicing had fallen silent, and she was freezing. Silence spread into every inch of the room, an intent and thoughtful silence, a waiting for the truth of the last fairytale of all, for the whispering of the prompter. The grey-green oven, the old shipping trunk and the white, empty bed – in this draining silence, they all shrank to backdrops and waited to be inflated again. Despairingly, the cross flashed above Southwest Africa, defending itself to the last against the panting breath of the despairing.

The grandmother had turned her head away from Ellen and was thinking. A story, a new story – surely it couldn't be so hard to find. Wrapped up in the blanket, arms propped on the side of the bed, Ellen waited. She waited silently and imperturbably, as all silence always waits for the fulfilling word, for the skipping heart at the centre. Like a miserable soul, she cowered on the edge. "Tell me, grandmother, tell me! Didn't you say yourself that we can find every story in the air, if we just reach out for it?"

"I can't think of anything, not now!" Gripped by fear, the grandmother turned away.

"Yes, precisely now," Ellen murmured.

"There'll still be enough fairytales for you, you're young!"

"How is that supposed to help me?" Ellen asked.

"Let me off telling this one!"

"I can't do that."

"You're young," the grandmother repeated, "and cruel."

Ellen bent down and put her forehead against the grandmother's. She had no answer. Uneasily, the old woman turned around. Where were they all, those stories which she had pulled in hundreds from her coat pockets, from under her hat, and in emergencies from the unstitched silk padding, from as many hiding places as a hamster has for fat? The great police had come upon her, the darkness had devoured everything. That darkness which is always yawning without holding her hand over her mouth.

The grandmother groaned. She leafed back through the disintegrating album of her memories. And she found Ellen sitting on a white, gleaming stool, with her mouth opened in a question, three years old.

"Grandmother, what's a sparrow?"

"A quick little miracle."

"And a pigeon?"

"A fat miracle."

"And a chestnut roaster?"

"A chestnut roaster is a person."

Then Ellen was usually silent for some seconds before she started again from the beginning.

The white stool had been burned long ago and the picture had yellowed. But the questions hadn't fallen silent.

"A story, grandmother!"

But are there really any new stories? Aren't all the stories old, ancient, and only the rejoicing of the person who embraces, the breath of the world, creates them again and again? While Ellen was demanding a story she was demanding of her grandmother, and in the middle of a black, dangerous night, the readiness to live.

Right, either she'll find the story, so after that she won't want to die anymore. Or she won't find it, so she'll lose the bet and the poison will belong to me. But what will I do with it? I'll throw it into the darkness. It won't kill the darkness.

"Grandmother!"

But the grandmother still couldn't think of a way to start. She was still struggling in vain for words and the crumpled map was hanging below the cross, a piece of paper and no more. The oven demanded fire, the bed demanded warmth, and the night demanded her command. She was gripped by impatience, because the morning was already threatening, blessing the fulfilled with hope and spurning the unfulfilled. And nothing was happening, still nothing was happening. Things were maturing in the silence, and whoever couldn't wait remained immature. So the night waited and Ellen waited, while the grandmother became sleepy. A stroke, she was thinking, my God, a slight stroke, before they come! But God does not strike on request. Ellen chewed tensely on a piece of bread and didn't give up hope. "Once," the grandmother stammered, "once upon a time –"

"That's right," Ellen called out excitedly, threw away the bread and bent down further, to hear what was coming from far away. "Go on, grandmother, go on!" But again the stammering trickled away to nothing. Telling stories wasn't so simple. They demanded opened hands and narrow gaps between the fingers in order to flow through. And they demanded open eyes.

The old woman repeated the four words several times more, but didn't go on to the fifth or the sixth. The stories could be found in the air right enough, but they were sleeping, and the moment they woke up they began to mock, drifted close to the lips and fled again. "The poison," she said clearly, after a while. Ellen shook her head. The grandmother lifted her hands pleadingly, whispered a final "Once upon a time –," was abandoned by all the tormenting powers and dropped into sleep.

"But, no," Ellen said helplessly. She turned on the night light, and flinched. What was lying there was as strange, as far away and as drawn in upon itself as if it had never been her grandmother. What was lying there was breathing as heavily and gasping as if it had never known the comfortable calm of a peaceful citizen.

"Hallo!" Ellen said uncertainly and put her warm face against the cold one in the pillows. The gasping subsided gradually, the breaths became easier. But everything else remained far away.

"Then," Ellen said with decision, "then it'll be me who tells the story!" She didn't know why she began with Little Red Riding Hood, nor did she know who this fairytale was for, for the night, for March or for the damp cold which was seeping through the cracks in the window. After all, the grandmother was sleeping, with her eyelids just twitching from time to time in the weak glow of the light.

"Once upon a time there was a mother," Ellen began, raising her eyebrows thoughtfully, "in America. She was working in a club there as a waitress. This mother had a great longing. And the longing was red." Ellen fell silent and looked around challengingly, but there was no-one there encouraging her, and no-one contradicting her. In a softer voice, she continued: "When she came home from work late at night, the mother was very weary, no-one was waiting for her. And she began knitting. And out of her longing she knitted a round red cap with a long bobble for the wind. She knitted every night, but the longing did not diminish and the cap became as big as a saint's aureole, but red, and the bobble became as thick as a ball, a toy for the storm." The night listened, leaning against the window. The window rattled. "Whether it was quiet outside," Ellen said, throwing a glance across the bed at the dark glass, "or whether the wind off the sea blew against the windowpanes, she kept on knitting. When the cap was finished, the mother broke off the wool at her heart, packed the cap into a box and sent it across the ocean. Yes, I almost forgot, she put some cake and wine in too, and a basket for the grandmother." Again Ellen looked around, as if someone was doubting her veracity, but the night at the window just laughed quietly, and her tears fell silently too. "God knows how it all got through the checks," Ellen said, "but it any case it was delivered." She was speaking faster now. "Only the paper was a bit scorched and the cake smelled burnt, because the cap was glowing. The child picked it up and pulled it quickly onto its head. But when the child tried to remove the cap that evening, it wouldn't come off, but stayed there like a saint's red aureole and kept on burning. You shouldn't envy anyone a saint's aureole."

At the window it was still raining, the old woman was breathing more regularly and the floor was creaking, as if Ellen's voice had just woken it up. But Ellen didn't let herself be distracted, she was silent only for a moment, as if she was embarrassed before this big audience, then continued immediately: "The bottle had a leak, but Little Red Riding Hood put it into the basket all the same along with the burnt cake, and set off to visit the grandmother. The grandmother lived in the same room, but nevertheless it was a long way through a dark forest. Once the basket knocked against a tree and what was in the bottle leaked out. The next time the cake fell onto the ground and the war ate it up. The war had a long shaggy dirty coat, almost like a wolf. – Where are you going? – I'm going to my grandmother. – And what are you taking her? he asked mockingly. Look, your basket is empty! – I'm taking her the longing. – Then the wolf became angry, because he couldn't eat longing, in fact it would burn his tongue. He ran away in fury, always a little ahead, and Little Red Riding Hood ran along anxiously behind him. But the wolf was faster and got there first. The grandmother was lying in bed. But she looked quite different."

Ellen paused. She grabbed her grandmother by the shoulders and stared into her face. She lifted the bed-lamp and shone it over the old bed. She jumped up and searched for words.

"Then Little Red Riding Hood said: But grandmother, why do you have such big ears? – The better to hear you with! – But grandmother, why do you have such big teeth? – The better to bite you with! – But grandmother, why do you have such thick lips? – The better to swallow it with! – The poison? Do you mean the poison, grandmother?"

Ellen had jumped off the bed, she was standing barefoot in the middle of the room and trembling with cold and fear. The old woman was sleeping, and didn't move. The poison on the table was gleaming, Ellen left it there. With one jump, she was in her bed. She pulled the blanket over her, put her head on her arms and searched for the final question. "Grandmother, why do you have such cold hands?" But she didn't find an answer. She wiped the tears from her cheeks and sighed. After a while she fell asleep, exhausted.

Then she saw a pale soldier stumbling out of the high old building of the northern railway. He was carrying a rucksack on his skinny back and cursing softly to himself, so softly and so helplessly that all-knowing God thought it was a prayer. His feet were frozen, so he stumbled again and again. His uniform was in shreds and his paybook was forged. From time to time he looked around and stopped in a shadow, as if he was expecting someone who was expecting him. But no-one was expecting him. Then he went on again for a while. He passed under the little viaduct in the direction of the fields. He trod in all the puddles of this night which held the promise of spring and splashed an old sergeant who was returning from his patrol in the meadows. He was trying hard to remain inconspicuous, so that he made himself very conspicuous. He staggered towards the river, turning back half-way there. He shook the loose-fitting but still locked doors of the coffee houses and hung around one of the stations on the children's railway for a while, as if he felt like journeying back into his childhood and slinging his boots away. But no train came. Finally he went back towards the city. He lost his cap on the way and bent down, but he couldn't find it anymore.

The hair on his head was light brown, short and fluffy and cried out to be stroked. The nails on his fingers were bitten down and his scarf was checked. But no-one was expecting him. He went back to the northern railway and strayed for some time like a lost animal around the yellow walls. At last he decided to go home, although that was particularly dangerous. As he crossed the old marketplace he had the distinct feeling that he was being followed, and stood panting between the booths. He hid between two potato sacks behind a stack of onion crates, but no-one came. He took off his rucksack, picked it up again and lurched on. Now and then he took his forged paybook from his pocket and looked at it attentively, as if it was the genuine one – yes, as if all forged paybooks were genuine and all the genuine ones were forged. Then he put it in his pocket again. When he reached the square in front of the church, he knew for sure that someone was behind him, and hid in the shadow beneath a stone saint. "Intercede for me," he prayed, "intercede for me!" He didn't know the name. As he ran away again, it looked in the moonlight as if the saint was moving and blessing him with an old, enigmatic gesture.

The boy ran both hands through his hair, he had lice. Again he heard footsteps behind him, but now he didn't turn around. He zig-zagged like a hare, coming at last to the high, quiet building with the badly blacked-out window. Someone is behind me – no, no-one is behind me – no-one – the emptiness of the world. The little soldier shook the broad ugly door, but the door remained fast. He knocked and thumped and beat his fists bloody. He pushed at it with his boots, which were in shreds, but that only damaged them more.

Ellen jerked awake. She sat up, stared confusedly into the darkness and forgot the dream. She forgot it immediately and as completely as if it had never penetrated her heart, as if it had never driven salt and water into her closed eyes. She got out of bed quietly and bent out of the window. But you couldn't see down. Somewhere in the hallway footsteps dragged, the door to

the building opened. Ellen heard squeaking and groaning. "No,"
she said hoarsely. She took a step towards the grandmother's
bed and stopped. She moved back three steps and forward two
again, it looked like an old-fashioned dance. But there was no
time left for dancing. They're coming up the staircase – they're
taking three stairs at once – four stairs – five stairs – "They're
taking you away, grandmother!" Ellen cried out. She put her
fists into her mouth and bit on her fingers. She wanted to think
every thought at once but couldn't think a single one. The poison on the table was shining urgently, in a strange light. The old
woman awoke, sat up and grabbed for it with both hands. She
seemed calm and not at all surprised. "Give it here," she said.
Ellen squatted at her feet, staring in astonishment into her quiet
eyes. "Good for you! You're grown up, grandmother, the wolf
can't devour you!"

"Give it to me!" the grandmother repeated sharply.

"No," Ellen stammered, "no, I'll get you out of this, I want
to hide you – come up to the storage loft, quickly, or into the
wardrobe here, and I'll defend you – yes, I'll knock them down
and you'll see how strong I am!"

"Be quiet," the grandmother said dismissively, "don't make
such big talk, do what I tell you!"

"Be good to me," Ellen begged.

"Yes," the grandmother said, "afterwards."

"No," Ellen screamed, "you won't have any time left afterwards!"

"Hurry up!" the old woman urged.

Ellen stood up. She turned on the light, went over to the table, took the poison in her left hand and a glass of water in her
right and moved with them towards the grandmother.

"More water!"

"Yes," Ellen replied. Her movements were stiff and careful.
She filled the glass anew.

"Don't spill any of it!" the grandmother said. Ellen held the
glass to her lips. Then she fed her grandmother the poison the
way a sparrow feeds one of its fledglings and promptly collapsed beside the bed.

"Stand up!" the grandmother said. Ellen stood up. Woodenly, with arms hanging down, she stood beside the bed. A strange voice emerged from the pillows, detached, abandoned by everything around it, belonging to itself no longer. "When they come now, open the door, be polite, don't say anything and don't try to stop anything."

"They'll drag you out of bed, grandmother," Ellen said, but what had fallen silent lay crouched and heavy in her voice too.

"They'll drag my bones, not me!"

"They'll kick you when they discover that you've taken poison!"

"Their feet can't reach me."

"They'll insult you, grandmother."

"They'll be talking to the wrong number, everything they say will be to the wrong number. I've changed my number."

"Yes," Ellen said, fearfully, "I think you've got a secret number now!"

"Go and listen to what's happening in the hallway!" Ellen went and listened. She leaned on the door to the hallway and held her breath. At first there was silence, but then footsteps approached. She heard them feel their way slowly, fall silent and feel their way again. "Drunk –" Ellen whispered, "they're taking their time, they think they've got us for sure!" Triumph suffused her. "What I did is good, it's good, it's good!" And the astonished angry faces of the hunters appeared from all the corners. Ellen fled back into the room. "It's good, it's good –" and she buried her head in the grandmother's sinking shoulders.

"They'll move to grab you, and you'll take a little step, grandmother, and they'll fly into empty space – a little step – just a little step. And you've taken it!"

The grandmother sat up and propped herself on her elbows, her face was glowing. She grabbed Ellen's hands. They sat there like children on Christmas Eve, like children who have looked through the keyhole and are trying to feel triumphant. "We've outsmarted them – we've outsmarted them! Look at their trembling jaws, their shaking knees, their puffed-out cheeks!" Again, the disappointment of the hunters appeared from all the corners.

"Do you see them, do you see them? Now they're climbing the last steps. And now they've stopped. They're lurching and holding onto each other. They're checking the names on the door to the hallway. They're seeing the star and jeering. But they've taken the wrong path. They're killing a thousand innocent children, and none of them is the right one. Now they're searching for the bell – the bell doesn't ring – they're raising their fists, and now –"
Everything remained quiet. The old woman sank back down.

"No," Ellen said a second time. She opened her mouth wide, tried to scream, but the air balled itself up into a lump and threatened to suffocate her. She ran out, groped her way to the window to the hallway and opened it cautiously: dark – pitch dark, not a sound – not a breath – nothing. With trembling fingers, Ellen began searching for the keys. She turned on the light and unlocked the door. She stepped out and said: "You can all come – come on – don't hesitate to come!" She stood on the threshold and extended her arms helplessly. "Come and take us away, God permits it – my grandmother has taken poison and I want to go with her, I want to go to Georg!" But no-one came.

"No," Ellen said once more. "They've forgotten something, they'll come back!" She crouched down and waited. Time drained away. But no-one came back. A moth fluttered in front of her face and settled on her hand, Ellen shook it off. She stood up and locked the door again. She smoothed down her nightgown and made the fastening tighter. Then she put the keys back in the drawer and draped a coat around herself, a black coat which didn't belong to her. She pushed the drawer shut, put the chain across the door and crept back into the room. Her bare soles made a little dull sound. The half-empty glass stood under the bed-lamp. "Too close to the edge," the grandmother murmured. Ellen pushed it into the middle. "It's working slowly," the grandmother whispered.

"You'll fall asleep," Ellen said, "and when you wake up –"
The old woman waved her hand dismissively.
"Grandmother!"
"Yes?"

"It's your birthday next week. So I wanted – I wanted to tell you –"

"This week," the grandmother said clearly, "this week is a much better day."

"Be good to me," Ellen said, "you promised, afterwards, you said, and now –" Her mouth quivered. "It's ringing," the old woman smiled. Ellen didn't hear it. It was a different ringing.

"They're coming," the grandmother sighed inaudibly and closed her eyes. Her head fell suddenly on one side.

Ellen clung to the dying woman with both arms and searched for her face.

"Grandmother, spit it out, don't die – don't die, grandmother!" The withered lips in the half-dark were distorted, the head lifted and sank back down. That was the final attempt.

Ellen jumped onto the bed like a young cat. She grabbed the grandmother by both arms and tried to sit her up. She shoved and shook despairingly. The old woman groaned in protest.

"Dear God, what can you do to stop death?" The old bed made cracking sounds in every joint. "Grandmother, wake up, pull yourself together – people don't die if they don't want to!"

With eyes opened, the night heard this curious sermon against death. The core of her duty seemed to be coming closer.

Ellen lifted her round, black head and trained her senses on the darkness, thinking carefully. Now the old woman's death-rattle began. Ellen knelt over her and listened; all her senses were awake. There was something the grandmother still wanted – she was demanding something and seemed insatiable. Her hands freed themselves from Ellen's grip and began to dance restlessly over the blanket again.

"What are you searching for? Do you know what you're searching for, grandmother?" Ellen asked. "One time it was your handkerchief, then another time it was your opera glasses, and finally it was the poison. But didn't you want something quite different? Grandmother, why didn't you think carefully?" Ellen was trembling with fear. She grabbed the restless hands, but they weren't to be stopped. She took the thin, white braid and pulled on it, but the grandmother gave no answer.

"What are you searching for – tell me what you're searching for, I'll give you everything! Grandmother, then at least say: don't make such big talk – grandmother, why don't you answer, grandmother, do you want to live?"

The breaths fled the dying woman's half-open lips as if something was hunting them. Ellen lowered her head to listen, pressing her fingers into the mattress.

"Do you want to live?"

"Yes," the night sighed on her behalf and put her hands on the old woman's shoulders.

"Then I'll give you life," Ellen said with decision, and still the cross was flashing above the map. A consuming will flooded through her, tore a hole in her heart and opened her ears. But in this great storm no voice could be understood. Ellen jumped onto the floor and took her black thick prayer book from the old wardrobe, the prayers for the dying were on the last page. She began, was frightened by the sound of her own voice and dropped the book again. The death-rattle was becoming quieter. "Stay," Ellen whispered, "stay here, let me think. Didn't I give you the poison? Don't I have to wake you?"

In this instant she was struck by the idea of running for the doctor. But he lived a long way away and you weren't allowed to fetch another one. And even if the grandmother was alive when he came, what could he do? A tube, put a long tube into the stomach – Ellen knew that. But were these dancing, insatiable hands demanding a tube? Ellen shook her head. She pressed her knees against the side of the bed and was silent.

"By the rivers of Babylon, there they sat down, yea, they wept –" the night said suddenly. Ellen heard that and she saw them sitting by the rivers and she saw how the rivers grew ever larger from their tears. But they didn't jump in. They were waiting, they were still waiting and singing strange sad songs and still speaking in a sing-song. Four of them stood up and moved towards the old bed. In a moment they would grab the grandmother and they would carry her out to the last cemetery, which was sleeping fearfully in the greying light of morning. And they would pray, sing and weep, but their prayers remained lying on

147

the ground like empty tubes, silent and sad. The wine has been drained from those wine-skins. This cemetery had the oldest secret number, but its watchmen had forgotten the number, and everyone who lay there suffered because of that. Just like Ellen's dying grandmother, all their lives they had demanded all kinds of things which they didn't want at all, they had rung up all kinds of numbers, but in essence they had always been talking to the wrong numbers, for none of them was the secret number. "Wait, all of you," Ellen called out feverishly, "maybe I know the number, maybe I can give it to you! Do you want to live?"

"Yes," the night said for the second time. "Yes," she said impatiently, because the morning was already climbing like a conqueror over the roofs. The grandmother's nose became sharper and more prominent, her cheeks collapsed. The hands of the master himself made the final gestures, extinguishing what was extinguishing itself. Ellen opened her eyes wide, she made shapes with her hands as if she could tear the word which would wake up the grandmother away from the twilight. Crouched to spring, she lay at the foot of the bed and waited without speaking, in the silence of readiness.

The grandmother's nightgown was in shreds, the blanket cast off. With her last shadows, she replaced the night.

"Grandmother, what are you searching for? Grandmother, do you want to live?"

With a small movement, the cord on the bed-lamp was loosened. The light went out. Once more the dying woman's head jerked back in the face of the imminent darkness, the body reared. Ellen sprang, she grabbed the half-empty glass. Three swallows had been taken. And she poured the remainder of the water over the white square forehead, over the neck and the chest into the stiff pillows, and into the middle of the last lonely death-rattle she said: "Grandmother, I baptise you in the name of the Father and of the Son and of the Holy Ghost, amen."

The night sank into the arms of the day.

During this night, towards two o'clock, a little, despairing deserter had come home and been arrested in the morning.

Dream of Wings

Three minutes before the train's departure the engine driver forgot where the journey was headed. He tore open his tunic, pushed his cap to the back of his head and wiped the sweat from his forehead. He jumped down and ran a little way ahead. He stopped, extended his arms and walked slowly back, talking loudly to himself. He had to find it, oh yes, he had to find it. In the dark behind the line of the headlights. That was where it was hidden and that was where it would be for as long as men's trains raced through the night and no-one thought to turn off the headlights and walk a little way alone. That's where it would be, silent and unmoving in the face of their racing, that's where it would be for as long as they thought their sad blacked-out stations were great bright destinations, for as long as they put names where wisdom should be, for as long as they made detours to avoid the crossing point which lay in the middle, for as long as they confused departure and arrival, for as long as, as long as, as long as – – but now it was too late. No time left, my God, no time! Three minutes before departure.

Why are you all in such a hurry? Come on, get out, help me to search! Where we're heading, where we're heading.

But this train was a freight train, a munitions train, a train which had to take weapons to the front, and the weapons didn't get out. Despairingly, the engine driver ran along the train. You're not coming? Why? You don't want to. You'd rather go to the front. Where's the front? The front is the place where you curse where you're heading, the front is always, the front is everywhere, the front is here. The man was panting. One of the stokers threw a surprised glance at him.

"Don't depart, don't depart," the engine driver whispered, turning back, "you won't get it under the wheels, it'll always be the same distance away. A trick. You push waggons all across the country and back, around the earth and back, waggons are

149

pushed, that's all. There and back, there and back, names, names, nothing else. New waggons are coupled and you uncouple the old ones. And when it turns dark, you start shooting. And all your borders are called the front. Names, nothing else, none of them hits the black of the bullseye. And I'm supposed to help you? No, I won't help you anymore. I've travelled this route long enough, there and back, there and back, the whole thing is a swindle, a waiting game, a way of filling in time for people who are bored, not for me. I want to get to where the journey is headed. Late by three minutes – we can make that up. Late by a whole life, do you hear, that's more serious."

"Hallo," the station master shouted, shocked, "where are you running off to?" With the signal in his hand, he ran behind the other man with long strides.

"Where are we travelling to?" the engine driver shouted back and doubled his speed. "Do you know where we're actually travelling to?"

Again he tried to get behind the line of the headlights, where the place they were heading was hidden.

"Stop!" the stationmaster shouted. "Stop where you are, at once! Where are you running to?"

"Where are we travelling to?"

"God in Heaven," the stationmaster panted, shocked.

"Yes," the engine driver laughed, stopping and smiling, "you see, that's what I thought too. That's why I got out. You get there quicker on foot, I think. We have to find a new route, we have to build a new route, an unfamiliar route, one which no-one has travelled before, the route without a terminus, the route to where we're heading."

"Oh," the stationmaster shouted in horror, grabbing him by the sleeve, shaking him back and forth and hitting him on his skinny shoulders with the signal to calm him.

"Come to your senses!"

"*You* come to *your* senses," the engine driver repeated aggressively, as if there was no possibility at all that his superior the stationmaster was in his right senses or even anywhere near his right senses. "Where are we travelling to?"

"Northeast," the stationmaster said, exhausted, "to the front." And he gave the name of a little town, a long, serious name which he mispronounced.

The engine driver shook his head. He had absolutely no memory of it. He had cast off all his memories like false teachings, all these old memories of names and signals, of things which lay within the light, within the circle cast by the headlights. And he had taken the great forgetting upon himself like a completely new memory.

"It's important," the stationmaster shouted indignantly, "it's hugely important, do you hear? Weapons, weapons, weapons! Weapons to the front, you'll pay with your head!"

But the other man didn't move from the spot, shaking his head as if it wasn't firmly attached at all, as if he didn't mind paying with his head as long as he didn't pay with his heart. In his sad condition, it was completely impossible to explain to him how important twenty heavy guns and three minutes were in this situation, because he no longer believed in this situation.

"Cleared for departure!" the stationmaster shouted, beside himself, lifted the signal and hit the engine driver on the forehead with it. "Cleared for departure! Help, help me!"

He raged and stamped his feet. "Help me!" He was shouting as loudly as if the little engine driver had control of at least one heavy gun, and was determined in the next second to shoot him onto the moon with it, where it was very lonely, where there were no names and no signals and you got time to think. And that was about the worst of all things an official could imagine. No timetable and no whistle in the top left-hand pocket, no regulations. Anything but the moon, for God's sake, anything but the moon! The stationmaster was shouting like a madman. The engine driver didn't move.

People came running from the station buildings. They were shouting too, and moving their arms agitatedly.

"Come on!" the stationmaster urged. "I won't tell on you if you come now."

"You can only tell what you know," the other man answered, unmoved.

"I'll pretend that nothing happened," the stationmaster declared, exhausted.

"That's what you've always pretended," the engine driver said. He wanted to say more, but they had already grabbed him and were dragging him back angrily towards the engine. They fired questions at him and tore his cap from his head.

"Gone off your rocker, have you?"

"Yes," he replied, "gone in another direction," and he managed to pick up his cap again. He stopped and dusted it off. They threatened him and pushed him in the back. Not knowing what to do next, they stood in a half-circle around the engine.

The stoker bent far out over the tracks. He was laughing quite loudly.

"Police!" the stationmaster raged, "inform the police. At once!"

"A major operation," the engine driver said. The stoker laughed more loudly.

"Railway security! Where are the duty policemen?" the stationmaster panted.

"Cannot be located."

The stoker's laughter cracked. The engine driver joined in cheerfully.

"They'll shoot you, they'll stop you along your route and shoot you in open country."

Again they raised their fists against him.

"All your routes are open," he said. "Didn't we arrive on an open route and don't we have to leave again on an open route?" The stoker fell silent.

"All your routes are open," the engine driver stammered, opening his eyes wide, letting his arms hang down and staring into the distance beyond them.

The stationmaster pulled down his tunic to straighten it. "Fortunately there are handcuffs, there are green vans with barred windows and walls with barbed wire." His voice was trembling solemnly. "There are gallows and there is a scaffold, there are regulations and –"

"There's a Hell," Ellen shouted threateningly across the roof of the third waggon, "and there are engine drivers who don't know where the train is going! A sealed envelope, that's all. Don't accept that! Don't depart, don't depart until you know!"

She jumped down. As if something was hunting them, the duty policemen raced after her. The train stood in silence.

"Don't depart, don't depart, don't depart until you know! Think, don't depart!" The voice was becoming weaker, and the policemen's shouting was being lost in the fog too.

Confused, the engine driver blinked into the headlights. Think, about what? What don't I know? The direction? "Northeast," he stammered reluctantly. Play blind man's buff, turn around, that's your compass. A white handkerchief over your eyes.

The face turned pale. The rails gleamed icily.

The regulations, my God, the regulations. Your conscience, your God, your conscience. You have to build a new route, you have to find your own regulations. You have to lay better rails. Get to where you're heading, get to where you're heading, think, don't depart – where you're heading!

The voice fell silent.

"Excuse me," the engine driver said, looking around the circle, "excuse me, I'm sorry, just what was I doing? Are we very late?" And he gave the name of a little town, a long and serious name which he mispronounced.

"That's what I thought." The stationmaster was angry. "I suppose you've been drinking. Get in now and get going. And don't ever think again about where you're heading. By the way, you haven't heard the last of this."

Silently, the engine driver climbed back onto his seat.

"In love?" the stoker asked. "Who was the girl?"

"Never seen her before."

The stationmaster lifted the signal.

Once again a black swift shadow slipped into the light of the headlights.

Where we're heading, where we're heading!

Ellen jumped to the side of the track, and leapt over it just in front of the departing train.

The policeman staggered and stopped. The departing train gave Ellen a lead on them.

The stationmaster wiped the sweat from his forehead. The police bit their lips until blood came, counted the waggons, miscounted and reached for their rubber truncheons.

A heavy gun whose barrel was poking cheekily over the edge of the last waggon took a bead on the anger in their eyes and was frightened. It would have liked to bend the silly, young barrel down to protect it from the policemen's gaze. But that did not lie within its power.

Fog enclosed them. The engine driver pushed his cap lower over his face. The train raced into the night.

The signal dropped. It wanted to say: The train has passed. But it wanted to say a lot more: Run, run, run! Run, all of you. No wheel nor propeller, no train nor even aeroplane will catch up to the secret. Those who are called are tender burning feet, your feet, your own feet, your reluctant feet. Run, run, run, till you're out of breath, it's an order. Away from yourselves, into yourselves. The train has passed. Run, Ellen, run, they're behind you.

A street urchin was playing in the coalyard.

Run too, you street urchins, and run, you policemen. The tracks are free; free to be jumped over. Hear how they're singing: Jump over us, jump over us! They demand that you do. Run, you policemen, catch up to the secret! Take off your caps and drop them without a second thought, you won't catch the secret as you catch birds. Catch up to the secret! Run blindly, run with outstretched arms, run as children run after their mother. Catch up to the secret.

Left or right, left or right? Separate in order to encompass, separate in order to embrace! Only don't forget why you separated. Don't lose yourselves.

The signal trembled gently for another moment and fell silent. The railway embankment stretched out endlessly.

Ellen was running. Behind Ellen the two policemen were running. And behind the two policemen a street urchin was running who didn't know exactly what was going on. Around the woodpile, straight through the shed, across the footbridge.

He knew exactly that he didn't know exactly. He had always known that it was difficult to catch his breath, that woodpiles are more than woodpiles and a railway square more than a railway square. That it was important to be weary before the night came. Run now, run, they're behind you! Keep your lead, what is a lead? Cursed mercy, meaningless mercy. Left or right? Neither one, mercy without a result.

Ellen was running, she was running like a deposed, beaten king, her blind followers at her back: these poor people, who like all pursuers became the followers of the pursued.

Smoke, there was a smell of smoke, of fires lit on endless steppes after the potato harvest, of a lost glow. Uncatchable, trucks and hearses had turned around the final corner. Neither Georg nor the grandmother waved back.

Ellen was running and the two men were running and the urchin was running. And they were all running together after the secret, after this flood which had receded.

Come after me, come after me. For a woodpile is more than a woodpile.

Twilight lay in wait silently, sitting on their shoulders like an unfamiliar rider and urging them on. Run, run, run, make use of the long break. Make use of the fast life. Interregnum between coming and going. Don't build a fortress in between!

Run, Ellen, run, someone is leading the race. The count was finished long ago. Whoever is pursued leads the race. One, two, three, four, five, six, seven, you're allowed to be It. Drag them along with you, drag them along, the chain of pursuers! Straight across, No Entry, straight across yourself.

A watchman's booth – up the steps – a chicken coop. Jump, jump, shadows fall. Lanterns in the way. Jump over, it's nothing. Dark lanterns, a brighter dark, God is dimming His light, you can't endure Him. Can you endure yourselves?

Go on, go on now! Up the barriers, down the barriers, drums, drums, filled with fuel. Bump into the drums, how powerful the sound is! The fuel is gone, leaked out, used up. Swindling, trickery, everything that's empty sounds powerful, the drums are rolling far behind you.

Do you hear the noise? The lead is shrinking. An empty waggon, through it, through it. Do you hear them whistling? Poor pursuers. Drag them along with you, behind, to where you're heading. The lead is growing.

Shouting, groping, shouting. They're running in circles. They stumble, they fall, they stay behind. They stand still.

Ellen hesitated, she turned around. Compassion came over her, an unfamiliar compassion with her pursuers, who had lost their way. The signal fell. For whom? No-one was leading anymore, no-one was being pursued, no-one was on the road, no-one was heading anywhere. No, no, that can't be, the chain isn't allowed to break. She breathed in deeply.

It was a long, shrill and wild whistle, a whistle on five fingers. Longer than the Milky Way and shorter than the last breath of all. It startled the railway watchman's chickens. A few boards fell off the woodpile. The uncoupled waggons on the side tracks stood even stiller. Ellen whistled to her pursuers. Stop, listen, hold your breath.

The policeman under the bare poplar lifted his face to the fog. There, over there, the watchman's booth, up the steps, you're not there anymore. Shed full of tools, aren't you a tool, an unfamiliar tool among the hammers, among the pliers, among the drills, you're not there either.

The policeman was freezing, while the sweat ran from his forehead. His fingers were stiff with excitement. He was still a very young policeman, inexperienced in the procedures and not at all sure of himself. And although he had learned how to knock people over with a single movement and force them onto their knees, he still hadn't learned how to be knocked over and forced onto his knees. And although he had learned how to shoot and to duck when the others were shooting, he still hadn't learned how to be shot or even to be alone just a little.

He was running, but his boots were too tight. He was moving very uncertainly.

Twice more the whistle sounded from the twilight. More threatening than his colonel's order, more enticing than his beloved's wish and much more mocking than the mockery of the street urchins on his beat. While he ran, the blood rose to the young policeman's head. The last means of getting to where he was heading: Stop, listen, hold your breath!

Nothing moved. The rails lay in wait in the shadow of the signals. Doubt enveloped him like a hair shirt. Wasn't it ridiculous to attack the nothingness?

What else do you people attack, besides the nothingness? – the poplars on the embankment whispered.

Angry and lonely, the policeman moved forward. His eagerness was growing. And then, he thought, and then, when I've got it, got something, got someone, the shadow in the light, then I'll be praised, then I'll become indispensable to this world, then I won't have to go to the front, then I won't be allowed to die, then there'll be no shadow in the light but my own anymore.

Cursed fog, pushing itself forward like a forgotten backdrop, lying like thin milk between the undecided people. Uneasily, the moon shifted among the clouds. The young policeman ran with his tongue out, his head pushed forward at an angle and his nose pointing to the ground like a dog tracking a scent. The track, the track, along the rails. As if there weren't more tracks than rails, tracks which crossed, tracks which combined, more tracks than rails and no-one to switch the points, that was why.

But then, when I've got it, the scent of the shadows, everything will come right. "Stop or I'll shoot, stop, stop or I'll shoot! Stop, or I'll have to shoot!" His voice cracked. Ellen was right in front of him. He stretched out his arms, but his arms were too short. Like a dancing bear, he remained behind the shadow. "Stop or I'll shoot!" But he didn't shoot. Once more he threw back his head, as if he was calling out to a comrade.

A woman walked slowly across the eastern footbridge. Three sleepers further on a bird flew into the air. The policeman prepared to jump, jumped and grabbed at emptiness. Dizziness overcame him. Dull and blue, the lights of the station shimmered in the distance. He was trembling with rage. He threw himself onto the ground, jumped up again and turned around despairingly on his own axis like his mother, the earth. He stamped his foot, hit out with his arms and stood still at last. He lifted himself onto the tips of his toes, his boots grated on the bare ground, new boots, gleaming boots, he really was still a very young policeman. "Is there someone here?" his voice said, the voice of a boy. He felt for a cigarette. Red flared. Who goes there? Qui vive? An old question, a ridiculous question. You yourself, are you no-one?

Ellen didn't move, her eyes flashed green underneath the waggon. Red and green, red and green, the signal for the last train. She drew her knees up to her chin. The policeman was very near. It was tempting to put her hand through the spokes and tear the boot from his foot.

"Is there someone here?"

It was tempting to throw back his question and to comfort him. Yes, yes, yes, be quiet, dear man.

It began to rain suddenly. The policeman was freezing. "If there's someone here," he said loudly, "I order him – I order him – –" he interrupted himself, "I ask him –" He broke off.

From a long way off he heard the shouting of his comrades. Back and forth, back and forth, ordered to find, yes, ordered to search, no. It was like playing "The emperor sends out soldiers" when he was a boy – don't send me, please don't send me!

"Who goes there?" the boy whispered, agitatedly and for the last time, and then: "You see, I can wait, oh yes, I can wait for a long time. We had a lot of exercises in the last few days, and I'm tired. In three days I'm going to the front. To the place where the horizon is set fast. I can wait for three days, three days –" His shoulders lifted; it was good that none of his comrades was nearby. No-one saw you, no-one heard you, no-one, no-one – – run, be a hero, catch the shadow in the light and take it to the guardroom. It's a long way in front of you, why are you wasting time? Wait till I've got you, shadow in the light, whistle in the silence, mockery in the night!

Out of breath, the policeman stumbled across the dead tracks. Anger shook him, pleasant anger, strong anger. His cigarette fell to the ground, he trod it into shreds. As if dogs were on his scent, he rushed forward.

Ellen stretched her head out from underneath the waggon and followed him with her eyes. He was running blindly, his arms were flailing, his cloth helmet wasn't sitting very securely. The insignia on his back gleamed defensively. Ellen crawled onto the pathway. Crouched to spring, she remained on the damp ground. Run, they haven't discovered you, run in the other direction, quick, run home. Through beneath the footbridge, towards the street, and there's a place, you know, where there's a break in the embankment. Disappear before they find you! But besides that there was another voice, which was as hard to hear as it was hard to ignore. And then the first one again: Stay, turn around, stay, you're running in the wrong direction!

Ellen was following the policeman. Fleetingly, her feet touched the wooden sleepers. As if across the sods in a ploughed field, she jumped from one to another. And with every jump she overcame the tormenting stiffness of her sleeping limbs and with every jump she jumped over herself. Like a black rebellious flag, her hair was blown around in the encroaching fog.

The young policeman was running in front of her. He had taken his helmet from his head and he was running quickly. For any price, for God's sake, for everything in the world. Shadow in the light, woe betide you! Noiselessly, Ellen stuck to his heels.

The policeman lengthened his stride, his eyes burned restlessly into the black coolness. There, over there, nowhere. His glances were like little captured birds, leapt from dark to dark, seemed to strike glass and turned themselves hostilely towards him. His head jerked uneasily in all directions. Threats leapt like bubbles from the foam on his lips and burst in the damp air. His anger grew. His feet hurt. His shirt was sticking to him and his collar was askew. Needle-pricks rained from the sky, his own back attacked him from behind. A few more strides and he had lost the game. Reporting as ordered, sir! Nothing, nothing at all. It's raining, fog is closing in, the night is coming.

Wasn't someone calling there? Or was he dreaming after all? Nothing, there was nothing to dream about. The platform over there, the comrades, the guardroom. His head dropped forward, bereft of courage. Three more strides, two more, a half. The others were leaning under the tin roof at the exit.

"Captured her?"

"Caught her?"

"Nothing," the policeman shouted angrily, "nothing, nothing, nothing."

A strange hand placed itself over his mouth. A strange hand grabbed for his collar. "Nothing," he stammered in confusion.

"Only me," Ellen said, and let herself be dragged unresistingly to the guardroom.

Past the stern faces of the unfeeling, past eyes which looked like damp spots in grey walls, past piles of things, blunt darts which bounced off. Through passageways, through the bodies of swollen snakes, twisted reluctantly under black lights, and across strange sleepers as across poison teeth.

The policemen's fever demanded resistance, demanded cursing and begging, but Ellen complied, let herself be led unquestioning through the questionable, as if it was only a matter of trying an old step in a new dance. It seemed to the policemen as if they too were dancing for the first time in these passageways. The guardroom was at ground level, was in a heavy half-sleep like all guardrooms, dreaming evil dreams, and unable to be woken. The guardroom guarded its own sleep, watched jealously over its heavy dreams and willingly let the miasma of evil settle upon it.

Shredded by drawing pins, the map was stuck to the wall between the locked windows. Shredded everywhere: in the blue abysses of the oceans, the shimmering gleam of the plain, the dark swirling of the settlements, the image of their world was shredded. For the names of the cities have turned into the names of the battles, coast or front, city or battle, boot or wing, who thinks they can tell them apart?

All the shutters were locked, no light was allowed to escape. The unauthorised could find comfort in this inconsolable bleakness. War, there was a war on.

Poor guardroom. Blue smoke merged with the yellow light of the lamps to create the virulent green of the uniforms. Ellen narrowed her eyes in surprise. A conference was in progress. The men fell silent. Behind the closed shutters you could hear, like something gone forever, the swift steps of people passing by.

"What have you brought us?" The one in the middle straightened up.

The policeman stood bolt upright. He threw back his head, opened his mouth and failed to produce a single word.

"Your report?" the colonel repeated impatiently. "We have no time to lose."

"Sir!" the young policeman said, "we have much more to lose." He said it in a high and very uncertain voice. There were deep circles under his eyes.

The second one jumped into the breach. "Sir! There was a child among the weapons."

"Sir!" the boy interrupted him, "there are children among the weapons everywhere."

"The munitions train almost stayed behind," the second one called out angrily, "the engine driver forgot the direction of the journey."

"Sir!" the boy said, "none of us knows the direction of the journey."

The colonel took his glasses from his eyes, fiddled with them and put them back on.

Ellen was standing calmly among the green uniforms. Little drops flowed from her hair down her shoulders onto the dusty floor.

"It's raining," she said into the silence.

"Everything in the proper order," the colonel remarked sharply and moistened his lips.

"Sir!" the second policeman shouted, "there was a shadow in the light."

"Sir!" the boy said quietly, "it's always your own."

"We caught it," the second one called out, out of breath.

"Catch hold of *yourself* !" the colonel shouted. He pressed the palms of his hands against the edge of the desk.

The men shuffled their feet uneasily. One of them laughed out loud. Storm drove drops at an angle against the locked shutters, like a foreign army.

Open up, open up, open up to us!

"Shut the door," the colonel told the two policemen, "the draft is ice-cold."

"Sir!" the boy said stiffly, "I'd prefer to leave it open. I don't want to pretend to myself anymore. In three days I'm going to the front."

"Take him away," the colonel said, "at once."

"The draft is ice-cold," Ellen repeated.

"Silence," the colonel shouted, "you're not at home now."

"Sir!" the boy whispered, exhausted, "none of us is at home now –" They had grabbed him.

"Let him say what he was going to say!"

"If he's started to think," the boy said calmly.

"Otherwise you have nothing to report?"

"Nothing." He relaxed his arms. "Nothing," he repeated, drained of strength.

"Everything," Ellen said, and her voice flew ahead of him down the black passageways. But she didn't follow him with her eyes.

The lamp swayed. Ellen bent and picked up her scarf, which had slid to the floor.

"Put her in the middle."

The floor trembled.

"What's your name?"

Ellen gave no answer.

"Your name?"

She shrugged her shoulders.

"Where do you live?"

Ellen didn't move.

"Religion – Age – Familial status?"

She made the fastening tighter. You could hear the policemen breathing, otherwise it was quiet.

"Born?"

"Yes," Ellen said.

One of the men boxed her ears. Ellen looked up at him in astonishment. He had a black moustache and an anxious face.

"What are your parents' names?"

Ellen pressed her lips together more firmly.

"Record of interview," the colonel said wildly. "Take it all down!" One of the men laughed. It was the same one who had laughed before.

"Quiet," the colonel shouted, "don't interrupt!"

His fingers were drumming rhythmically and sharply on the wooden barrier.

"What's your name, where do you live, how old are you and why aren't you answering me?"

"You're asking the wrong things," Ellen said.

"Girl," the colonel said, panting, "do you know what's waiting for you?" His glasses had misted up. His forehead was glowing. He pushed open the barrier.

"Heaven or Hell," Ellen said, "and a new name."

"Should I write?" the clerk asked.

"You should write," the colonel shouted. "Write everything up."

"He's writing it down," Ellen said quickly, "don't write, don't write, you have to let it grow."

"Paper is stony ground," the clerk said, shocked, and squinting as he stared around him, "truly, I've made too many notes, my whole life long I've made too many notes." His brow furrowed. "I drew my conclusions from what I observed, and my conclusions collapsed. I let nothing grow, I suppressed nothing. I had no ideas, or at least I abandoned them. First I captured butterflies and pinned them down, and later I did that with everything else." He grabbed the pen and threw it from him. The ink liberated itself and splashed across the floor, dark blue tears dried up and turned black. "I'm sorry, I don't want to write anything up anymore, no, I won't write anything down anymore." The clerk's face was glowing. Dizziness rose to his temples. "Water," he said, crying as he laughed, "water!"

"Give him something to drink," the colonel said. "Give him something to drink," he shouted.

"Water," the clerk smiled, comforted. "Water is transparent like invisible ink. At the due time, everything will become visible."

"Yes," Ellen said.

"What's your name?" the colonel shouted. "Where do you live?"

"One must go in search of oneself," the clerk whispered.

"Where's your home?" a fat policeman said, bending down to her.

"The place where I lived," Ellen said, "has never been my home."

"So where's your home?" the policeman repeated.

"Where your home is," Ellen said.

"But where is our home?" the colonel shouted, beside himself.

"Now you're asking the right things," Ellen said quietly.

The colonel closed his eyes. When he removed his hand from his eyelids, the light in the guardroom was paler. The barrier was dancing before his eyes. I could give an order now, he thought despairingly, for this barrier to disappear.

This dancing barrier between the ones who are detained and the ones who are doomed, between the ones who break in and the ones who are breaking down, this swaying barrier between the robber and the cop.

"Where is our home?" the fat policeman repeated.

"Be quiet!" the colonel shouted. "Speak when you're asked a question."

164

The rain was still playing on the closed shutters. "Anyone who wants to ask has already been asked for," the clerk said fearlessly, and overturned the inkwell.

Ellen stood quite still.

"Your name!" the colonel said and moved threateningly towards her. "Who are you?"

"Names are snares for the feet," the clerk whispered, "traps in the wet grass. What are you searching for in the dark garden? I'm searching for myself. Stay where you are, you're searching in vain. What's your name? Somehow –"

"Be quiet, that's enough," the colonel shouted, putting both hands over his ears, "it's enough, it's enough!"

"No, colonel," the clerk said, "it's not enough. I was given the name Franz. What's my name? Franz. But what does my name mean, who am I, what do I mean? A hundred and one. Why don't you all ask more questions? You're caught in the snares for your feet, do you hear, there's laughter behind you! All your names mean that you need help. Tear yourselves loose, tear until your feet bleed, run, keep searching!" The clerk was raging. He had swung himself up onto the table and was stretching out his arms. The policemen stood as if they were awaiting his more enlightening order.

"Enough," the colonel laughed, motionless. He took three steps and stood in front of Ellen. "What's your name, for the last time, who are you?"

The door was torn open.

"My scarf is sky-blue," Ellen said, "and I long to be away from here."

Cold rushed like a foreign dancer into the hot guardroom. Defend yourself! Resistance of dragging feet, oh you unequal pairs, and the sound of fists striking, the Devil's applause. "Bibi," Ellen called out. Her lips were trembling. Before she could catch hold of herself, a wet, bloody bundle landed at her feet.

"What's your name, for the last time?"

"Ellen," Bibi called out, "Ellen, help me!"

"Her name's Ellen," the clerk said.

"Quiet," Ellen said, "just be quiet, Bibi." She helped her up, pulled off her own scarf and wiped the blood from the smaller girl's face. The man in the doorway was rocking back and forth with anger. As he was about to throw himself onto them, he noticed the colonel and stood still. The colonel didn't move.

"Ellen," Bibi said, "I didn't go with the others. They'll shoot us, that's what Kurt said, and by next summer the cherry trees will be growing over it. That's what Kurt said, and all the time we were in the camp that's all he said. Until it was too much for me."

"Yes," Ellen said.

The policemen moved back a little towards the wall. The two girls remained in the middle of the raw dusty floorboards. "Go on," Ellen said.

"It's too much for me," the man at the door bellowed.

"It's a lot more," Ellen said.

"Georg distracted them," Bibi whispered, "he helped me. On the last day, when we were supposed to be loaded –"

"Shut the door," the colonel called out over the tops of their heads.

"You made it!" Ellen said.

"Yes. I don't know myself anymore how. But Kurt said, they'll shoot us and the cherry trees will be growing over it. And you know, Ellen, I'd still like to go dancing, I don't want to be a cherry tree."

"Bibi," Ellen said, "there are dancing cherry trees too, you can believe me."

The smaller girl lifted her head towards the pale, swaying lamp. "Six weeks I was in hiding and now –"

"Bibi," Ellen said, "one, two, three – coming, ready or not! Do you remember, that time on the quay?"

"Yes." Bibi smiled for a second.

The man at the door moved as if he was about to jump at them. Bibi flinched, cried out, and began to cry again.

The colonel shook his head imperceptibly. The man at the door stood still.

"But someone reported me, Ellen, and they found me. And they dragged me out from under the bed and down the stairs. There, he was the one, the policeman –"

"The policeman is asleep," Ellen said contemptuously. "He's missing, he's disappeared without trace, but he doesn't know it. Poor policeman, he finds everyone else, only he can't find himself. Missing persons, nothing but missing persons!"

Bibi closed her eyes and, shaking with fear, pressed her head against Ellen's shoulder. A threatening murmur arose among the policemen.

"Prisoners," Ellen said, "poor prisoners. They can't find themselves, they're preoccupied by themselves, their mortal enemy has occupied them. They're in league with the Devil, but they don't realise it, their wings are broken." She drew breath. "Factories which make secret weapons, but they can't enter, they hang on the gates and shake them. Their wings are broken!"

"We have to help them," Ellen said, "we'll liberate them."

"Liberate," Bibi repeated, lifting her head. "Ellen, how do you think you can do that? – Ellen," she looked around in surprise. "Ellen, what are you here for?"

"I've been asking that long enough," the colonel complained, "and I'll have had enough of it very soon."

"Can't you explain it?" Bibi asked.

"Explain?" Ellen called out unwillingly, stroking her hair back from her forehead. "How much of it all can someone explain?" Anxiously, the smaller girl grabbed her arm. Ellen tore herself loose. A glow fell from her face into the low-ceilinged guardroom. "Why did you all break your wings and exchange them for boots? You have to cross the border barefoot, you can't occupy it, this country. Whoever yields will gain the victory. The sky is on the move," she said, "but you're holding it up. There are too many flagpoles in the air. Your wings are broken."

"Wings," the colonel said, "which wings are we talking about here?"

"Always about the same ones," Ellen said, "all the troops are at the borders. The troops should be withdrawn from the edges, there's no-one in the middle."

"Are you talking about military secrets?" the colonel said mockingly.

"Military secrets," Ellen laughed, "no, there are secrets and there's the military, but military secrets, there's no such thing."

"We'll find proof against you," the colonel declared.

"The fire is hungry," Ellen replied calmly.

The glow in the little iron oven crackled as it settled down.

"The tea is overflowing," the fat policeman shouted, shocked.

"Everything is overflowing, except for your eyes. Be on your guard, we learned in the last lesson, for the Devil is as a roaring lion."

"Speak in the proper order," the colonel said threateningly.

"In the middle nothing's in the proper order," Ellen answered, "in the middle everything's at once."

"And I'm asking you now for the last time: Do you have parents, do you have brothers or sisters and who are you living with? How were you able to get onto a munitions train? What came first?"

"Wings," Ellen said, "and the voice upon the waters, lots of brothers and sisters and I'm living with all of them."

"Yes," Bibi said absently, "that's true, once we fled to Egypt together too."

"To Egypt?" the colonel repeated. "But the train you wanted to take didn't go to Egypt."

"Names," Ellen said dismissively, "Egypt or Poland. I wanted to get to the bottom of it, I wanted to go across the border, to the place where Georg is, Herbert, Hanna and Ruth, following my grandmother –"

"Where is your grandmother?"

"Into the middle," Ellen said, not letting herself be interrupted.

"That's why I got onto the train."

"Following the dead people?" the colonel said.

"Away from the dead people," Ellen called out angrily, "away from the grey buffalo, away from the dreaming people. Names and address, that can't possibly be all of it!"

"Take me with you," Bibi said, clinging onto her, "please take me with you!" Tears ran down her face.

A whispering arose among the policemen, a growing, imploring murmur, and it was as if the wind had come across the mountains, and it was as if the tide was coming across the grey sand. The virulent green uniforms swayed slightly.

"I can't take you with me," Ellen said, looking thoughtfully at the smaller girl, "but I've got a better idea: Let me, for you."

Again the wind moved across the crowns of invisible hills, again the tide washed the gold out of the sand.

"Let me, for you!" Ellen repeated impatiently.

"No," Bibi said, rubbing the tears from her eyes with her fists and stretching out both her arms, as if she was just waking up, "no, I want to go, I want to go alone. To the place where Kurt is and the buffalo have faces." She smoothed down her coat and lifted her eyebrows impatiently. "Follow me, if you want!"

Lights leapt in a circle.

"Take me with you," the policeman at the door jeered.

"Take him with you," Ellen said, "take him with you a little way, accompany him to your train!"

"Come," Bibi said to the policeman.

"Go with her," the colonel called out, "go!"

There was a rustling in the walls. The bricks behind the whitewash were knocking against each other. The movement among the policemen gathered in the direction of the open door, as if they were being forced against their will across secret borders, following the captured child.

Silent and shocked, Ellen stood under the pale lamp. Using his back, the colonel blocked the door. "You all have the possibility of going to the front." He wiped the sweat from his forehead. "Death is open to all of us."

"No," Ellen shouted. "Life is open and none of you is allowed to die before you're born!" She jumped onto the nearest armchair. "Where's the middle? Where's the middle? Do you travel on weapons trains or do you travel in an aeroplane, do you travel for a year or do you travel for a hundred years?" She threw her hair back from her forehead and considered. "Everyone travels differently and finally you all have to go. Listen to where the call is, that's where you're called to. It's calling in your middle. Free yourselves!" She jumped off the armchair. "Free yourselves, free yourselves!"

"It's going too far," the colonel said.

He couldn't understand how it had come to this. Against all precedent, a quick and extraordinary conference was running quickly and extraordinarily. In a few rapid sentences it was jumping over the drawing pins on the map. The burst seams on the brightly-coloured tunic were demanding a lighter-coloured thread. A feverish policeman pushed a strange child through the door and all the conclusions which had been drawn so far proved to be false statements. The guardroom was threatening to wake up.

What was left for him to do? He had to take action now, quick, composed and well-considered. Strange voices were rising among the men again.

"Quiet," the colonel said calmly, "quiet now. Gather all your wits. Don't look to the left or to the right, or up or down. Don't ask where you come from, and don't ask where you're going to, because it goes too far." The men were silent. "Hear and see," the colonel said, "but don't listen and don't look, you don't have time for that. Be satisfied with names and address, do you hear, that's enough. Have you forgotten how much it means to be registered in the proper way? Don't you all know how good it feels to walk in your ranks and files? Don't dream, or you'll speak in your dreams. Catch and hold and sing in between times, and when it turns dark, then sing more loudly. Don't think that one man is one man, remember that many men are many men, it reassures you. Catch the saboteurs when the nights are bright, don't look too much at the moon! The man in the moon remains alone, the man in the moon carries explosives on his back. I'm sorry, we don't have the power to detain him.

But we do have the power to forget him. Anyone who has a pocket mirror doesn't need a mirror in the sky. All faces look the same."

"As who?" the clerk whispered, shocked.

"I didn't ask you," the colonel said, "and it's not for you to ask me. Questions get in the way of duty."

"Yes," Ellen said.

"Now as to you, your cup is overflowing. Accused of sabotage by questions and by undesirable statements, suspected of the strange fever and suspected of having said nothing about the greatest part."

"Yes," Ellen said.

The colonel paid no attention to her. Once again he turned towards the policemen. "It's your fault. There were important things to discuss and I was authorised to take you into my confidence. Instead of that you took me into your confidence and the things were delayed. I came here for a fleeting inspection, prompted by a vague suspicion of all these widely scattered, ground-level guardrooms. And what do I find here?" He shoved the armchair back and closed the barrier, pushed up his cuffs and looked at the clock. It was getting late.

Sir, it's raining, fog is closing in, the night is coming.

The policemen stood in silence, as if they were awaiting the old dark orders. Two of the most reliable ones, with the danger of harmlessness beneath their brows, were designated as sentries for the remainder of the night. Towards morning, Ellen was to be taken to the secret police. Without troubling to look at her again, the colonel left the guardroom with the rest of the men, tearing a leaf from the calendar angrily as he passed. Beneath the number on the next leaf stood: "St Nicholas's Day."

That's how it became apparent that this evening too was an evening before. The door closed. Ellen remained alone with the two policemen. One on the left, one on the right. Her hands on her knees, she sat between them, only glancing up at them fleetingly from time to time and then trying to look just as serious and just as much at a loss as they did, without quite managing it.

The difference was: Ellen knew that there would be snow later in the night, and the policemen didn't know.

An evening before. What is an evening before? Doesn't it lie like one of those braided-looking pastries between the windows of your apartment? But don't leave it lying there. Expect the unexpected. Don't expect that your clocks will run precisely to time and that your collars will sit in precisely the right way. Don't expect that it will become quiet outside behind the shutters when the storm eases. Expect that the singing will begin. Hear it! Not quickly, as soldiers sing who are ordered to be cheerful, not loudly, as girls sing who are driven to be sad, no, quite softly and a little hoarsely, as little children sing when fog is falling. Do you hear it? It's coming from far away. It's coming from the place where you came from. Too far, the colonel says. The colonel was mistaken. Silently, Ellen sat between the policemen. The policemen stared straight ahead.

Quick, cover your ears, before it's too late! You're allowed to hear, but not to listen, the colonel forbade it, to hear, not to listen, where's the border? You won't get across, you have to walk barefoot. Put your boots in the window, for tomorrow is St Nicholas's Day. Be happy, be happy! A name has fulfilled itself, a name has forgotten itself, a name has become a song for you. Listen to where there is singing, behind locked shutters, go in to yourselves, there's singing in your middle. The far is becoming near, put your boots in the window. Apples, nut and almond and a strange song, the colonel was mistaken.

Ellen sat as upright as a candle. The policemen squeezed their hands between their knees. The colonel was mistaken. You have to sing softly when it turns dark, more softly, much more softly, just as children sing behind locked shutters. What are they singing, what are they singing? Ellen shifted her long legs quietly. The policemen pretended that they hadn't heard anything. The clock ticked, trying to establish control, but it was in vain: the directives hung around the walls were growing less direct from minute to minute. The instructions were only whispering now and finally fell silent before the strange song. What is the singing saying, what is the singing saying? Push open the shutters!

The policemen pressed their boots down more firmly on the hard wooden floor. One of them stood up and sat down again, shocked. The other brushed his hand up his forehead. They began speaking and coughed loudly, but nothing could help anymore. Push open the shutters, what are you waiting for? Tear down the black-out screens and open the windows. Bend far out, of yourselves.

They bent over the windowsill. Their eyes were dazzled, so at first they couldn't make out anything. Chains rattled, children gave embarrassed laughs and a bishop's staff knocked against the damp plaster. The sky was covered. The man in the moon had disappeared. The man in the moon had climbed down to the earth. Don't look into the mirror too much. Do you all know that you're disguised? White coats, black horns and a song in between.

The snow is coming, for tomorrow is St Nicholas's Day,
We're all so happy, for the snow is coming
And tomorrow is St Nicholas's Day,
Put your boots in the window, the Devil will take them,
For tomorrow is St Nicholas's Day,
And he's bringing you all wings,
Wings, lovely wings,
Wings, lovely wings,
Wings for the storm,
Wings for sale!

What does the last line say? Wings for sale!

The policemen laughed with the full force of their lungs. A draft attacked the backs of their necks and tore them back and forth. The guardroom stood darkly, abandonment danced around the swaying barrier. The door was open. Ellen had disappeared. Blowing horrified blasts on their short whistles, the policemen rushed along the passageways, shook the sentry on the corner, crossed many streets and turned back again.

And while one of them was running up the stairs, the other bent out of the window and heard once more, from far in the distance, that high rebellious voice: Wings for sale!

Marvel Not At This

The apple rolled over the edge. Darkly and expectantly, the lift shaft smiled. There were many things which it valued. Accommodatingly, it concealed the decision between good and evil. Poor apple. Tasted and rotted. Tasted and never eaten up. It's Adam's and Eve's fault, the rottenness is getting worse. And what falls weighs more heavily than any meal at the high table.

Ellen cried out in shock and looked down. The apple had disappeared. A rotten apple, nothing more? The pails in her hands swung and their joints groaned. They were groaning under the weight of the rottenness and they were groaning under the weight of the secrets. And their groaning was like the beginning of a rebellion:

Are we not laden too heavily? Created to serve, but they have made us into serfs. Who gives you the right to degrade us? Who gives you the right to subject objects to the power of the generations?

And the pails swung threateningly in Ellen's cold horrified hands. Did they sense that they were overheard? That one of their tyrants forgot herself so far as to understand their language, one of those tyrants who when lifted above the world of objects abused their rule? It was as if the pails sensed this, their anger grew and they screeched loudly like little foreign prisoners being led to work, they danced and resisted and threw their loads from them: orange peels like suns fallen from the sky, tin cans which, torn open and robbed, nevertheless still possessed the greater power to gleam. And they threw all caution far over the edge.

Give blindly, beloved, the commandment says.

Like one hunted, Ellen ran down the steps, but nothing helped anymore, the pails were raging in her hands and they were raging in the name of all locked boxes, of all enclosed beauty, of all violated things. And Ellen knew that vengeance was very near.

We are a parable, and what more do you all want? Is that your power, to grab what you can't hold, and to conceal what you won't let go? Don't rummage too deeply in your cupboards and don't cling too tightly onto the eaves of your houses, because they'll break off. Maybe you should go onto the little balcony again, which is bursting from the grey wall like a forgotten adventure, water your flowers again, look along the river and leave everything behind you. Measure the depths with your hearts. It's too late now for everything else.

Ellen ran straight across the factory yard. Her hands were trembling. Hammers were still singing as they fell onto stone and their song was sinfully sad. It was the song without trust, the song which no-one wants to hear.

A foreman who was passing by laughed:

"You'll lose everything!"

Ellen stopped and said:

"I'd like to lose even more!"

But the foreman passed on.

In the distance, fighter planes droned and hummed as they climbed.

Oh, you've overtaken yourselves and stayed far behind, the pails jeered. – Everything has been calculated exactly, but the only thing which can save you now is what you didn't include in your calculations! You've exploited everything down to the last piece – where is it, that last piece? It has to be given back.

Churned up by shadows, the sun lay across the sand. Ellen dropped the pails, her hands were burning. Using a big broom, she swept straw and scraps into the corner of the yard. Where did you put it, the last piece, it has to be given back.

"Faster, Ellen, faster, time is getting away from us!"

Ellen threw back her head and put her hands in front of her mouth like a funnel.

"What did you say?"

High-pitched and lonely, her question climbed into the shreds of the sky.

The people in colourful fluttering clothes on the flat roof bent a long way over the black railings.

"Come up here, come up here at once, the heavy guns are over there! We have to get ready, then we can get away from here. You can dream your dreams to the end later! We want to go home. The major alarm is coming!" Like blind white gravel, their voices fell into the waiting depths.

Ellen leaned the broom against the wall again. "Where is your home? The major alarm is in all your dreams, but where is home?"

Again she heard the others calling angrily high above her. But who was calling her, who was calling her really? She listened intently. To the left and the right, the two little pails stood defiant and battered, in the name of all things, liberated from the last piece, filled with bright dust and hidden wisdom, holed and incredibly relaxed.

Marvel not at the clouds of smoke on your horizon, the horrors you gave birth to are coming back. Your compulsion to grab is grabbing for all of you now. Weren't you seeking a replacement for the irreplaceable?

"Faster, Ellen, faster!"

Again the pails groaned under her grip and resisted. Rust tore at her hands and made them bleed. Dizziness attacked her. Tall and implacable, the chimney reared up. The knocking on stone had fallen silent. The sky seemed paler. The little green wooden door which led from the yard into the cellar swung half-open in the spring wind.

"What do you want from me?" Ellen said, shocked.

An imploring silence fell upon the wide, well-trodden yard. Anxiously, the warehouse stood in the shadow of the wall. Filled with hope, the siren on the roof opposite made no sound.

"Maybe I know," Ellen murmured. She gripped the pails, pushed open the cellar door and stumbled down the steps. Damp dark enveloped her. The silence upon the yard remained deep and disbelieving. And the siren still made no sound.

But this cellar was very deep. Here too, people's caution fell into the unforeseen and was enveloped by it: They trusted the depths.

Suitcases and bundles, suitcases and bundles. Their last things, oh, their very last things, but can the last thing be tied up with cords? Can it be had and held? Can it be watched over and locked away like an illegitimate inheritance? Shouldn't it break out, well forth and overflow into the emptiness which is searching? "Who's there?" Ellen called out, shocked, bumped her head on a beam and stood still. The bundles had been torn apart, the suitcases had been cut to pieces. Helpless, exposed and torn away from itself, the secret refuge lay in the dust.

"God bless all thieves," Ellen said.

"What do you mean?" the darkness asked. It had wanted to say: Hands up, but it came out differently. The darkness had two voices, a deep one and an even deeper one, and both were mistrustful.

"Hard to explain," Ellen said anxiously, searching for matches.

"You're mocking us," the darkness said.

"No," Ellen said.

"I'll make a light," the darkness said, but it couldn't find any matches. Nothing against itself.

"Hands up!" it said, defenceless.

"I'd better be going," Ellen said.

The men took the safety-catches off their guns. A piece fell off the wall. At that moment, the siren screamed despairingly and breathlessly across the city.

"Alarm," Ellen said, "but it's not the major alarm. The major alarm is different, completely different, and you don't hear anything before you're hit. But there's no doubt about it when you're hit."

"God bless you!" the darkness said.

"I'm sorry," Ellen said, "but I have to go now."

"Stay here!"

"No," Ellen replied. "The shelter is on the other side, underneath the warehouse. It's just the luggage here."

"And us," the darkness grumbled. The screaming of the siren stopped suddenly, and everything was quiet.

"I know," Ellen called out bitterly, turning towards the door, "but I can't wait any longer! The others will be searching for me."

"Careful!" the darkness threatened.

"I'm sorry," Ellen said again, "I'd rather have opened my suitcase myself. And I'd have picked it up and turned it around and then I'd have said: Take, everyone take! Whoever wants! – But not here. On the roof in the sun." She paused for breath.

"It's easy for you to talk, little one," the men laughed, "and why would you have done that? Tell it to your grandmother, she might believe you!"

"Yes," Ellen said, "she'll believe me." She was probably speaking right into the barrels of the pistols. From the south you could hear the bombs hitting the ground. Quite rapidly. One after the other.

"Let me go," Ellen called out, "I won't tell anyone anything!"

"You won't get back across the yard!"

"It's my fault," she murmured, "because I didn't come back. Why didn't I open my suitcase myself, before it was opened? Why didn't I hand out all my things before? I wanted to open my suitcase myself, do you hear?"

"Just be quiet," the darkness said, "it's getting closer and closer!" The anti-aircraft guns roared like hunted wolves, the sound interspersed with the gentle, horrible, inexorable rolling of what was falling from the sky. Ellen cowered against the wall and buried her head in her lap.

How did it go again? You have to distinguish between what's rising and what's falling. But they hadn't distinguished. Seeds in the dark shoots which thought they were fruit in the sun.

It was coming even closer. "Ssst!" the darkness hissed.

"I didn't say anything!" Ellen complained.

"You can't hear yourself speak anymore!"

"You never heard yourselves!"

"You shouldn't give answers now, this isn't the right time!"

179

"Oh," Ellen called out, "when the time has passed, you'll give them again!"

"That's what we don't know yet!" the darkness groaned.

"That's what we need to know," Ellen whispered, pressing her fists to her eyes. The droning was all around them. It closed above them, opened once more and closed again.

"Good God!" the darkness shouted. "Damn it, why did you keep us here? By all that's holy, if it goes on like this, the Devil can take you!"

"You're contradicting yourselves," Ellen shouted into the tumult, "you're still contradicting yourselves! Why are you contradicting yourselves?"

"They're above us!" A pistol clattered onto the ground. Ellen straightened up, jumped over the untied bundles and was hurled back by a strange power, a stranger's peaked cap hit her on the head. Then everything was quiet.

"Air pressure," the darkness sighed, and after a while: "Thank God, they've gone past!"

"Past?" Ellen said. "Above another building, do you call that past?"

"Come here, little one," the darkness said propitiatingly, in its very deepest voice.

"They're coming again," Ellen said calmly, ignoring it.

"Are you loyal to them?" the men asked suspiciously. Ellen gave no answer. What does that mean: to be loyal to someone?

"Come here!" one of them said again.

"Leave her," the other one said and began searching feverishly for matches again, "we have to get away before the alarm is finished!"

"And when will we divide it up?"

"Once we're somewhere safe."

"When will you be somewhere safe?" Ellen laughed.

Immediately she sensed dully that someone was moving towards her, noiselessly and in need of help. She flinched, felt her way around the corner and ran with long strides up the passageway, a long, straight passageway.

"Stop!" Ellen heard the men close behind her.

Beseechingly, the little yard above the passageway stared into the pale sky. And before anyone could realise what was happening, the air was filled by a howling and yowling, buildings collapsed completely and unquestioningly as if they were falling to their knees, the Devils were singing canons and the walls were exploding so that you could look out.

Ellen and the men were hurled back into the passageway, got mixed up together, rolled further and lay still, stunned. Horror and trickling dust forced themselves into their faces.

Swept bare as a desert, the little yard stared into the blue sky. Black paper-scraps floated cheerfully across it. The great grey factory had dropped to its knees, beams and rubble were still falling. And where the warehouse had stood, the warehouse underneath which everyone else had sought shelter, a huge crater yawned in amazement.

Colourful, silky scraps fluttered upwards, scraps from the kind of light clothes which girls wear when the sun breaks through, water welled up out of the earth and turned dark red. On top of the shattered pipe, torn loose from all desire, lay an open hand. Stones were torn down into the abyss, two pails rattled as they fell over the edge of the crater. And their rattling was like the sound of trumpets.

When the two burglars came to themselves, they remained motionless. Each concealed his conscious life from the other like a public disgrace. Quiet! We've had a bad dream, but that doesn't mean we want you to wake us. For the day is even more implacable.

Then Ellen made a movement between them, turning around and pushing out her head in all directions. A soft incomprehensible groaning reached the men. This groaning contained reproach and a great desire, it seemed to be trying to say something. What was it trying to say?

Carefully, the two men straightened up. They began coughing, everything hurt. Sand and slime came from their mouths, but the horror remained like a lump in their throats. Neither of them dared to speak. Only Ellen was bold enough to groan into the heavy darkness. Dust was still trickling down onto them.

Suddenly it seemed important to the men to know what Ellen was trying to say, more important than anything else. They grabbed her shoulders and felt for her face. One of them searched for his handkerchief and found the matches. With trembling hands, he made a light. They were lying on the untied bundles, and they were even lying comfortably. Ellen grimaced. The other had searched for the matches and found his handkerchief. He spat on it and rubbed her face, distributing the dirt evenly.

"Grandmother, leave it!" Ellen said reluctantly.

"What's she saying?"

"She's saying: Leave it, grandmother!"

"What does she mean?"

"My ears are blocked, this wretched sand!"

"Wake up, baby!"

"Now she's groaning again."

"Leave her! After all, that's what she's saying."

"She means her grandmother."

"I don't know. Now she's completely quiet."

"It's your fault, you idiot!"

"Check whether she's breathing!"

Ellen's lips were half-open and trembling slightly. The man bent over her and put his ear close to her mouth. Ellen didn't move.

"She's dying," he said, shocked. "Heavens, she's dying!" The other one pushed him aside. "Hallo, baby, stay with us!" He jumped up and said: "We have to get her out into the air!"

"And the other stuff?"

"We'll fetch it later."

"Later? We'll take everything with us."

"I'm all confused, light another match!"

"Where's the passageway?"

"There!"

"No, it was here."

"Another match!"

"The passageway was here."

"No, it was over there."

"But I'm sure –"

"Quiet, it was over there!" With an effort, the older one felt his way across bundles and stones. Silence ensued. Then he announced suddenly: "You're right, you're right, it's near you." That sounded relieved. The young one didn't say anything.

"And what now?"

He still wasn't saying anything, the match went out. Ellen began groaning again and breathed out loudly. He rushed over to her. Again he put his ear to her lips and listened.

"You come too close to everything," Ellen said dazedly and pushed him away. "Too close," she repeated softly.

"She's alive!" the young one shouted.

"What do you want?" Ellen asked in astonishment. "What do you want from me?"

"Light," the young one said and struck a third match.

"Ask her why God should bless us," the old one interrupted mockingly. It was only now he realised that the passageway had disappeared. "Why should God bless us?" he bellowed out of the darkness.

"You're using up too much air," the young one complained.

"Who are you?" Ellen asked in astonishment.

"Not your grandmother," the young one replied slowly.

"No," Ellen said.

"Nice woman, your grandmother?" the young one enquired.

"More," she said.

"Why should God bless us?" the old one shouted.

Ellen tried to stand up and fell back again. The young one had found a candle and placed it on a stone. Suddenly despair welled up in him too. He wanted to be gentle with Ellen, wanted to prepare her slowly, wanted to approach her as cautiously as something he was planning to steal, but he felt that it was beyond him. "Don't be frightened," he whispered.

"Easy to say," Ellen answered, putting her hand to her temples. She rubbed the sand out of her eyes and sat up, disconcerted. "Why's he shouting like that?" And she extended her forefinger into the darkness.

"He wants to know something," the young one replied. "You owe us an explanation. When you came into the cellar, I don't know why, you said – now, I don't know what for – maybe out of fright or fear or because you just couldn't think of anything better, maybe to flatter us, but anyway you said –"

"God bless all thieves!" Ellen repeated, and was completely awake. She pulled up her knees and wondered intently about the meaning of her own words. Yes, she had said it, her words had got ahead of her and now she had to catch up with them, she had to feel her way to the end with short, effortful steps, she had to explain it. The rat behind the great stone shifted attentively onto its hind paws.

"I don't want to flatter anyone," Ellen said darkly. "You'll have to give back everything, that's obvious."

"Even better!" the old one shouted and came closer.

"Much better," Ellen said, "but the others will have to give back everything too. The ones who aren't thieves."

"Aren't we allowed to hold onto anything?" the young one asked, confused.

"Hold," Ellen said, "hold things loosely. You both hold everything too tightly."

"Why should God bless us?" the old one whispered threateningly. "Don't bother with the rest of it!" He had picked up the pistol again and was playing with it.

Ellen stared attentively into the darkness, taking no notice of him. For the call to make things clearer was coming from the depths, where what was happening was definitely a matter of life or death, regardless of whether she was sitting on a sunny bench or on a bundle of rags in a bombed-in cellar.

The candle flickered, exposing the opened bundles, this little refuge without a safety-catch, to the mockery of the shadows.

"For the ones who aren't thieves," Ellen said hesitantly, "it's hard to give back everything, harder than for you, because they don't know who to give it back to. The police never come after them, they never have to throw away everything in order to save their lives, and they always save the wrong thing. People should help them, help all of us! People should come after us, attack us, rob us, so that we save the right thing. And that's why –" the candle hissed uneasily, "that's why God should bless you, you're coming after us!"

The rat behind the stone stretched out its head cautiously, as if it was meant too. Ellen was breathing deeply. She jumped up. "Time to go!" she said. Suddenly she felt stifled, everything seemed to be drawing in. "Air," Ellen said, "I can't breathe!" No-one answered her. She pressed her hands to her chest. The young one stood motionless.

"What's going on?" Ellen shouted.

"The air's running out," the young one said, "speak more quietly."

Furiously, the old one beat against the wall with the butt of his pistol. Ellen was horrified, and jumped in the direction of the passageway, bumping her head against something which didn't give way. The young one caught her. The candle fell over. With trembling hands, without speaking, they began to dig. Fragments of brick and wood fell indifferently, making room for new ones. Blood welled up under their fingernails. Their pulses were hammering like the secret signal on a door. "And you both let me talk –" Ellen whispered, exhausted, "let me talk and talk, as if that's what matters."

"Well, who knows now what matters?" the young one replied. They were whispering like children, as if surrounded by secrecy and not used-up air. And the old one was still beating away and throwing bricks at the ceiling.

"There's no point," the young one said in a voice of stone, "we're too far down."

"And on the other side?"

"No," Ellen said, "I know that cellar, it's just for luggage. There's no emergency exit."

"A vow, we have to make a vow, Mary mother of God!"

The old one dropped his pistol and sank in upon himself.

"Don't say a word," Ellen said, "be quiet, if you really mean it, or you'll swear to the Devil!"

"No," the old one whispered, "I'm not quiet, I hereby make a promise that I'll give back everything, a solemn promise. I'll start working again, in the brickworks on the river, like I used to do!"

"You'll start drinking again," the young one said. "Like you used to do!"

"No," the old one shouted, losing control, "you must believe me, do you hear, you must believe me! I'm going to give back everything, but you don't believe me!" His voice broke.

In the meantime, the young one had found a shovel.

"Give it back? Who to? To the others underneath the warehouse, will they care anymore? What do you mean?"

"I feel sick," Ellen said.

The old one was lying on the ground and trying obstinately to break bricks out of the wall. The young one's shovel had encountered a fair-sized block of stone, and now he was hitting it again and again. It was a high, split sound.

"We have to make a signal!"

"Yes," Ellen whispered dazedly.

"Stay calm," the young one said, "what would calm people do now?"

"Yell," Ellen said.

"We have to roll away the stone!"

"There's another one behind it –" the old one giggled.

"Roll away the stone from the tomb," Ellen murmured, "and in the morning he had disappeared – angels had accomplished it."

"You'll be waiting a long time," the young one replied.

"We should have started earlier," Ellen said.

"If only we had something to kill the pain!" the young one shouted. Ellen gave no answer.

"Help me!" he urged. Suddenly her face seemed to him like a window behind which it was twilight. His fear was growing.

"I'm cold," Ellen said, "I'm so cold here!"

"You're using up too much air!" The old one jumped upon her from behind and grabbed her by the neck. "We'll have to squeeze your throat tight!" Ellen fended at him, but he was much stronger than her. The young one tried to tear him loose, and when that didn't work he jabbed the shovel at his head, hitting Ellen. None of the three heard the new thing. The old one rolled down the bundles and approached her again. His eyes were blazing.

"You," the young one panted angrily, "you're not mad at all! You're just pretending to be, because it's easier, but if you try it again I'll knock you down!"

"I'm going to give back everything," the old one groaned, burrowing into the opened bundles.

"Give back yourself!" the young one shouted. With one jump, Ellen was between them. "Stop it! Don't argue."

"Quiet, you fool!"

It was quite clear now. They heard it as you hear footsteps one floor higher, and they didn't dare lift their heads. Frozen, they stood in the flickering of their shadows.

"White mice," the young one whispered, "some people see white mice, palms in the desert –"

"Stay where you are!" Ellen shouted despairingly. "It's going away, it's going away again! We have to do something, so that it doesn't go away again! Lift me up, lift me up, I want to bump my head on the ceiling, please lift me up!"

"Keep calm," the young one said. The old one sank in upon himself.

"It's going away, it's going away again!"

"It's coming again, there!" The young one took the shovel and hit at the stone like a madman. The moment he got tired, Ellen took his place. The old one was shouting with a long, drawn-out sound which sounded like a locomotive's whistle when night is coming.

When they fell silent in exhaustion, the tapping above them was almost tangible, seeming to rush towards them and in the next moment to break in. Suddenly they were overwhelmed by fear of the liberators.

"They'll find the cut-up suitcases," the young one said, "if they don't break through first and strike us dead with their good intentions."

187

It seemed to be coming from all sides now. At the same time a certain sequence could be distinguished clearly, a rhythm, the intention of being a signal. Dust and small fragments of rubble slid along the wall, quickly and forgetful of themselves: Look at our example, don't think yourselves so important, forget yourselves!

We have too much to forget!

Much too much is still too little, so stay calm.

One false move up there, and everything will fall on top of us!

So if you know that, why did you grasp indiscriminately at everything when you were still one floor higher?

One beam dragged away when it shouldn't be, and everything collapses! But how many beams have you dragged away when they shouldn't have been, taken them for yourselves, when you were sent out on rescues?

One false step up there and everything is lost!

How many false steps have you made, and thought that you've gained? And how does it come about that you're still alive? That's what we're asking ourselves.

If you ask yourselves, if you just ask yourselves –

Resigned, the sand ran into the depths, blissful and pulverised, having become intangible.

For you will only possess what you have not grasped, and you will embrace what you have not touched. You have as much as you give life to with your breath, and you will give life to as much as you sacrifice. A strange sacrifice, to a strange price, listen, your fortunes are failing, to a strange price! What is your currency? Gold for which you murder, oil which banishes you, work which kills the pain? Is your currency not hunger and thirst and did your fortune not end in death? But love is the value, is the fortune won in God's market, that is everything.

"They'll find the cut-up suitcases, the punishment for looting is death. They'll shoot us!"

"Me too?" Ellen asked, shocked.

"Yes," the young one jeered, beside himself, "you too! You led us here, you showed us the place and you lighted our way!" Ellen didn't move.

"Or maybe you want to tell them that you came to conciliate the sirens, the dung-pails and the artillery outside the city? That you came to open your own bundle and to hand out your last things on the roof in the sun? Who's going to believe you?" the young one raged. "God bless all thieves, but how will you prove that you don't belong with us?"

The knocking was coming from the passageway now, very near. "I can't," Ellen said, frozen, "no-one can prove that about themselves."

"Stay with us!" the young one groaned and collapsed.

The old one was shaking with laughter. Like a man possessed, he bent his body in all directions and fended with hands spread wide at the invisible thing which was compelling him to laugh, that was telling him bad jokes and threatening to tie him up with his own shadows. Horrified glances flew back and forth like black butterflies between Ellen and the young one. Distant high voices could already be distinguished in the direction of the passageway, the kind which would ask without waiting for an answer, the kind which would answer without being asked – distant high voices which weren't silenced by the closeness and the depth of all darkness, the voices of their rescuers.

"Quick," Ellen called out, "hurry, before they come!"

As white as the stump of an arm, the remnants of the candle grew up from the stone. "Give me the shovel! Fill the suitcases with stones and cover everything with rubble! Hurry, why aren't you moving?"

"Fill us with stones," the young one whispered, "sew us up and throw us into the well. Wolves' stomachs are insatiable, didn't you know?"

Without speaking, the old one pushed Ellen aside. Shoes and brightly-coloured silk shirts flew fearfully into the air. He had torn open the remainder of the bundles and snatched whatever he could for himself with both arms. Ellen threw herself against him despairingly.

189

"Stop that, do you hear, stop it! The punishment for looting is death, they'll shoot us all!" But the old one shook her off. His mouth was contorted with greed, he tore more and more things out of the bundles, stuffing himself like a dead beast of prey. The young one remained motionless.

"Hold him, bind him, throw him down!" Ellen shouted.

"And you, what about you, what will you say when it turns light?" Everything began spinning around.

"The air pressure tore it open," the young one replied.

"And filled the old one's sacks?" Ellen held fast to his arm. "If each of you keeps putting it on the other, if –"

"No-one is responsible for the old one!"

"You," Ellen shouted, "you and me and the people up there who are trying to save us, and the people even higher up in their aeroplanes, we're all responsible for the old one, don't you understand, we have to give an answer – there, they can hear us now, come on, get up, help me, prepare yourself!"

But this light was brighter than they had realised. It burned their eyes, split their gaze and entangled itself in their hair like an unfamiliar comb. It prickled on their skin, parched their throats and dried their tongues. It laid traps for them, made them stagger and stumble and seemed to be laughing behind them like the old one, who was lying in the great crater with a bullet in the back of his neck. And this light cast their own shadows like dead men in front of them. The young one dragged Ellen onwards. Gradually their rescuers' shots died away behind them. Blind swift shots which were frightened of themselves.

"They're aiming at their angels!" the young one jeered. The sky was pale like a late-arriving spectator who couldn't make sense of the show. Ellen and the young one forced their way through an unfamiliar garden, overturned a pram full of potatoes and mingled with the other people, no longer offering a target. Laden shadows slid past. Muzzy in a black haze, the city lay before them. A gust of wind came from the east.

They ran along the street which led down the hill, disturbing a queue of people who were standing with big shopping bags outside a little shop, waiting to fetch the last supplies. You people there – isn't there something else to be fetched? A new supply before the siege begins, and a greater reserve? Jump out of the queue, you have to catch up to yourself, you're called up to the last sector of all, you're included in a new calculation, jump out of the long, snaking queue, you have to shed your skin! Run, catch up to yourself, tear yourself out of the packing! Horrified, they stared in their wake. But the young one and Ellen were already far away.

The old one's laughter was coming after them, it was jumping up at them, taking their breath away and driving the blood into their temples. And it jeered at them: Didn't you save the wrong thing after all? Don't you despise them again already, your deadly fear and the foreign words in the darkness? Don't you regret not taking anything? Don't forget – the old one's laughter groaned. – "Don't forget me, help me, roll away the stone from the sepulchre!"

They sought shelter in the empty hallway of a building.

"We were lucky!" Ellen looked into the young one's grey face and flinched.

"Been away for a thousand years!"

"Us or the others, who should we ask?"

"Save your breath!"

"I don't want to save anything anymore, they'll take away its value again."

"Be quiet now, rest yourself. We're out of the cellar. You'll never preach to me again!"

"Just wait till the next time you're bombed in!"

Dust drifted in from the courtyard. The caretaker appeared behind the panel and shook her fist, threatening them fearfully.

"Sliding panels," Ellen said contemptuously, "sliding panels in the door. Who's outside there, please? Robber yourself! Aren't you afraid of yourselves?" The caretaker opened the door a crack and threatened them with a broom. They ran off.

191

Carts with refugees were blocking the streets. People with bundles or bundles of people, you couldn't distinguish clearly between them anymore.

"The bundles are angry," Ellen said to the young one, "tied too tightly, everything will go bang."

"By itself?" he asked mockingly.

"Like explosives," Ellen said. "Don't touch them!"

Little round smoke-clouds were rising at the outskirts of the city. Leather thongs were slapping the mangy backs of the draft horses. The young one and Ellen managed to climb up, hiding a little of themselves under the tarpaulins; a child screamed, but the people up the front didn't notice. The bundles kept bumping against each other in the half-dark of the cart, as if they knew what the point of this escape was: The point was to join the journey for a little way in an unknown direction, to be taken along without taking anything along, no more and no less.

Ellen and the young one fell silent, exhausted. Tormented by hunger and thirst, they jumped down near the customs office. Didn't you all know? The world is suffering a haemorrhage. A spring has burst forth, run and drink! Catch the blood in pails, for God has performed a miracle. God has turned it into wine. In response to the siege, the city's cellars had been opened. Three men were rolling a barrel across the horizon. The barrel slipped from their grasp. The young one stopped it. The three men followed it, panting.

"Where did you get it from?" Ellen asked. But they had already taken the barrel and left, she received no answer.

Yellow frameworks rose from the low grey. Only part of the customs office was still standing. They ran with the others, their thirst was immeasurable. To drink. The fear of coming too late broke from their pores. That's what they all believe: The world could bleed to death before they drank.

The young one climbed a ladder, Ellen after him, to below the hole-riddled roof, onto the flat, sun-dried boards of the customs office. "There!" Ellen said. Jugs and pails were lying in a corner, lying silently and mockingly, ready to pay duty and pass into a never-discovered land, prepared to be filled and to shatter.

Red flowed swiftly from the barrels, and the people couldn't keep up. Dampness splashed around their limbs, redness climbed into the hems of their clothes. The sun rose higher, the better to look down. White and jeering, the moon remained at the edge. They were setting their roofs alight down there again. The moon's light had become too soft for their nights. Behind the gardens, their arsenals were waiting to be blown up.

A tender sky stood above what had been poured away, a shocked whirring hung in the air and blacked itself out. Black butterflies brushed the eternal lamp. Foreign fliers.

The thirsty people rioted around the barrels, drunkenness rolled imperiously over the low customs house. Surprised, the things abandoned their relationship to each other, the sky became entangled in veils.

Someone pushed Ellen away from the spigot on the barrel.

"Look out," the young one shouted, "robbers, thieves!" But it was already too late. Ellen grabbed for the filled pails, but staggered and grabbed at the air. The silence of lost shells was droning in her ears, the surf of the red sea.

"No!" Ellen shouted.

Roaring filled the space between Heaven and earth. Everyone was forced to listen to it. The red sea receded. The bullets from the low-flying planes punched holes through the roof. People who were fleeing pitched forward onto their faces. A barrel tipped over.

Marvel not at this!

The young one crouched and dragged Ellen down. Wine and blood flowed over the faces, concealing them. Blue lips appeared, sank and came again. And the silent wonderment of the dead flooded through the customs house.

Don't move, preserve the secret, do you all hear: Preserve the secret! Let the thieves march through, through the golden bridge.

Boards were missing, new light broke in.

And now: Heaven or Hell? Are you crying or are you laughing?

But the laughter could not be suppressed any longer, this crazy laughter of the survivors. It raged, swung itself up onto the barrels and set them rolling and jumped between them, screaming all the while. Being pushed itself, it pushed at the silent people.

Are we alive? Are we alive again? Shaken between Heaven and Hell, the soles of our feet burnt and the brows on our faces transfigured, whirlpool amid the rivers! Why are you all lying so quietly? Give us something to eat, we're hungry! Heaven or Hell, give an answer: Aren't you hungry anymore? The bread is going mouldy in your larders, the telephone is ringing in your bedrooms. Why are you all lying so quietly? Help your friends, help the survivors! Because right now they're carrying their beds into the cellars, they're settling down there again, as if they're staying. And they're calm again. The siege is starting, but they won't acknowledge that it exists. Besieged since they were born, and they don't know the extent of it.

Leave your beds, you people who are locked in, leave your larders! Jars are shattering, milk is flowing into the gutter, light-coloured fruits are dancing across the people who are fleeing.

Don't give us anything to eat, our stomachs are in revolt. Don't give us an answer. What could satisfy us is being torn to shreds, and what doesn't tear us to shreds leaves us greedy.

"Back home, back into the cellar!"

"Haven't we been away for too long?"

Again the humming was in the air.

"Bumblebees, are they gathering honey?"

"Blood," the young one stammered. The ladder leading down to the street had collapsed and they had to jump.

"I'm hungry," Ellen said.

"Didn't you know: The slaughteryards are open, the slaughteryards are being attacked. They're playing the fairytale about Hans in Luck again!"

"Let's play with them!" the young one said.

When they came into the slaughteryard the sky above them had become gloomier. The young one was bleeding heavily. They were holding each other's hands. Artillery grumbled in the distance. Sirens screamed mockingly in between: Alarm – Peace – Peace – Alarm –

Packed together in clumps, shouting, with fists raised, the people rolled onto the black killing floors.

Go on, scrabble in the abundance of your mortality, it will never satiate you. You deaf people, you dumb people, you people on the brink, don't your stomachs ever revolt when you try to satiate yourselves, you forgetful people?

But no-one heard the grumbling of the things within the grumbling of the artillery. The great herd wished to be sacrificed to themselves. Give us to the wolf!

A young foreign shepherd was leaning at the gate of the slaughteryard, strumming gently on his shawm:

Now give it back, now give it back,

For that which you should have,

You have it not.

Under the sign of the defenceless people, the song challenging the wolf. They flowed past him heedlessly.

Now give it back, now give it back!

Ellen turned around to him, but was dragged along with them. Steps led down. Far below soldiers were forming a chain. The chain of sweat and anger, the last ornament of this world, the last chain.

Stony and pitted, their young faces stared towards the attackers.

The order was: Hand out the last reserves! But you can't put your hands on the last thing.

What was the order?

Fire!

Isn't someone laughing there? Shots cracked. Isn't someone crying there?

Ellen cried out. The young one's hand slipped gently out of hers, he fell.

195

The chain broke. A raging mob stormed the slaughterhouse. Heavy cold crashed against them in waves. Matches flared up and died helplessly away. The first people fell, others trod them down as they raced on. Ellen slipped, staggered and regained her balance again. Animal carcasses piled up in heaps, meat gleamed whitely and icily above the looters, the bait in the trap.

Ellen was sent flying into one of the stalls. Fat penetrated her clothes. Ice made her freeze, salt bit into her skin. Now she only distantly heard the shouts of the others, who were losing their way, who were slipping, falling and being trampled to death. She snatched meat, her own booty, to her.

Up at the old gate, the young shepherd played on undisturbed:

> Now give it back, now give it back,
> What you won't leave,
> Won't leave you ever.

But Ellen didn't hear him.

And you, what are you bringing them when you return from Hell? She grabbed without thinking, grabbed for the smooth thing, for the white, defenceless meat and dragged it along with her. People who had stormed the slaughteryard after her tried to tear it away from her, but she held on tightly, again and again it threatened to slip out of her hands, but she held on tightly. She dragged it up over bloody stairs.

"Where are you?" She called out to the young one, but noone answered her. Pale and horrified, she stood in the great raging slaughteryard. The sun had disappeared.

"What do you want for it?" a woman said, looking greedily at the meat.

"You!" Ellen said darkly, holding it even tighter.

Then she heard the foreign shepherd singing above the tumult:

> Give blindly, beloved,
> Hold nothing too tightly.
> Now give it back, now give it back,
> For what you take,
> Is denied you forever.

The dark fell. Two men drove a cow ahead of them, whipping and shouting. Ellen began to cry.

"Hey, why are you crying?"

"For both of you," Ellen shouted, "and for me!"

The rolling of the artillery was very close now. Impatiently, the men pushed past her and towards the gate. The meat slipped out of her hands. She let it lie there.

The Greater Hope

As Ellen was crawling out of the cellar, she noticed a horse off to her left. It was lying there with the death-rattle in its throat, the sweetish smell of putrefaction already rising from its wounds, and it had its eyes focussed on her with boundless faith.

"You're right," Ellen said urgently, "you're not allowed to give it up – don't give it up –" She turned away and vomited. "Why –," she said to the horse, "why is it all so disgusting, so degrading? Why must we suffer such humiliation and contempt before we set out on our search?" The wind had shifted and was blowing a warm and pain-killing rottenness into her face, all the rottenness in the world.

The horse bared its teeth, but no longer had the strength to lift its head. "You're not allowed to give it up –," Ellen repeated helplessly. She swayed on her feet, crouched down and reached for the horse's mane, which was sticky with blood. There was a bright spot in the sky, clouded by the smoke from the fighting. "The sun is camouflaging itself," Ellen told the horse comfortingly, "you'll see – you mustn't be afraid – the sky is blue, can you see?"

The sky was easy to see. The building opposite had been blown away. At the edge of the crater, cowslips threw up their fresh blossoms heedlessly from the churned-up earth. "God is mocking us," Ellen said to the horse, "why is God mocking us? Why?"

But rather than giving an answer, the horse just looked at her once again, its expression now changed to one of deadly fear, and then, to prevent any further importuning, shuddered briefly, threw out its legs and lay still.

"Why," Ellen shouted, to drown out the howling of a shell, "why were you afraid?"

From the depths of the cellar she heard once again the high and rather ridiculous voices of the adults, calling her back. Purposefully, she straightened up from her bent position and ran towards the city. She ran quickly and easily, with light, even strides, not looking back once. She was running towards Georg, towards Herbert, Hanna and Ruth and the dancing cherry trees. She thought she was running to the Atlantic coast and the Pacific coast, the shores of the holy land. She wanted to get to her friends. She wanted to get home.

Rubble rose up like hurdles and tried to stop her, burnt-out ruins with blasted-out windows which stared – like blind soldiers – into the timid sun, armoured cars and foreign orders.

"What can possibly happen?" Ellen thought. She ran between heavy guns, ruins and corpses, between noise, chaos and all that God had abandoned, and she was shouting softly with happiness. That lasted until her strength abandoned her. The barrel of a heavy gun reared up from among brightly-coloured lilac bushes. She tried to get past. A foreign solider dragged her to one side, quickly and roughly and carelessly, with his left hand. Some order or other came from the direction of the gun. The soldier turned his head and let Ellen go.

The park gates had been destroyed here. Dense, wild undergrowth caught her and released her again. The grass stood tall and green. In the distance a uniform was hanging on a young beech tree, but it was no longer possible to tell if the uniform still enclosed the body of a man. Apart from that there was no-one to be seen. Once again, something heavy hit the unbroken ground close behind Ellen. Lumps of stone and earth sprayed up and struck her on the shoulders. It was as if a pack of little boys had thrown things at her from behind a bush.

But the further she moved into the middle of the garden, the quieter it became.

The noise of the battle receded, as if it had never existed. The spring evening fell like a gentle artillery shell and struck everyone at once.

Ellen jumped across the stream. The wooden footbridge had collapsed. The white swans had disappeared, and with them the supreme carelessness of their desire. What was left to be fed no longer let the children give it bread. The glass on the weather clock had shattered and the hand had stopped, pointing forever to "Changeable." There were no white-clad nannies anywhere on the gravel pathways. There was no longer anything to suggest that park keepers had ever existed.

In the sandbox in the playground there were three dead men. They lay there in no particular order, as if they had played for too long and not heard their mothers' calls. Now they had fallen asleep, without seeing the light on the other side of their tunnel.

Ellen ran up the slope. Suddenly, she heard the clinking of iron quite close by, they were digging the graves. Ellen threw herself onto the ground. She crouched between the shadows in the doubtful light.

The foreign soldiers were using big shovels to shift the loosened earth. This earth was black and damp and gentle, it gave way easily. The soldiers worked without speaking. One of them was crying.

Light wind broke through the silent bushes. Now and then the earth trembled as heavy artillery shells exploded in the distance. Ellen lay quite still. Now she was lying pressed close to the ground, at one with its trembling and its darkness. The statue on the fountain, the one whose arm had been shot off, smiled fixedly in the direction of the open graves. The statue was carrying a pitcher on its head. The pitcher was stable even though the statue wasn't holding it, it gave the statue substance. The fountain had run dry long ago.

When the soldiers took the corpses from the sandbox, Ellen stayed behind alone. She lifted her head from her arms a little and followed their movements. They were running down the slope in great leaps. Ellen could see how they lifted the dark things from the white sand. She didn't move. Like a high-flying piece of shrapnel the evening star rose and, against all expectations, remained fixed in the sky. Heavy and reluctant, the dead men hung in their comrades' arms. They couldn't make things easier for them, it wasn't that simple. Defiantly, the hill curved.

Just before the soldiers had reached the top again, Ellen stretched out at full length like a rolled-up carpet and span down on the other side. She closed her eyes and landed in a shell-hole. She pulled herself out, stood half-upright and ran across the lawn towards the tall trees. The trees stood calmly, accustomed to serving as cover. Individual branches seemed to have snapped. White and fragile, the wood shone through the damaged bark. When Ellen had reached the middle of the lawn, she heard someone calling her. Her feet hesitated. She couldn't distinguish whether it was the grandmother who was calling her, a jaybird or the hanged man. And she didn't think about it any further. She wanted to get home, she wanted to get to the bridges. And she mustn't let herself be delayed any longer now. She bent down and kept running.

It was almost completely dark. The motors of heavy trucks droned in the distance, behind the low wall. They were bringing new supplies up towards the canal. Towards the same canal on whose banks the merry-go-round stood serenely in the last light between the fronts. Do you want to fly? And do you want music while you're flying?

A few paces before the trees took her into the deeper shadow of their canopy, someone called again. The voice was much closer now, and could be made out clearly against the roaring of the silence, which from time to time even enveloped the droning of the armoured cars; a harsh, very loud voice. Ellen jumped into the shadow, threw her arms around a tree trunk and kept running.

The people in the cellar had just finished their game of cards. "Ellen," they called peevishly, "Ellen!" – "Where are the children?" The children were crouched at the cellar's hatch, which had been enlarged by an exploding artillery shell, and arguing noisily about who was allowed to look through. You could see rubble through the hatch, and the sky with the first star. But Ellen wasn't with the children anymore. She had run after the star, and she had run quickly, with the burning enthusiasm, with the last breath, which childhood permitted her.

"Someone should inform the police, but where are the police?"

The shadow of the trees moved back. Ellen felt giddy, stumbled over an abandoned helmet and knew suddenly that her strength was at an end, consumed in her expectation, burned up and drained away. She cursed. Why had she run out of the cellar? Why hadn't she listened to the councillor, to the neighbours, the caretaker, to the people who never ceased to value reason and contentment above all else? Why had she followed the irrepressible thing which had commanded her to run, and to search for what could not be found?

Unbridled anger took hold of her, anger against the compelling silent temptation which had led her here. White and lonely, the little stone benches stood beside the dried-up river. Shadows weave themselves into a wire rope. No – there wasn't one rope, there were lots of ropes, but which one of all the ropes was the one that mattered? Which one of all the ropes would hold? Ellen swayed on her feet. Flashes of light flooded the dark garden. The earth reared, the hanged man began to dance and the dead men turned uneasily in their fresh graves. Fire tore the sky to shreds. All the flames are one fire. The ones which burst out of the windows, the ones which live in the lamps, the ones which shine from the towers. All the flames are one fire. The ones which warm their hands, the ones which shoot out of the gun barrels. One fire in the middle of the night.

The soldiers beside the pond threw themselves onto the ground. The position was protected. Covered by the slope, it seemed better suited than any other for making a fire quickly and resting from the battle beside it. But still it was as if the pond had cast its light into the sky, blackly and deceitfully, as if this one fire had the power to make water boil and to destroy.

They straightened up and filled the kettle once more. The kettle sang and the soldiers began to sing again too. Their song sounded deep and concealed. It was like hearing a truck rolling in the half-dark. Some of them ran up the slope, listened to the distant noise of fighting, and bent to observe the shadows of the trees, the lawn and the sky. Blinded by the flame, it seemed to them at first that the darkness was impenetrable, so that it was better to rely on the things which revealed themselves in the sky. That's why the guards only noticed now, quite suddenly, that Ellen and the sentry from the other bank were standing in front of them. Up here the grass was wet and high. So it seemed to the soldiers as if two tall, dark blades had shot out of the ground in front of them, with the light shining on their faces against their will.

There was a soft clicking as the soldiers' fingers tightened on the triggers of their rifles.

"What's your business here?"

"She ran across the lawn," the other one said, "she ran across the lawn as if it was Sunday." He laughed. "When the explosions started over there, I saw her. I called to her. She kept on running, towards the trees. As if everything would be alright again if she reached them, as if it was Sunday!"

They took Ellen to the fire.

The lawn sloped down towards the pond. The lilac was in bloom here, white and wild and luxuriant. The music pavilion on the hill opposite stood silently. Round and eager to please, its dark roof rose towards the firelight which was shining from around the bridges. It was so bright now that Ellen could make out the music-stands huddled like a crowd of anxious civilians in a corner of the dance floor. The dance floor was half-destroyed, and covered in stones. Smoke drifted across the trampled-down grass.

The officers consulted uneasily. The fire flickered, pushing their shadows into each other and throwing Ellen in between them.

"What's your business here?"

Ellen was trembling with cold. When she noticed a loaf of bread, she offered no further resistance, and said: "I'm hungry." The foreign soldiers didn't know much of the foreign language, but they knew that word. They commanded her to sit down. One of them cut off a piece of bread. Another one shouted something to her which she didn't understand.

"She's weak," the one who had found her said, "give her something to drink!"

"Is she carrying her papers?"

"Give her something to drink," the other one repeated, "she's weak."

They gave her wine. They chucked the empty bottles across the pond. The water threw up silver splashes before closing over them again.

"She's not carrying anything," he said.

After a few minutes the blood rose to Ellen's head. She straightened up and called out: "Have you seen peace?"

The other one laughed and translated. The soldiers said nothing, astonished, then suddenly burst out laughing. One of the officers looked wonderingly into her face. But no-one gave her an answer.

Ellen began to cry. Again a small explosion shook the ground. "Have you seen peace?" she called out. "We, we were supposed to be peace, every one of us ought to be peace! Just let me wash my face in the pond!" Dark and agitated, the water was throwing itself against the banks. "I want to get to my grandmother," Ellen said, "my grandmother is in the last cemetery. Can't one of you go with me?" She cried even harder. Clouds of smoke from the fighting came from the north and surrounded the moon. The rumbling of the artillery could be heard from the river. "Didn't you at least see Georg," she murmured without hope, "Herbert, Hanna and Ruth?"

The other one had stopped translating.

"Be quiet!" he said.

"She's putting on an act!" The soldiers rose threateningly. "Who knows why she's here?"

One of the officers jumped up and came around the fire.

"They say that you're putting on an act, do you understand? They say we should arrest you!" His speech was harsh and broken.

Heavy fighter planes flew low over the garden.

"I want to get to the bridges!" Ellen said.

"Didn't you just say that you want to get to the cemetery?"

"To get home," Ellen said, "it's all on the way."

"Where is your home?"

"On the Island."

"They're fighting for the Island. Do you understand?"

"Yes," Ellen said, "I understand."

The soldiers assessed her suspiciously. Like a sigh, the barrel of the heavy gun reared into the cold sky.

"This city is besieged," the officer said, and even he wasn't sure why he was continuing this debate for so long and explaining things which couldn't be explained. Angry shouts clashed above the fire. "This city is besieged," he repeated, "it's nighttime. Anyone not involved in the battle is supposed to stay in a cellar. Don't you know how dangerous it is?"

Ellen shook her head.

He said a few words to the others, it sounded conciliatory.

"What did you say?"

But he gave no answer. The third explosion was heavier than all the previous ones. It must have been very close, on one of the connecting roads which led to the bridges.

The fire was threatening to go out for good, sparks were spraying across the pond. This time they didn't fill the kettle again, they only consulted briefly. The officer turned back to Ellen.

"I have to get to the bridges, you'll show me the way. Maybe I can take you home. Come on," he said, "come on now, we've lost enough time because of you."

He walked with long strides. Silently, Ellen ran along beside him. Serenely, the pond stayed behind. Distant and dismissive, saturated in moonlight, the towers of the inner city reared up. When he got close to the graves he paused, and seemed to think. Then he ran on without paying any attention to her. When she stayed behind, he called out something in his own language and took her by the hand.

"Now we both have to get to the bridges!" Ellen laughed. He gave no answer. Both to the bridges! The walls threw back the echo. A board was laid across two heaps of rubble, the board was wobbling. "You'll have to hold tight," he said. Ellen clung onto his wide belt.

A few streets further on, the battle seemed to be over. "Over –," he laughed. "Over!"

The night was very clear.

The ruins stood like silhouettes made by a magician. Sharper and firmer than by day, inhabited by those without bodies. Resigned to the incomprehensible, freed from the citizen's question: Why me? And the blackness from the burnt-out holes was no blacker than the blackness from the rooms of those who slept. The buildings which were still standing had little round bullet-holes. In the moonlight that looked like a new decoration, like the architectural style of those who were to come.

He took a handful of sweets from his pocket and offered them to her.

"Thank you," Ellen said, without taking them.

"Have you had enough to eat?"

"I feel sick. I haven't had enough to eat."

"Really?" he laughed evasively. "Is that possible?"

"That's how it is," Ellen replied, "you don't have enough to eat. You just feel dizzy all the time. That's why I went out searching."

"Who do you expect to believe that?"

They ran along the sides of the buildings, as if they needed to protect themselves from the rain which wasn't falling.

"There's always something left over," Ellen explained eagerly.

"Because it's not allocated properly."

"That's not what I mean," Ellen said, "not things you can allocate."

"You're insatiable!" He smiled suspiciously.

Blood had flowed across the pavement, spreading red and dark. They jumped over it. Ellen slipped and fell backwards. He lifted her up. He called to her and shook her.

"We have to keep going, do you hear? To the bridges!"

His breath was above her face, his medals gleamed uneasily. Ellen held onto him and pulled herself up.

Three metres further on, a cork sprang out of a champagne bottle and hummed past them, just over their heads. In a half-lit gateway, a short soldier rested his rifle on the stone floor and laughed. The officer seemed to know him. He parleyed with him briefly and turned back to Ellen.

"He'll lend us a car."

They pushed it out of the gateway. It started with difficulty and winked cunningly with half a headlight. Ellen climbed onto the seat. The front mudguards and part of the door had been torn off. A scrap of the tarpaulin roof hung down in front of their faces, stiff with dirt.

At the intersection, the shattered traffic signal was blinking with black lights. That was the only signal left, everybody was responsible for warning themselves. They overtook two tanks, swerved around a collection of barricades and approached the bridges from the other side. He was driving faster now. The car was swaying and throwing them against each other. Shortly before their destination the roadway was torn up, and they had to retreat. Their star seemed to have abandoned them. A few moments later the left front wheel got stuck in a shell-hole.

"Help me," he said, "we have to keep going!"

The car groaned and seemed immovable. When it did move at last, it sank even deeper. The officer had snatched his cap from his head, his damp, light-coloured hair hung down over his forehead. Ellen jumped into the crater, she worked hard without talking. The car offered obstinate resistance, but suddenly it rose as if it had achieved salvation, giving way so unexpectedly as to startle them. The moon had re-emerged, jumping over the light of the fires and entangling itself in the wheels. Far behind them, a building was blown into the air.

Where are we travelling? We're travelling along the Gold Coast, and where are we travelling to? To the Cape of Good Hope. Ellen closed her eyes. You could believe that. But she didn't dare say anything, she just clung onto the iron even more tightly.

Soldiers passed them, their footsteps echoing. Windows rattled, fragments glinted brightly. Without fear, no longer worried about preserving themselves. And retaining their jagged radiance.

When she opened her eyes again, the street was illuminated by fires like the driveway to a party. Where the street ended, the flames combined into one. The man beside Ellen thought for a second. His feet probed at the pedals, his hands enclosed the steering wheel as if it had the power to steer him. He looked straight ahead and increased his speed. Fiery red fled across his forehead, intensified and seemed to stay put. He grimaced, laughed a little and had just enough strength left to bring the car to a stop in a side street. Blood seeped through his tunic. The steep roofs sloped down considerately towards the old street. The last little street, it seemed, passed over and almost undamaged, calm in a silence that did justice to the noise all around. The street was preserving this silence like the last ton of fuel.

"To the bridges," Ellen stammered. She jumped down.

"Help me!" he said. "No, don't help me. You have to go on to the bridges alone, you only have to pass on a message –"

Ellen opened his tunic, tore a strip from his shirt, but couldn't see anything. "I have to get help," she said. But she feared the foreign soldiers, whose language she didn't understand.

"Stay!" he grumbled weakly. "What's your name?"

"Ellen. What's yours?"

"Jan," he said, then laughed into the darkness, as if that was the solution to all the world's puzzles.

"Wait," Ellen called out, "wait!"

She jumped onto the pavement and stumbled through a shattered doorway. The hallway was dark. It smelled of abandonment, of decay, of the possibility of complete collapse. Ellen felt her way along the walls and caught hold of a door. She threw herself against it and fell inside, the door had been open. That gave her the courage to strike a match. Light flared up, allied with the silence and the open door, and created everything anew. The light-coloured walls and the dark floor, the gleaming doors, and the cracked mirror which absorbed the dark of the hallway.

This apartment had been abandoned by its inhabitants. They had abandoned it as the soul abandons the body. They had left it as foreign guests leave. When the sparks flew across the roof, they had noticed that it was getting late. Alarmed, they had called for the car and driven off without saying goodbye. They hadn't worried about the host at any point. The apartment had been abandoned in haste.

Jan straightened up and attempted to get out of the car. He tried to call out, but his voice was quieter than usual. So that's how it is when you're hit, he thought. He supported himself on the seat, extended his legs, stood in the middle of the street for a second and fell with his back against the radiator. The street was spinning around like a top under the whip. Angrily, he took three steps towards the pavement. Ellen caught him. "Come on," she said, "come on, Jan!"

He was carrying some candles and their light seeped through the unfamiliar, abandoned apartment. Cupboards and tables, blankets and beds, and everywhere the silence slept, that misused, that most wounded of all the casualties. You who are my creator, why do you permit it? Why do you create this race who must destroy me in order to know? Why do you create them ever anew?

Jan's boots left black marks on the floor. His head bumped against the gloomy chandeliers, the glass tinkled. Exhausted, he dropped into an armchair. His shirt was soaked with sweat, silently the blood seeped through. Half-conscious, he felt the bandages being applied, the brightly-coloured cloths being placed around his wounds, cool and maternal, ready to stop the unstoppable.

The light has a green tinge, as green as grass in the sun. That's good for the eyes, that's good, Jan! But this light made his face even paler.

"Jan," Ellen said, "it'll be better soon, everything will be fine." Better or fine? Deciding that suddenly seemed important to her.

He asked for something to drink, he was freezing. Ellen found wood under the kitchen counter. After a long search she found a copper saucepan. She turned on the tap, but it had been dry for ages. The drinking water was in a covered barrel in the corner. She dipped the saucepan and filled it. The stove smoked reluctantly, but settled down gradually like a horse beneath an unfamiliar rider.

Jan lay still. The armchair was soft and deep. Through the walls he heard footsteps, the splitting of the wood and the rattling of crockery. It was possible to imagine that it had always been like this and that it would always remain like this. If the people before them had been capable of believing that, then they'd be capable of it too. Silently, Ellen held her hands over the stove-top. It was possible to imagine that all of this was the first and the last time. If the people before them hadn't been capable of believing that, then they still would be capable of it. She poured the boiling water on the tea leaves and put the cups on a tray. She heard him calling out.

"In a minute!" she said.

He lifted his shoulders from the chair-back. His wound had stopped bleeding. His cap had slipped off his head, and in the moonlight his hair looked even lighter than before. She let him drink and looked at him.

Everything which had been torn to shreds came together again like a game. Red flowers, a handful of sweets and an open wound. Everything united with everything else. The wide world suddenly had the face of a young foreign officer, a bright, triangular face with cheeks which ran sharply down to the chin, lines which diverged gently from the big ruler like those drawn by a child. All the pain coalesced in a hidden glance. The invisible was looking Ellen in the face. She took him by the hand.

"Say that it's you!"

"That I'm who?"

"The one I meant when I wanted to get home!"

He lay in the armchair and looked at her. She held his hand more tightly. "When I laughed some time, then I always laughed because you laugh, and when I played with a ball, then I was

210

always playing with you too. And when I grew, then I grew so that my head reaches your shoulders. I learned to stand up and to walk and to talk for you!"

She jumped down in front of him and stared into his face.

"It's you. Say that it's you."

She clapped her hands.

"Peace –," she said, "I mean peach ice-cream, veils in the air and you."

"Veils in the air and me," he said wonderingly.

He stood up and put his arm around her. He was swaying a little, but he could stand. He took his cap and put it on her dark, dangling hair. He tried to laugh, but his laughter was help-less, like a damaged mask. Far-off singing accompanied this coronation.

Ellen maintained her composure. The crack in the mirror split her face like a sword's blow. Her knees shimmered palely beneath her short coat. The wind howled like bagpipes. The flickering light of a fire danced up the wall and cast a fleeting gleam onto her cheeks.

"How long have you been here, Jan?"

"Since yesterday."

"And how long will you stay?"

"Until tomorrow, maybe."

"From yesterday until tomorrow, Jan, that's as long as any of us stays!"

Ellen was freezing, sadness was taking her breath away. She pushed the cap off her head. A shiver stroked her hair.

"What's the matter?" he cried in despair. He grabbed her arm and dragged her to him. "What do you want?"

"To get home!" Ellen said.

He pressed his fingernails into her arm. She didn't move. He hesitated. Tormented, he put his face against hers.

"Jan!" she said. Her trust made him defenceless, he pushed her away. There were tears in her eyes.

Suddenly he seemed weaker. The wound in his shoulder was hurting and began to bleed again. Ellen was frightened. She wanted to change the cloths, but he wouldn't permit her.

"I have to get help!" she said.

He didn't want help, he wanted something to eat. She brought him what she could find. She spread a white cloth over the table, cut the bread for him and poured fresh tea into his cup. He watched her thoughtfully. Her movements were quick and yet preoccupied, serious and playful. They were both very hungry. While they drank the tea, he kept gazing at her calmly over the rim of the cup. She drank silently, looking at her knees. He offered her a cigarette. She made an effort to finish it.

He lifted his shoulders from the chair and sank back down. "It looks," he said, laughing bitterly, "it looks as if we'll be staying here!"

"It looks like that sometimes," Ellen said. "You have to get your strength back, Jan!"

"I have to get to the bridges!" he shouted.

"To get home," Ellen said.

To get home? His thoughts were becoming confused. "Do you mean to the place where the plain cries in its sleep and the children screech like wild birds in the fields on the left and the right? To the place where the little towns lie on invisible borders and the crooked station buildings wisely let the express trains go by? Do you mean to the place where the green towers are round and only come to a point when everyone has stopped expecting them to?" His hands made the shapes of roads and railway embankments, tunnels and bridges. He assured her of his love for young ravens above the fields after the harvest, for wood-smoke, for wolves and lambs and broke off suddenly.

"What am I telling you here?" He stretched out his arms, wanting to draw her to him. "Come on," he said. She didn't move.

"Do you mean me, Jan?"

"Yes, you!"

"You're wrong, say that you're wrong!"

He stood up, supporting himself with a hand on the table.

"Don't forget the bridges!" Ellen said.

"Don't be afraid," he said. He stood right in front of her, looking into her face. "You!" he said, and began to laugh. He

212

laughed so much that she feared his wound would start bleeding again.

"Keep calm," she said despairingly, "keep calm, Jan!"

He asked for his tunic and felt in the pockets. "Why do you want to get to the bridges?" he asked again suspiciously.

"To get home," Ellen replied steadily. She could have said it again and again. It was much clearer now than before.

"It's important," he said to her.

"I know," Ellen answered.

"What do you know?"

"That it's important!"

"What's important?"

He took a crumpled envelope from his pocket, wrote some words on it and pushed it across the table to Ellen. It lay there. So still and as it had lain forever. Always rediscovered, always with the expectation of being passed on. The covering for the longing, the message for the bridges. She knew it without him needing to explain much to her. But he had developed a kind of trust in her now.

"We have to go on," he said calmly, "before the day comes. And if I'm too weak, you'll deliver this thing here for me."

Ellen nodded.

"I'll show you where!" He took his hand off the table and walked carefully towards the door.

"Where are you going?"

"Just upstairs a bit!"

"You're too weak," she said. He shook his head.

It was very dark in the hallway. Ellen ran back to fetch a candle. She left the others burning in the unfamiliar apartment and the door wide open behind her, so that there was light for the first part of their way. Spring wind whistled through the shattered windows. The lift was stuck half-way up the shaft, some of the apartment doors stood open.

Jan tried to walk, but couldn't manage it. After two floors they had to rest. They sat on the dark steps as if they'd come in from playing. But when were father and mother coming home?

213

He was panting, they didn't talk. When they climbed the final stairs he had to lean on Ellen again. The wind blew out the candle. The windows in the hallway higher up were nailed over with boards. Darkness danced around them and prevented them from seeing how high they had already come. They climbed up the iron ladder.

There was the roof. Resigned, it lay on the border of their impatience, on the edge of their exhaustion, flat and silent, surrounded by night and fire, troubled no longer. Sparks flashed across it as if a swarm of glow-worms had been disturbed. Fire pressed itself upon the silent roof like an impatient suitor: Take me! Take me! You shall have a golden dress! No more gravel, no boards, no mortar, just light forever! Take me!

Jan forgot the pain, he pulled Ellen up. He encircled her with his uninjured arm, he laughed. It was the wound that was making his face composed and his movements easy.

The chimney stood as quiet as a gravestone. It was the only fire-watcher left on this roof. The railing curved mysteriously around the corner, a forgotten apron waved faithlessly in the light of the fires. They walked around the chimney and bent over the railing. From up here everything was further away and much quieter than it actually was. From up here it seemed simply as if a stone had fallen into the water. From up here it was all one.

Jan still had his uninjured arm around Ellen. They saw the street deep down below, and they saw that fires were burning, and they saw the moon. The lights were combining and dying away. And their eyes allied themselves with the depths. They looked at each other and laughed softly. It was like the first time and it was like the last time and it was like always. It was one and they were one and on the other side of the river there was a great party.

They were setting off fireworks there, they were celebrating dying there. They were knocking down all the prizes there, the ones belonging to the owner of the great shooting booth, and they were changing the red lanterns from second to second as from eternity to eternity. It was only a long way away that the fires drowned in the dark of the eyes.

They leaned back on the chimney. Their eyes sought the bridges. How far away was the battle? As far as the moon or as far as the next roof?

"Look, Jan, where that explosion is now, that's where we used to live. And where it's burning over there, that's the last place we lived. And where the smoke's so white, that's where the cemeteries must be!"

"And the bridges!' he shouted impatiently.

"Here!"

He put his hand over his eyes and assessed the shifts in the battle once again, the shifts Ellen didn't understand. He showed her which bridge he meant. Again sparks flew across the roof. He threw his coat around her, she pushed it away forlornly. As if in a dream, they crept down the iron ladder, as if in a dream, they stumbled down the dark steps.

"Our fire!"

The water had boiled over, the wood had got wet. Ellen laboured desperately to light a fire with it again. Haze and smoke filled the unfamiliar kitchen, gentle sleepiness and gnawing anxiety, staying and going. Ellen began to cough, the smoke brought tears to her eyes. Fire, she thought confusedly, fire from the bridges, the wood is too wet!

"You have to warm yourself, Jan, before we drive on."

He was leaning on the door, but the door wasn't firm enough. The door gave way. But we're not on the roof, Jan thought, no, we're not on the roof anymore, I shouldn't be so dizzy. We're further down, a long way down, and you can't fall from here. That's an advantage.

Ellen straightened up and stroked back her hair. Once again her shadow threw itself across the floor, as if it was fainting. Jan saw this shadow through the open door. Casually, fleetingly, it repeated her movements. It grew high up the whitewashed walls, covered them like a climbing plant, leaned to one side, disappeared and came back again. Defined, but already dissolving, still visible, but no longer tangible, dancing and divorced

215

from any purpose. Jan assessed this shadow, as if the battle was revealing itself here in a different way.

When she turned around to him, his eyes were closed.

"Jan, what's the matter? Wake up, Jan, don't fall asleep, Jan! Can you hear me?"

One step, one step! Wasn't the next step the only thing that ever mattered? How could one step become so impossible, when millions of steps had been possible? Millions of steps hung on his feet, impeding him. One step, one step, seven-league boots for this one step!

"Wake up, Jan! What will I do without you now? What should I do?" She rubbed his temples and tried to make him drink. "Can you hear me? Didn't we want to get to the bridges?"

"To the bridges," he repeated and straightened up. They burned into his mind again. The letter shimmered palely, shadows danced around it. His weakness overpowered everything.

"Wake up, Jan! Wake up, get up –"

Ellen bent over him. His face was serious, resigned to the completely different thing of which he knew nothing when he was awake. Red and heavy, his head hung to one side. She lifted him back onto the cushions. Reluctantly, he creased his forehead and reached with one hand for his belt.

Wind threw the curtains inwards. Ellen shuddered. Who gave her the right to disturb him? Who gave her the right to share her fear with him. Stay – she thought – stay.

"When the sun comes up, you'll comfort me, Jan. When the sun comes up, I won't have to be afraid anymore. Didn't you say yourself that it looks like we're staying? Aren't we even allowed to act as if it's true, Jan?" Ellen folded her arms. How simple it was to be paralysed. To be anaesthetised against the mystery and to wipe away the pain like foam from a beer glass. Behind me, in front of me, to my right, to my left, everything is alright! A teapot is a teapot, a heavy gun is a heavy gun and Jan is Jan.

How simple. A teapot is just a teapot. Everything is as simple as a soldier's curse, as simple as freezing to death. The place it stops hurting is where it gets dangerous, the old man said. Oh, who cares about the old man.

The place it gets dangerous is where it stops hurting. That's better. Overturn the trams and use them as barricades, everyone, you're right! Don't admit that your hearts are becoming a battlefield. Don't let the reasons attack you from within. Join together like I folded my arms, that's better. Don't try to stay here through yourselves. Believe that you'll stay here in your sons, that makes it much simpler. Forget the risk of being alone!

Ellen put her hands over her eyes. Forget, forget! Where do you want to get to? Home? You have to believe them when they say: It is here and it is there. What are you searching for? It can't be found. Stop searching, Ellen, accept things as they are. A teapot is just a teapot, accept that! Ellen lowered her head. Forget, forget!

Then she heard him breathing. She lifted herself onto her knees. Suddenly she understood that all the world's heavy guns had been manufactured to drown out people's breathing, these unveiled sighs, this unveiled brevity. It was quite still now. Ellen could no longer hear anything else.

How seldom do you hear yourselves breathing! And how unwillingly do you hear each other. Either – or, either – or!

"Didn't we want to get to the bridges together, Jan?" He gave no answer.

"Or do you think," Ellen said, "do you think we have to get to the bridges alone? You alone and me alone, each of us on our own?"

He moved uneasily. She touched his hair gently. Still sleeping, he brushed away her finger. The candle burned weakly, flickering.

"Jan, it's past midnight!" She reached for the hand which was hanging down. He murmured something in his own language which sounded threatening.

"Jan, it's spring, Jan, the moon is getting bigger!"

His lips were parted, his forehead was damp. Ellen wiped away the sweat.

"Jan," she whispered fearfully, "you have to understand me. Aren't we all like the towns on the border? Aren't we all like the green towers which come to a point where everyone has stopped expecting them to? Aren't we all like the station buildings blown crooked by the wind which wisely let the express trains go by?" With her last strength, she defended herself against the sleeping man. "I'm only one of the many trains which go past you. Jan, when you wake up, don't reach for my hand!"

She spread her coat over his knees.

"When you wake up, everything will be better. When you wake up, the sun will be shining on your face!"

He breathed quietly.

"You have to understand, Jan. Didn't I crawl out of the cellar so that I could get home? Out of home to get home. Away from so many desires, into the middle, Jan, to the bridges!"

Once again she tried to explain everything.

But it seemed to her while she was speaking that it couldn't be explained, yes, she had the feeling that everything she was saying was producing no sound in this silence, that she was moving her lips like a dumb woman. What she was doing couldn't be explained, because it carried its purpose within itself. You had to get to the bridges alone.

Ellen put her cap on and took it off again. Just for a moment she stood quite still.

It was the hour before morning, that hour between black and blue, at which many die and many are afraid, that hour at which the unknowable looks over the sleepers' shoulders. Don't throw yourselves onto the other side! That won't achieve anything.

The night moved on. All the fires were burning down.

The fire in the stove had almost gone out too. Ellen poured water over it. She cleared away the cups and put the teapot back in the cupboard. She bent over Jan once again.

She took the letter. Then she opened the door, closed it quietly behind her and didn't look back. She walked through the unfamiliar apartment, beneath the glass chandelier, past the potted palm and the cracked mirror. In the kitchen she took a piece of bread. She nodded to the hat-stand and slipped into Jan's coat. No-one would stop her if she was wearing that.

"I'll see you there, Jan!"

She jumped down the steps. In the hallway, she stood wondering what to do. She felt her way down the stairs to the cellar and hammered on the door. Frightened faces stared at her.

"There's a wounded man upstairs," Ellen said. A man and a woman went with her.

"Where the light is," Ellen said. She watched as they went up. The desire to go with them flashed through her once again. But the letter was burning in her hand.

She ran down the street and across the square.

Unfamiliar activity assailed her from all sides. Shouts were flying into each other like dark stars. Horses were being unharnessed. Everything was like a thousand years in the past and a thousand years in the future. The image in the mirror was shattered. The image must be a symbol. Soldiers were stamping out the fire, one of them called to her as she passed. Ellen didn't look back. She slipped between two horses and was gone. Deep in the distance the Island was burning, perhaps the bridges were burning too. She began running again.

Like windows on Christmas Eve, the red emerged out of the grey. The morning was very cold. Far away, the mountains rose untouched above the chaos. Behind those mountains, it was turning blue.

"Whatever happens –," Ellen thought. She kept close to the wall. How many times had she run like this. And hadn't someone way behind her always called out: "Stop! Don't run so fast, or you'll fall. Wait till I catch up with you!" Now a call was coming from way in front of her: "Run faster, run even faster! Don't stop, or you'll fall, don't think anymore, or you'll forget! Wait till you catch up with yourself!"

You had to make the leap eventually. Ellen knew that she'd run out of time. She knew that she would jump soon. It had all been one big run-up, father and mother, the consul and Franz Xaver, the quay and the English lessons, the grandmother, the colonel and the men who broke into the bombed-in cellar, the dead horse, the fire beside the pond and this last night. Ellen rejoiced softly. She would have liked to shout it into all their faces one more time: It's a run-up, somewhere it's turning blue. Don't forget to jump! She held the letter like a sign.

She felt like she was flying on the old merry-go-round for the last time. The iron chains made cracking sounds. They were ready to let Ellen fly away. They were ready to break. Ellen ran towards the quay, towards the bridges where the battle was continuing. She ran after the king of peace on his way to the cross. No-one tried to stop her anymore, no-one could stop her. A sentry took the letter from her. A woman in a light-coloured coat shouted: "Don't go there!" Her coat was spattered with blood. She reached for Ellen's hand, but Ellen tore herself away, found herself in a cloud of acrid smoke and rubbed her eyes.

Blinking, she could make out numbers of figures running here and there, girders and heavy guns and the grey-green, churning water. Here, there was no more chance of sorting out the confusion. But beyond here, it was turning blue.

Once again Ellen heard the shrill shocked shouting of the foreign soldiers, she saw Georg's face above her, brighter and more transparent than it had ever been.

"Georg, the bridge has collapsed!"

"We'll rebuild it!"

"What shall we call it?"

"The greater hope, our hope!"

"Georg, Georg, I can see the star!"

With her burning eyes fixed on the splintered remains of the bridge, Ellen jumped over a piece of destroyed tramline which was jutting up from the ground, and before gravity could draw her to the earth again she was torn to pieces by an exploding shell.

The battle for the bridges continued. Above them stood the morning star.

Translator's Note

My source text for this translation was the edition of Ilse Aichinger's *Die größere Hoffnung* published by the *Fischer Taschenbuch Verlag* in Frankfurt am Main in 1991, and specifically the twelfth printing issued in May 2012. An earlier English translation of *Die größere Hoffnung* was published by Atheneum in New York in 1963. The title was *Herod's Children*, and the translator was Cornelia Schaeffer. I made a deliberate decision not to consult Schaeffer's translation (which in any case was quite difficult to obtain) until I was in the final stages of editing my own translation. Although it transpired that Schaeffer and I had produced very different texts, I should acknowledge that I have adopted her translation of individual words or phrases on various occasions, most notably by rendering "bürgen für" as "to vouch for."

Geoff Wilkes
University of Queensland
Brisbane, Australia

Family tree

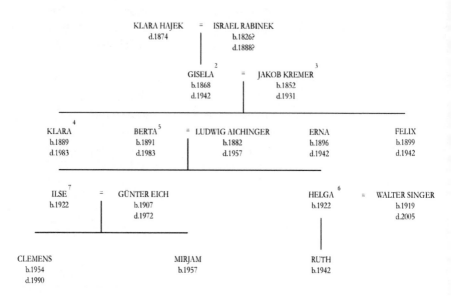

1. Israel Rabinek: According to Ilse Aichinger her great-grandfather Israel was an extremely gifted man, an engineer who worked on the Serbian northbound railway line. At some point he was also stationmaster at Auschwitz.

2. Gisela Kremer: Jewish grandmother much loved by Ilse and Helga; lived in an apartment with Erna and Felix at *Hohlweggasse* 1. Deported in May 1942 to Minsk. Murdered.

3. Jakob Kremer: A captain in the Imperial Army of Emperor Franz Joseph. Realised that the career advancement of his children would be facilitated by their baptism into the Catholic church.

4. Klara Kremer: The only child who did not convert to Catholicism; linguist, worked in London; gifted photographer (cover of this book).

5. Berta Aichinger: One of the first female graduates in Vienna; a devout Catholic (Ilse and Helga baptised). Divorced from Ludwig Aichinger in 1927. With her twin daughters she then lived at *Hohlweggasse* 1, the family home.

6. Helga Aichinger: Educated with Ilse at Sacre Coeur. Her aunt Klara left Vienna in 1938, and Helga escaped on the last Quaker transport (4 July 1939), joining her aunt in London.

7. Ilse Aichinger: After the closure of borders (1 September 1939) designated a *Mischling 1. Grades* under the Nuremberg Laws (1935).

Source: Ruth Rix and Gail Wiltshire, 2016

Afterword

In 1980, Peter Härtling proclaimed: "Ilse Aichinger's novel has been waiting for us for a long time, for far too long. It is [...] as patient as its author" (178).[1]

The veracity and poignancy of this statement almost four decades ago constitute a clarion call today. The literary contribution of Ilse Aichinger's œuvre has not been widely acknowledged. Indeed, the minimal recognition of her work represents an inexplicable, undeniably tragic loss to both German and non-German worlds of a literary giant who, surviving one of history's most barbarous times, the Holocaust, did not define the perpetrator, judge the atrocities or indicate the topographical area of her protagonists' persecution. Probably most widely celebrated for this, her seminal novel *Die größere Hoffnung* (the manuscript of which has not survived), Aichinger explores the experiences of the Jewish teenager Ellen who, like her author, is classified as a "Mischling ersten Grades" in Nazi-occupied Vienna. Only now, with this new translation, can this literary masterpiece, obscured and retained exclusively within *Mitteleuropa* for a German reading public, transcend linguistic boundaries and captivate the imagination of an English audience. Just as Ellen transits the socio-political borders of captivity, through this translation the genius of *Die größere Hoffnung* will receive global recognition.

Aichinger introduces Ellen in a "sailor's cap" (7), dreaming of victimised, defenceless children whose caps bear the gold lettering of the "*Training Ship Nelson*" (10). War-torn Europe, departure and undesignated destination, govern the dream-images of the central character, who awaits an audience with the apparently omnipotent consul, the arbiter of freedom from a domain where chil-

---

[1] With the exception of the quotation from Michel Foucault on p.227, all quotations from secondary sources in this afterword have been translated by Geoff Wilkes. All quotations from *Die größere Hoffnung* are from the present translation, and all quotations from Aichinger's *Kleist, Moos, Fasane* have been translated by Geoff Wilkes. All quotations from interviews with Aichinger are from the volume *Es muss gar nichts bleiben. Interviews 1952-2005*, and are identified with the abbreviation *GN* and the relevant page numbers; the editor of that volume has requested that these quotations not be translated.

dren, like the shark which accompanies them, are hunted and persecuted. Gifted with speech in the tradition of the fairytale, the shark is also hounded: "He told the children that he was being hunted" (8). On awakening, Ellen demands a visa which will facilitate her crossing the Atlantic Ocean to the Statue of Liberty, a physical symbol of freedom, thereby initially establishing "The Great Hope" (Chp. 1). Although the protagonist's grandmother has warned her that no-one will vouch for a Jewish child, Ellen pleads that the consul sign her travel document. With this initiative, however, Aichinger's central character and audience are aware that the visa to be signed is intrinsically personal, a sketching board holding a white page "bearing the heading 'Visa' in big, awkward letters" (14). The highly-coloured flowers, stars and birds around the edge immediately indicate that Aichinger denotes no common politico-administrative document or fugitive. The child's commitment and quest will eclipse physical and topographical frontiers into the spiritual and metaphysical realm "where everything turns blue" (13).

Aichinger, who was born on 1 November 1921, did not expect to survive the Holocaust. As she has indicated in several interviews, she originally decided to record and report on the Nazi occupation of Vienna. In 1985, for example, she stated that: "Ich wollte zunächst eigentlich nur einen Bericht über die Kriegszeit schreiben. An ein Buch habe ich gar nicht gedacht [...]. Als das Buch dann bei Fischer erschienen ist, stand noch immer viel zuviel drin. Ich wollte am liebsten alles in einem Satz sagen, nicht in zwanzig" (*GN*, 110). In 1993, the author reiterated that: "Im Roman *Die größere Hoffnung* [...] dachte ich zuerst, ich schreib' einen Bericht, damit man weiß, was geschehen ist" (*GN*, 67). Nevertheless, Aichinger's subsequent fictionalisation of the particularised time-space of her putative report in *Die größere Hoffnung* (which was originally published in 1948) reflects and supersedes the totalitarian *Zeitgeist* of Nazi-occupied Vienna, the closure of borders and the persecution of the Jewish minority. Luzia Stettler affirms that Aichinger's work is "an autobiographical novel, a story of children and being a child in the Third Reich" (43). Referring to authorial influence, Alfred Frankenstein also comments that "the fates in the novel are formed from personal experience and personal suffering" (174). And Lutz Grübel describes Aichinger's novel as "the last ten stations in the

225

life of a half-Jewish girl in a city in the area controlled by Germany during the Second World War," noting that Aichinger uses the perspective of the protagonist Ellen to describe "the situation of the times: war, persecution, deportation and the ever-recurring fear" (160).

Aichinger's œuvre also includes short prose fiction in the volumes *Der Gefesselte* (1953), *Eliza Eliza* (1965) and *Schlechte Wörter* (1976), radio plays and dialogues in *Zu keiner Stunde* (1957) and *Auckland* (1969), and poetry in *Verschenkter Rat* (1978). Her personal and semi-autobiographical writings include *Kleist, Moos, Fasane* (1987), *Film und Verhängnis. Blitzlichter auf ein Leben* (2001) and *Unglaubwürdige Reisen* (2005). Importantly, she has been awarded the following prizes: Immermann Prize (1955), Grand Literature Prize of the Bavarian Academy of Fine Arts (1961 & 1991), Anton Wildgans Prize (1968), Nelly Sachs Prize (1971), Roswitha Prize (1975), Trakl Prize (1979), Petrarch Prize (1982), Kafka Prize (1983), Weilheim Literature Prize (1988), Grand Austrian State Prize (1995), Austrian State Prize for European Literature (1995), Joseph Breitbach Prize (2000), and most recently the Grand Art Prize of the State of Salzburg (2015). *Die größere Hoffnung* has been translated into French (1956), Italian (1963), English (1963), Japanese (1981) and Dutch (1987), and the late 1990s saw a small wave of new translations (Bachleitner, 137).

In spite of prestigious awards and limited translation, most significant is the dearth of secondary studies in English, which contributes to the prevailing unfamiliarity with Aichinger's texts. Indeed, her work within the Germanic and international literary sphere has disappeared from personal and commercial bookshelves, classrooms and university language departments. The overriding dilemma, however, remains the paucity of an international audience aware of the creativity of Aichingerian virtuosity. It has been argued that Aichinger's writing is highly complex and her meaning is multi-layered. She does not belong to any particular school, and it is impossible to categorise her œuvre within a specific genre. Gisela Lindemann argues that Aichinger's work cannot be aligned with that of her contemporaries and members of the "Gruppe 47" (20), who included Alfred Andersch, Heinrich Böll, Uwe Johnson, Wolfgang Hildesheimer, Günter Grass and Ingeborg Bachmann. Having been invited to join the "Gruppe 47" by Hans Werner

Richter, who aimed to encourage young writers of the postwar German republic, Aichinger received the Group's prestigious prize for her short story "Spiegelgeschichte" in 1952, just four years after publishing *Die größere Hoffnung*. Aichinger's composition does not belong to the verisimilitude of the literary tradition of forensically recording external details of time, place and character, but originates within the realm of the affective, emotive, metaphysical and non-rational, and the stylistic quality of her work has been compared with that of Franz Kafka. Walter Jens refers to Aichinger's "Kafkaesque technique" (170), and Dagmar Lorenz writes that her "visions of an inescapable, guided universe" can be "traced back to Kafka" (3). The juxtaposition of dream episodes and non-realistic narrative sequences in *Die größere Hoffnung* parallels Wolfgang Borchert's surrealist radio and stage play of the *Heimkehrer*, *Draußen vor der Tür* (1946), and it has also been argued that the "utopian quality" (Lindemann, 24) of Aichinger's style is similar to that of Erich Fried's novel *Ein Soldat und ein Mädchen* (1960). In later years, Aichinger asserts that "my language is a form of anarchy" (Stettler, 45), and Lorenz affirms that this "positive anarchy" (7) generates the mysticism inherent in the author's works. Other critics have identified a surrealistic element, with Hermann Schreiber suggesting that *Die größere Hoffnung* can best be characterised "through a comparison with surrealism" (158).

Aichingerian scholarship and analysis notwithstanding, Aichinger's original intention of recording a personal report on the Nazi occupation of Vienna metamorphosed into a dynamic prose piece. But this does not mean that the personal element was eliminated. As Michel Foucault emphasises in "The Death of the Author," "it is not enough to declare that we should do without the writer and study the work itself" (208). While postmodern literary criticism tends to ignore the significance of the relationship between author and text, my discussion of *Die größere Hoffnung* focuses on the synchronicity between Aichinger and the commentary revealed in published interviews. Structure, narrative imperatives, the symbolism and imagery of *Die größere Hoffnung*, form and internal relationships – the elements which constitute Aichinger's novel – intrinsically pertain to the author.

Imperatives Underlying *Die größere Hoffnung*. "[D]u würdest dich jetzt zu mir setzen und mir eine Geschichte erzählen. [...] Eine Geschichte, [...] eine neue Geschichte!" (*GN*, 164) The artistic merit of *Die größere Hoffnung* within the context of the western literary canon is irrefutable. "Lesen kann man also das Buch noch, und das ist ja wohl nicht selbstverständlich für Literatur aus dem Jahr 1948" (*GN*, 17), Heinz Schafroth maintained in 1972, and the same can be said today. When Aichinger was asked at that time if she could write a novel similar to *Die größere Hoffnung*, she stated unequivocally: "Ich könnte heute *Die größere Hoffnung* nicht mehr schreiben, so wie ich den gestrigen Tag nicht mehr erleben kann" (*GN*, 18). In 1986 she commented succinctly: "[I]ch würde [den Roman] natürlich nie mehr so schreiben. Aber ich möchte auch nichts davon zurücknehmen" (*GN*, 44). The author also recounted that it was Hans Weigel who gave the manuscript to the Fischers "als sie in Wien waren" (*GN*, 44). Commenting on the reception of *Die größere Hoffnung*, Peter Zimmermann acknowledged that "[d]er Roman hat zwar die Kritik begeistert, aber der Verkauf...," to which Aichinger replied: "Nein, der war nicht gut [...], es braucht seine Zeit, so wie das Zuhören. Das Lesen braucht seine Zeit. Es braucht ja auch das Schreiben seine Zeit. Und das Lesen ist ja auch eine Art zu schreiben – wenn man richtig liest" (*GN*, 54).

Although – in interviews with Karina Urbach in 1991, Brita Steinwendtner in 1993, Christina Brecht-Benz in 1995, Iris Radisch in 1996 and Cornelius Hell in 1997 – Aichinger reiterated her original intention to present a report on Nazi occupation and tyranny, her responses in fact afford new insights into the magnitude of her writing, the personal element, the suffering which permeate her text. She accentuates suffering: "Zum Beispiel all d[as], was meine Familie durchmachen musste. Das hat damals den Anstoß zu einem ersten Roman gegeben [...]. Meine Erlebnisse gaben die Anregung zu diesem Roman. Aber ich habe darin auch die Geschichten meiner Freunde verarbeitet" (*GN*, 64). Moving beyond the conception of a report, Aichinger became aware of the subjective dimension of her writing: "Es hat mir ermöglicht, auf der Welt zu bleiben" (*GN*, 67). Emotionally and spiritually her opus "war notwendig, für mich jedenfalls" (*GN*, 67). The indelibility of the *Angst* of persecution and terror remains such that: "Es wäre schlecht, wenn sie nicht wiederkehrte" (*GN*, 70). Again, Aichinger reinforces the impact of the annihilation of her family on her seminal work: "Ich möchte berichten [...]. Berichten, was damals, als der Krieg begonnen hat, in unserer Familie passiert ist" (*GN*, 88). Aichinger further suggests that the writing of *Die größere Hoffnung* spanned three years "weil es in dem Buch darum ging, das Leiden zu definieren" (*GN*, 101). At the age of eighty-three, she recalled: "Nach dem Krieg wollte ich nur mir selbst erklären, was geschehen ist. Dadurch ist *Die größere Hoffnung* entstanden" (*GN*, 216). Describing Aichinger as "eine der bedeutendsten Schriftstellerinnen des 20. Jahrhunderts," David Signer asked her in 2005: "Gibt es im Alter so etwas wie eine Engführung auf die zentralen Themen des eigenen Lebens?" (*GN*, 230) Aichinger's answer established that "diese Themen waren schon immer da" (*GN*, 230).

Childhood. "To play. It was the only possibility remaining to them, composure before the incomprehensible, grace before the secret." (110)

The discourse of childhood and the role of the child are vital to any reading of Aichingerian literature in general, and of *Die größere Hoffnung* in particular. The timeframe of the novel encapsulates 1938 to the liberation of Vienna by the Allies in 1945. In 1938 the author was only seventeen years old and, writing from the perspective of a child, she projects the incomprehensibility of the brutality of the Nazi occupation. In 2004 Aichinger stated: "Die Perspektive des Kindes erlaubt, das Überleben während des Nationalsozialismus als Spiel darzustellen, als Spiel im Angesicht des Todes, während der Verfolgung" (*GN*, 212). Erich Boetticher declared that it is not by chance that Aichinger chose children as her protagonists, "[h]aben doch die Erwachsenen im Chaos versagt und wissen nicht mehr um Gut und Böse" (*GN*, 12). When Manuel Esser asked Aichinger to comment on the synergy of children and play, she replied: "Aber der Verlust der Kindheit ist damit nicht zu vergleichen. Weil das Spielen und die Kindheit die Welt erträglich machen und sie überhaupt begründen" (*GN*, 51). Distrust of adult hypocrisy, betrayal and inherent cruelty stand central in her novel, and Aichinger was aware of this mistrust even as a child: "Mir haben als Kind die Erwachsenen so leid getan. [...] Sie sprechen über

229

nichts. [...] Es war mir immer, als wären sie gar nicht existent. Als Erwachsener wird man konform, man gibt sich zufrieden, nicht nur mit den eigenen Schwierigkeiten, auch mit denen der anderen" (*GN*, 77). In "The Fear of Fear" (Chp. 5), Herbert defines the alienation of the child from the adult, declaring that "the adults at our place speak in foreign languages!" (92) And Leon confirms the convictions of the author: "They always do that, [...] they've been doing that for ages" (92). What is more, the recollection of the pleasure, glee, indeed *Schadenfreude* of the excited spectators, the adults who witnessed the deportation of Aichinger's family, has never left her: "[D]a haben die Leute ganz vergnügt zugeschaut" (*GN*, 108). She also recalled "die Leute um mich herum, die mit einem gewissen Vergnügen zugesehen haben" (*GN*, 113). And in 2004, she reiterated: "Eines Tages zerrte man [die Großmutter] und ihre Familie aus dem Haus. Die Wiener haben sich gefreut" (*GN*, 212).

Anna has warned the children that adults will deceive them and lead them astray: "Don't ask the adults, they'll deceive you, as Herod tried to deceive the three kings" (101). Compellingly, Aichinger generates the potent theatre dynamic of persecuted Jewish children who are actors, and Nazi perpetrators who are their audience: "Leon, who gave us such terrible roles? [...] [And] what a dreadful audience we have, a dark maw which devours us, people without faces!" (109) The vividly depicted brute pleasure, the barbaric celebration of the pack governs Kurt's negation of Leon's beliefs – Leon the idealistic producer and angel in "The Great Play" (Chp. 6), whose image of an audience "with pale faces which shine a light in the darkness" is demolished by the horrendous reality of Kurt's exposition: "Don't you see how red their faces are and how bright their eyes? And don't you hear how they're already laughing, how they'll laugh when we're being led across the bridges?" (110) The untarnished intuition of childhood aligned with a candid acknowledgement of adult hypocrisy, cruelty and greed synthesises the tenets of the author, who as a child suspected the sincerity and emotional integrity of the adult.

The *Kindertransport*. "The last *Kindertransport* had left long ago. The borders were closed. There was a war on." (49)

Readily discernible are the obvious biographical analogy and significance of the *Kindertransport*: "The boat set sail from Hamburg. The boat was carrying children. Children who had something or other wrong with them. [...] Children with long coats and very small knapsacks, children who had to flee. [...] Children with the wrong kind of grandparents" (7). Helga and Ilse Aichinger, identical twins, were separated for the first time when Helga travelled on the last Quaker transport out of Vienna before war was declared. Ilse's Jewish family – her mother Berta (a pædiatrician), her maternal grandmother Gisela, her Aunt Erna and her Uncle Felix – were trapped within the confines of Nazi imprisonment. Aichinger explains: "Meine Schwester und ich sind identische Zwillinge. Wir sind gewissermaßen Klone, Doppelexistenzen. [...] Meine Schwester war mit einem der letzten Kindertransporte nach London gekommen." She continues: "[D]ass meine Schwester und ich so zum ersten Mal getrennt waren, die in England, ich in Wien. So waren wir zum ersten Mal zwei verschiedene Personen" (*GN*, 154-156). Furthermore, as the twins' father Ludwig was not Jewish, Aichinger was classified as a "Mischling ersten Grades." In 1997 she recalled: "[I]ch habe 39 die Matura gemacht, und da haben wir in Biologie gelernt [...]. Juden und Zigeuner wären das Schlimmste, aber noch schlimmer wären Mischungen. Das wären entweder Idioten oder Verbrecher. Also, das war ja so primitiv, man kann sich das heute gar nicht mehr vorstellen" (*GN*, 126-127).

Aichinger transfers her "Mischling" status to her protagonist Ellen, who is thus marginalised within her Jewish peer group. Ellen must ask: "Let me play with you!" (27) three times before she can join the group on the quay, and her alienation from the others is also emphasised during her entrance to "The Great Play":

"Why didn't you open the door?"
"You didn't know the signal!"
"You didn't tell me it."
"Because you don't belong with us!"
"Let me play with you!"
"You don't belong with us!" (108)

The categorisation of "Mischling ersten Grades" dominates the personal domain of Ellen and her author, who stated: "Meine Mutter war geschützt durch mich, weil mein Vater nicht jüdisch war" (*GN*, 42). Referring to the ration cards stamped with a large "J" for Jewish family and friends and a conspicuous, divisive red "E" which branded and separated her and defined her status, Aichinger recalls: "Das hat sich mir sehr eingeprägt. Und die Rolle, die man hier auf der Welt überhaupt als Mensch spielt, hat etwas von diesem Mischlingsdasein an sich. Deswegen hat es mir nichts gemacht, dass ich ein Mischling war" (*GN*, 43).

In Ellen's final bid to join the protagonists in "The Great Play," she is not only aware of her "Mischling" status, but also recognises the consequences of being identified as one of the doomed children. Superseding these circumstances, Ellen – like her author – is cognisant that physical survival transposes into the metaphysicality of a greater hope transcending death:

> "Let me play with you, go on, please, please let me play with you!"
>
> "Your grandmother has forbidden you to play with us" [...].
>
> "Because my grandmother still believes that people who stay behind are fortunate."
>
> "Do you believe that?"
>
> "Not for a long time," Ellen said. (108)

The Grandmother. "It's possible that I'll be taken away during the night." (133)

The polemic governing Aichinger's first creative work, and indeed to an extent her later writings, remains the brutal, tortured vision of a diminutive, frail figure, anonymous in a headscarf, flanked by her daughter Erna and her son Felix. Her face is turned from her granddaughter, who has run to Vienna's *Schwedenbrücke* in pursuit of the person she loves passionately: "Ich war sehr jung und hatte die Gewissheit, dass meine Großmutter, die mir der liebste Mensch auf der Welt war, zurückkommt" (*GN*, 113). Ilse Aichinger will not look on her grandmother's face again. She will not know the fate of the woman who provided unconditional love, security and refuge for the twin girls and their mother in her apartment in Vienna's *Hohlweggasse* after the breakdown of their parents' marriage in Linz. Dehumanised by the bestiality of the cattle truck and the jeering mob, this frozen image of her grandmother is engraved upon the memory and encapsulated in the creativity of Aichinger, the granddaughter who would become one of Europe's greatest twentieth-century writers, and the framed photo of Aichinger's grandmother stands on a table at the end of the author's bed today. Aichinger remembers: "Das Lager, in dem zuerst alle gesammelt wurden, war über den Brücken im früheren Ghetto, eine ehemalige Schule [...]. Und da musste man in den Lastwagen, in denen sie dann abtransportiert wurden, endgültig, über eine Brücke fahren. Dort bin ich gestanden und habe sie gesehen, mit einem Kopftuch. Und irgendjemand hat gerufen, schau, hier ist die Ilse. Aber sie hat sich nicht umgedreht" (GN, 42). Again, in 1996 Aichinger reiterated: "Das erinnerte mich daran, wie meine Großmutter während des Krieges in einem Lastwagen über die Schwedenbrücke deportiert wurde" (GN, 108). In the same year, Iris Radisch asked the seventy-five-year-old Aichinger what she had not survived. The answer defined the psyche of the writer: "Den Anblick meiner Großmutter im Viehwagen auf der Schwedenbrücke in Wien" (GN, 113).

The young Aichinger believed that her grandmother would return after the war, but:

Es war so eine Illusion. Ich dachte, meine Großmutter und die jüngeren Geschwister meiner Mutter kommen aus diesem Vernichtungslager Minsk zurück. Ich habe sie noch über die Schwedenbrücke in einem offenen Lastwagen fahren gesehen, und es war ja vollkommen klar, dass niemand mehr zurückkommt. [...] Darum war die Zeit nach dem Krieg – so zwei, drei Jahre nach dem Krieg – eine sehr unglückliche Zeit, weil ich eben Illusionen hatte. (GN, 125-126)

In the last interviews of 2004 and 2005, Aichinger elucidated her final impressions: "Angeblich wurde sie in Minsk ermordet, eines der schlimmsten Lager. [...] Ich dachte lange, sie kommt zurück, aber von dort kommt niemand zurück" (GN, 212).

Asked fifty years after the deportation of her grandmother: "What would complete happiness on earth be for you?", Aichinger answered: "To see my grandmother, who was murdered in the extermination camp in Minsk, again" ("Fragebogen," 25). For the granddaughter of Gisela, "bei der [Ilse] aufwuchs" (GN, 182), the resonance of memory transmutes into an abiding presence: "Meine

233

Großmutter hat existiert und existiert deshalb auch noch heute" (*GN*, 108). What is more, Aichinger declared: "Ich glaube an die Präsenz der Lebenden und der Toten. Ich weiß nicht, ob sie wirklich erreichbar sind. Aber ich spüre eine Präsenz" (*GN*, 114). For Aichinger, the polarities of life and death merge. When Julie Kospach suggested in 2003 "dass der Tod mancher Menschen – zum Beispiel Ihrer Großmutter – deren Präsenz für Sie noch verstärkt hat," the writer replied: "Bei ihr habe ich schon das Gefühl, dass sie noch weiter existent ist" (*GN*, 207).

Aichinger constructs her fictional grandmother within a framework of personal memories, experience and a subjective observation of events which were to commandeer her imaginative, subjective consciousness and, most importantly, her artistic authority. Nourished by the belief that her grandmother could return, the original report of a young author burgeons into a literary masterpiece. It is impossible, indeed naïve, to ignore the parallels between Aichinger's grandmother and Ellen's. In line with her originator, Ellen is nurtured by her grandmother who, when the motherless, displaced and dreaming child is falling through space, catches her and "put[s] her back in her bed" (18). The owner of the shooting booth enquires where Ellen lives, and she replies: "With my grandmother [...]. She's one of the wrong kind, but she's alright" (32). Both grandmothers, actual and literary, are compelled to wear the "Judenstern" and are aware of imminent extirpation, by means not yet disclosed. Ellen's grandmother leaves the apartment in search of information, in an exit which employs the maritime symbolism that permeates Aichinger's œuvre to sombre effect: "She had gone around the corner like a rolling ship. For as long as you could still see her, her umbrella stood out like a black sail against the wet wind" (83).

"The Death of the Grandmother" (Chp. 6) constitutes one of the novel's most impressive narrative episodes. Aichinger establishes a playing area, a stage, pre-empted by the presence of an audience, the personified night, who carries "the strongest lamp of her lord, the darkness" (127). Falling like an asbestos curtain at the conclusion of a tragedy, the darkness delineates the separation of playing space and spectators. Critically, the night "cut off the stage from the audience. She fell like a sword through man and separated the player from the spectator and cut him off from himself" (127).

Aichinger demands an objectivity of her audience, the reader, who – through the literary prism of the anthropomorphised night – witnesses the suicide of Ellen's grandmother. The impoverished, sparsely furnished room designates the set and Aichinger carefully catalogues the limited theatrical properties: oven, beds, wardrobe, bedside table, shipping trunk and the rosary whose cross trembles, at this crucial point in the dramatisation, above a map of Southwest Africa, reinforcing and sustaining the compelling introductory image of the novel, "the Cape of Good Hope" (7), the topographical and metaphysical trajectory of a greater hope.

Aichinger devises a *mise-en-scène* for the meticulously constructed poetic drama of the grandmother's death. The author also powerfully portrays the vicissitudes of age. Immediately rejecting and ashamed of her thoughts about "decay" (130), Ellen, feigning sleep, watches her grandmother search for "a little glass vial" (135) which will release her not only from the decreptitude of time, but more importantly from the terrifying uncertainty of the time of her death: "It's possible that I'll be taken away during the night" (133). Ellen, like her creator, would do anything to save her grandmother. Aichinger had faced the horror of this situation with her mother Berta: "Ich dachte immer, wenn die Männer die Mutter holen, gehe ich mit" (*GN*, 42). The author's protagonist would accompany her grandmother, and pledges that she will carry the suitcases "[w]herever you go!" (133) Could her grandmother not be hidden from the secret police? "I'll get you out of this, I want to hide you [...], and I'll defend you – yes, I'll knock them down" (143). Ellen strives to prolong the life of her grandmother by invoking the cultural and familial instrument of the power of the fairytale.[2] She urges her grandmother to remember past stories, for example the conversation of the Turkish mocha cups under the cover of darkness, what the fat dog in the farmyard tells the pigeons and the riddles of the sparrow, the pigeon and the chestnut roaster. Repeatedly, Ellen desperately urges the old woman to "tell me a story" (133), believing that were her grandmother to do this, her subconscious allegiance to historical tradition and cultural memory would compel her to choose survival, the continuity of

---

[2] Ruth Rix, Gisela Kremer's great-granddaughter and Ilse Aichinger's niece, recollects that Gisela was a gifted storyteller and read fairytales to Ilse and Helga.

235

life. The elderly protagonist's confusion and extreme fear are such that she cannot recall the fairytales which existed within the emotional parameters of the security, love and joy of past times: "Where were they all, those stories which she had pulled in hundreds from her coat pockets [...]? [...] She leafed back through the disintegrating album of her memories" (137).

Aichinger reinforces that, without doubt, the audience witnesses a theatrical and stylised enactment of the death of the grandmother:

> Silence spread into every inch of the room, an intent and thoughtful silence, a waiting for the truth of the last fairytale of all, for the whispering of the prompter. The grey-green oven, the old shipping trunk and the white, empty bed – in this draining silence, they all shrank to backdrops and waited to be inflated again.
> (136)

The author's fictional grandmother manipulates her own fate. Free will triumphs. She is not dragged from her apartment and manhandled onto a cattle truck. In spite of fragility and overwhelming fear, Ellen's grandmother controls her destiny. Her death is a victory, which eclipses decay, physical negation and jeering crowds. The incubus of the grotesque cattle truck diminishes. Death and rebirth coalesce in the symbol of metamorphosis, water, which simultaneously facilitates departure, the absorption of the poison, and arrival, the baptism, whereby Aichinger evokes the interface of Judaism and Christianity. It is significant that the title which Aichinger originally proposed for her novel was "The Baptism of the Grandmother" (Herweg, 32). Arguably, the fate of Ellen's grandmother is tantamount to a restaging of the personal tragedy of 6 May 1942.

Central staircase in *Hohlweggasse 1* apartment

Mosaic tiles featured in *Hohlweggasse 1* apartment

The Grandmother's Apartment.
"Didn't you just say that you want to get to the cemetery?"
"To get home," Ellen said, "it's all on the way." (204)
"And where the smoke's so white, that's where the cemeteries must be!" (215)
"Didn't I crawl out of the cellar so that I could get home? Out of home to get home. Away from so many desires, into the middle." (218)

The significance of personal and inhabited space, that is of the apartments in *Hohlweggasse* and of the grandmother in *Die größere Hoffnung*, contributes to Aichingerian constructs of space. When interviewed, the author described her emotional affiliation with and memories of her grandmother's apartment. She related how, after her parents' divorce, she and her sister and mother "kamen [...] relativ rasch zu unserer Großmutter, weil es keine andere Möglichkeit zu wohnen gab. Es war ein sehr stiller Kosmos. [...] Ich habe dann gemerkt, dass man irgendwo hingehört" (*GN*, 197). In 2004, Aichinger reminisced about her early years in *Hohlweggasse*: "Wir waren sehr glücklich. Ich hatte aber schon damals das Gefühl, dass dieses Glück wie eine Luftblase ist. Diese Wohnung schien mir eine gute, aber sehr fragile Erfindung zu sein" (*GN*, 211). Living with her mother and Aunt Erna, Aichinger also experienced great happiness in her grandmother's home. But again, this emotion is transitory, as traditional, familial behaviours and values are annihilated by the occupying military regime, which marginalises, separates, stigmatises and murders the Jewish minority. Thus *Kleist, Moos, Fasane* begins with the words: "I remember my grandmother's kitchen. It was narrow and light and ran in the direction of the railway line" (11). Peter Waterhouse notes the prominence of Aichinger's "descriptions of the kitchen [...], the connections between the freight-train line and the kitchen, [where] the death transports from Vienna began" (153). The resonance of the railway line reverberates through Gisela Kremer's kitchen: "[T]he railway set everything in motion. It moved the dusty seashells in my grandfather's drawer [...]. It shook beds and bottles, [...] the plates and glasses in the cupboards trembled and rattled" (12). The synchronicity of kitchen and railway suggests "a little intersection between the paths under the sky" (13). The apartment in *Hohlweggasse*, Aichinger declared, "ist für mich auch eine Art 'Herz der Finsternis' geworden, der dunkle Flur und der altmodische Salon mit den Bücherschränken" (*GN*, 182). Similarly, the vibrations of the nearby railway dominate the grandmother's apartment in *Die größere Hoffnung*. The pivotal image of memory and cultural heritage, the bookcase, which Ellen sees as possessing "a value which was determined by the dreams of people who were growing and people who had died" (56), reverberates with the passing trains: "It creaks! [...] And if a train passes over there, the glass here begins to rattle" (57).

In addition, through the powerful and historically ominous oven motif in *Die größere Hoffnung*, the image representing the nucleus of factual and literary abodes, Aichinger foreshadows the grandmother's predetermined fate. Inherently, the motif of the oven sustains the paradox of sustenance and protection, extermination and death. The author introduces the oven, representing security and refuge, as Ellen's grandmother returns the dreaming child to bed. The anthropomorphised oven commands the scene: "The oven crackled and hid itself further back behind the dark green tiles" (18). Again, "eine große, stille Wohnung" (*GN*, 197) and Gisela Kremer's kitchen in *Hohlweggasse* formulate the atmospheric constructs of the familial apartment in *Die größere Hoffnung*. Central to Aichinger's geography of childhood, which within the strictures of artistic invention underscores the writer's manipulation of metaphor and symbolism, pulsates the powerful image of "the grey-green oven" (136), an allegorical precursor of the operations of death in the concentration camps. After the war Aichinger returned only once to the *Hohlweggasse* apartment, where she witnessed the "Abriss von dem Ofen, also seine Silhouette" (*GN*, 41). She commented: "Ich nehme an, es sind Nachkommen der Gestapobeamten, die dort eingezogen waren, nachdem man die jüdischen Bewohner hinausgeworfen hatte" (*GN*, 182). Factual and fictional, historical and imaginative living space and properties are aligned, indeed fused, within Aichingerian literary vision.

Erna. "Ellen couldn't find the word to conjure them up. But she felt that Aunt Sonja was here now [...]. She'd known for a long time that only the dead die, not the living." (133)

Scrutiny of biographical influence in *Die größere Hoffnung* must incorporate an analysis of the impact of Berta Aichinger's younger sister Erna upon the artistry of her niece Ilse. Dominated by a "Kinoleidenschaft" (*GN*, 157), Aichinger admits that her obsession with film originates from that of her musically gifted Aunt Erna, who was accepted as a pianist by the Vienna Music Academy in 1936. Aichinger recalls that Erna "war Pianistin, aber immer, wenn sie nicht üben musste, ging sie ins Kino" (*GN*, 156). The author concludes: "[Meine Tante] hatte über die Musik schwedische Freunde und hätte 1939 noch nach Schweden fliehen können. Aber sie fürchtete Verkühlungen und noch mehr die schwedischen Kinos. Sie wollte Klavier spielen und ins Kino gehen, beides um jeden Preis. Der Preis war dann ihr Leben" (*GN*, 156). Strains of music permeated the *Hohlweggasse* apartment. Every day "Erna hat sieben Stunden geübt. Aber plötzlich war sie weg. Sie war für drei, vier Stunden im Kino, und dann kam sie wieder" (*GN*, 188). The aunt figure is elusive. Indeed, "jedes Leben [ist] eine Chronologie des Verschwindens. [...] Es ist alles so fragil, dass man sich gar nicht vorstellen kann, wie ein ganzer Tag zustande kommt" (*GN*, 189).

The literary representation of Aunt Sonja aligns closely with the Erna of *Hohlweggasse*. When the dreaming Ellen searches for her absent mother, "[t]here was no-one in the next room either. The lid of the piano was open. Aunt Sonja must have just been practising. Maybe she'd gone to the movies. Since it had been forbidden, she'd been going to the movies much more often" (20). The motif of Aunt Sonja substantiates the auditory imagery which accompanies the vital physical and psychological metamorphosis of Ellen as she defies her grandmother and accepts the implications of branding with the "Judenstern." The reflection in the mirror conveys a greater hope:

> The mirror was like a great dark coat of arms. In the middle stood the star. [...] Ellen smiled thoughtfully at the star in the mirror. The grandmother wanted certainty. Between two mirrors. How uncertain all certainty was. What was certain was the uncertain, and it

had been becoming ever more certain since the world was created. (83)

As Ellen joyously adopts the yellow star which defames and stigmatises her race, contrapuntal music echoes from the floor above where Aunt Sonja is giving a piano lesson. Aichinger establishes the Sonja motif through the resonance of music: the aunt is not defined through direct speech; her character is mute. The mute pianist reinforces the metaphorical silent piano in the cataclysmic destruction of Noah and his attic by the Blue Dragoons as they search for a non-existent – and therefore mute – radio. Aichinger sustains the musical refrain as a child's monotonous, repetitive piano practice vibrates from an apartment below, delineating the metaphysical significance of the appropriation of resonance, in this instance of English, the language of freedom. The latter will never actualise because political borders are closed, and within the context of practical consideration the futility of this linguistic representation would again indicate muteness. However, a new language, like the reverberating music of the pianist Sonja, symbolises a greater hope:

"What is it, our life?"

"Practice," the old man said, "practice, practice!"

"It sounds odd."

He nodded. "It sounds odd, can practising change that? We're practising on a silent piano." (81)

"What does someone learn English for, if it's in vain? [...] What is your suspicion?"

"In the service of a foreign power!" the leader called out. "That suspicion is correct," the old man said. (82)

What do the thrushes whistle for, what do the clouds ride for, what do the stars shine for? Because elemental nature is in the service of a foreign power, Aichinger's visionary intonation of a greater hope.

The Sonja motif suggests illusion – an elegant figure who left the apartment only a short time before, wearing a grey fox fur, to have a hat remodelled. She does not return. Explanations are offered: she has gone into hiding or was visiting friends. Ellen refutes these suggestions because she is aware of the essential theatricality of her pianist-performer aunt: "She knew of Aunt Sonja's wonderful ability to disguise herself and to imitate people" (133). Manipulating Sonja's disappearance, the author again reworks and revokes the brutality of the death of a beloved family member, Aunt Erna, concert performer and devotee of cinematic illusion. In line with her creator, Ellen is reassured by the understanding of her aunt's "love for the horizon [...]. [Ellen] knew that Aunt Sonja was also capable of savouring death like a foreign country" (133).

Hope. "Man kann nicht ohne Hoffnung leben." *(GN, 26)*

As the implications, principles and manifestations of hope provide the quotidian of this novel, what has Aichinger disclosed in interviews about this multifaceted philosophical concept? In 1995 she explained that when she was writing *Die größere Hoffnung* "es [ging] um Leben und Tod, dennoch wollte ich mit diesem Buch noch etwas ganz anderes zeigen: das Glück, das in der Hoffnung liegt" *(GN, 85)*. In the following year she reaffirmed that the war was her "glücklichste Zeit," because "[d]ie Kriegszeit war voller Hoffnung. Man wusste sehr genau, wo Freunde sind und wo nicht [...]. Der Krieg hat die Dinge geklärt" *(GN, 110)*. Iris Radisch proposed that in the novel "die größere Hoffnung [besteht] vor allem darin, dass die Leiden des Menschen nicht vergeblich sind" *(GN, 113)*, and the author acknowledged that: "Diese Hoffnung ist im Krieg immer stärker geworden. Es war ein Triumph" *(GN, 113)*.

Furthermore, when asked to comment on the resistance to and annihilation by Nazi tyranny of the Scholl family and other members of the "White Rose" group in 1943, Aichinger recalled "dass von ihnen eine unüberbietbare Hoffnung auf mich übersprang. Das geschah nicht nur mir. Diese Hoffnung hatte, obwohl sie es uns möglich machte, in dieser Zeit weiterzuleben, doch nichts mit der Hoffnung aufs Überleben zu tun" *(GN, 25)*. Aichinger extolled the essence of non-Jewish resistance by adolescents whose physical and, more importantly, spiritual fortitude precedes and parallels her fictional Jewish child protagonists. The opposition of the Scholl family "war noch mehr als ein politischer Widerstand. Es war auch ein Widerstand von ganz innen her. Eigentlich ein Widerstand des Lebens, der Wahrheit, der Wärme und des Geistes vor allem" *(GN, 31)*. And so, Aichinger concluded, she was convinced that "was die Geschwister Scholl und ihre Gefährten getan haben, was Sophie Scholl getan hat, gerade sie als Mädchen, bleibt in der Luft und wirkt weiter" *(GN, 31)*. The same can be said of the perseverance and courage of the diverse and extraordinary ensemble, the child protagonists of *Die größere Hoffnung*.

Aichinger's perception of hope also evolves from her personal affiliation with the heterotopic otherness of the cemetery, of the fourth gate, the Jewish graveyard on the outskirts of Vienna in which her grandfather Jakob Kremer, husband of her deported grandmother Gisela, lies buried. "Es war offiziell den Juden und jüdisch Versippten, wie das so schön geheißen hat, verboten, sich auf Bänke und in Parks zu setzen, in den Wienerwald zu gehen, das engere Stadtzentrum zu verlassen" (*GN*, 46). Ilse and Berta Aichinger frequently visited Jakob's grave, which lies open to the fields and hills on the boundary of this impressive city of the dead. The author recollects: "Das war so ein merkwürdiger Picknickort [...]. Und so viel Hoffnung, wie ich dort gehabt, habe ich in meinem Leben sonst selten gehabt" (*GN*, 46). Aichinger recalls the nearby "Stoppelfeld" and the conviction that prevailed there, "[d]ie größere Hoffnung angesichts des Entsetzens" (*GN*, 63). She describes how "[e]inmal, am jüdischen Friedhof [...], trafen wir einen Ziegenhirten, der sagte: 'Wir werden es nicht überleben. Aber siegen wird *er* nicht,'" and both Aichinger and her fictional Jewish children could proclaim: "Dieser Friedhof ist uns zu einer Art Heimat geworden" (*GN*, 63). In her novel, the author immortalises this goat herder, a comforting figure to marginalised, defenceless children who are relegated to a place "[w]here the last farewell ends and the reunion begins" (44). Aichinger's fictional old man reassures not only his three goats (the designated number of the fairytale), but also the displaced Jewish protagonists:

> "It's time for you to go home" [...]. He said it tenderly; but he said it to the goats.
> "And for us," Leon murmured. (48)

The transition – indeed the fusion – of departure and arrival, despair and hope, death and life in *Die größere Hoffnung* is underlined by the motif of the colour blue. This signifies the intangibility, but nevertheless the potent expectation, of life beyond the brutality of Nazi domination, a dimension which supersedes corporeal fragility, non-survival and extermination. Aichinger's poetic vision reinforces this domain, a metaphysical, parallel universe where everything turns blue. The luminosity of the blue light signifies the topographical and spiritual destination of Ellen's mother, and at the very beginning of the protagonist's quest for a greater hope the consul reassures her "that somewhere there's a place where everything turns blue" (16). Similarly, Ellen begs the saint Franz Xaver: "Whatever happens, help me to believe that somewhere there's a place where everything turns blue!" (26) The persecuted Jewish children find sanctuary in the cemetery of their ancestors, "where what's near is far, and what's far is near, isn't it the place where everything turns blue?" (48) In addition, the hallucinatory journey to the holy land circumnavigates space where "[t]he sky was made of blue glass" (59). Finally, moving towards the dénouement of the transcendental quest, the search for a greater hope, Ellen comforts the dying horse: "[Y]ou mustn't be afraid – the sky is blue, can you see?" (198) And the mountain backdrop to the pandemonium of the liberating forces intimates an horizon, the co-junction of present and future, death and infinity, where there is the promise of a greater hope: "Far away, the mountains rose untouched above the chaos. Behind those mountains, it was turning blue" (219).

The principle of hope governs the imagery and symbolism of the poetic lyricism of one of Europe's greatest postwar novels. In the apocalyptic apotheosis of Aichinger's work, the paradox of departure and arrival is fused in the allegorical bridge. At her death, Ellen sees a vision of Georg's face which intimates the continuity of the spirit, a greater hope:

> "Georg, the bridge has collapsed!"
> "We'll rebuild it!"
> "What shall we call it?"
> "The greater hope, our hope!" (220)

Ilse Aichinger's magnum opus is definitively one of the great works of the human spirit.

References

Primary Sources

Aichinger, Ilse. *Kleist, Moos, Fasane* (1987). Frankfurt/M: Fischer Taschenbuch Verlag, 1991; 2004[3].

From: Reto Ziegler (Hg.). *Es muss gar nichts bleiben. Interviews 1952-2005* (2011). Wien: Edition Korrespondenzen, 2011[2].

--- Boetticher, Erich. "Den Frühling verstehen lernen" (1952). 11-13.

--- Brecht-Benz, Christina. "Genauigkeit der Träume" (1995). 85-88.

--- Cerha, Michael. "Hört jetzt das Schreiben auf, wird alles noch schwerer" (1990). 61-63.

--- Esser, Manuel. "Die Vögel beginnen zu singen, wenn es noch finster ist" (1986). 39-53.

--- Grabovski, Ernst. "Ich habe immer wenig ans Überleben gedacht" (2001). 195-201.

--- Graf, Guido. "Verschwinden, ein Leben lang" (2001). 186-194.

--- Hell, Cornelius. "Dazwischen sehr viel Schweigen" (1997). 122-144.

--- Kospach, Julia/Schneeberger, Peter. "Es muss gar nichts bleiben" (1996). 103-109.

--- Radisch, Iris. "Ich will verschwinden" (1996). 110-121.

--- Rathenböck, Elisabeth Vera. "Der Krieg war meine glücklichste Zeit, denn da hab ich noch alles erhofft" (2004). 210-219.

--- Reichensperger, Richard/Wittstock, Uwe. "Ich bin im Film" (2001). 154-158.

--- Reif, Adelbert. "Wir müssen die Barrieren unserer Gleichgültigkeit durchbrechen" (1996). 89-102.

--- Schafroth, Heinz F. "Teil eines stärkeren Widerstandes" (1972). 17-20.

--- Signer, David. "Ich bin ja gegen das Erzählen" (2005). 223-232.

--- Steinwendtner, Brita. "Ein paar Fragen in Briefen" (1993). 67-71.

--- Stuber, Manfred. "Man muss seinen Zorn wachhalten" (1993). 72-79.

--- Urbach, Karina. "Man muss seine Angst zähmen" (1991). 64-66.

--- Vinke, Hermann. "Sich nicht anpassen lassen" (1980). 25-32.

--- Zimmermann, Peter. "Es ist besser, man schweigt" (1990). 54-60.

Secondary Sources

Bachleitner, Norbert. "*Die größere Hoffnung* in englischer Sprache," in: *Internationales Archiv für Sozialgeschichte der deutschen Literatur* 37.1 (2012): 153-163.

Foucault, Michel. "What Is an Author?" (1969), in: *Aesthetics, Method, and Epistemology.* Trans. Robert Hurley and others. London: Penguin Books, 1994; 2000[3], 205-222.

"Fragebogen: Ilse Aichinger, Schriftstellerin" (1993), in: *Ilse Aichinger. Leben und Werk,* Samuel Moser (Hg.). Frankfurt/M: Fischer Taschenbuch Verlag, 1990; 2003³, 25-26.

Frankenstein, Alfred. "Zu *Die größere Hoffnung*" (1948), in: *Ilse Aichinger,* Bartsch, Kurt/Melzer, Gerhard (Hg.). Graz: Literaturverlag Droschl, 1993, 174-177.

Grübel, Lutz. "In der Düsterkeit nicht allein gelassen. Warum wir Ilse Aichinger Gleichaltrigen empfehlen?" (1988), in: *Ilse Aichinger,* Bartsch, Kurt/Melzer, Gerhard (Hg.), 159-162.

Härtling, Peter. "Ein Buch, das geduldig auf uns wartet" (1980), in: *Ilse Aichinger. Leben und Werk,* Samuel Moser (Hg.), 178.

Herweg, Nikola. "'Ich schreib für Dich und jedes Wort aus Liebe.' Der Briefwechsel der Zwillingsschwestern Helga und Ilse Aichinger," in: *Wort-Anker Werfen. Ilse Aichinger und England,* Görner, Rüdiger/Ivanovic, Christine/Shindo, Sugi (Hg.). Würzburg: Königshausen & Neumann, 2011, 27-43.

Jens, Walter. "Ilse Aichingers erster Roman" (1960), in: *Ilse Aichinger. Leben und Werk,* Samuel Moser (Hg.), 169-172.

Lindemann, Gisela. *Ilse Aichinger.* München: Verlag C.H. Beck, 1988.

Lorenz, Dagmar C.G. *Ilse Aichinger.* Königstein/Ts: Athenäum, 1981.

Schreiber, Hermann. "Die größere Hoffnung" (1949), in: *Ilse Aichinger. Leben und Werk,* Samuel Moser (Hg.), 157-159.

Stettler, Luzia. "Stummheit immer wieder in Schweigen zu übersetzen, das ist die Aufgabe des Schreibens" (1984), in: *Ilse Aichinger. Leben und Werk,* Samuel Moser (Hg.), 42-46.

Waterhouse, Peter. "An eine Papprolle gelehnt. Beginn einer Erzählung," in: *Wort-Anker Werfen,* Görner, Rüdiger/Ivanovic, Christine/Shindo, Sugi (Hg.), 147-159.

Gail Wiltshire

Coda: Geliebtes Helgilein: *Christmas 1945*

A previously unpublished Christmas letter festooned with intricate images reveals a further perspective of the greater hope as Aichinger writes to her beloved twin sister, Helga, in 1945.

Demolished by war, the Vienna of their childhood lies in ruins. The remnants of the *Jaquingasse* and *Prinz-Eugen-Straße* correspond with the skeletal remains of the *Hohlweggasse* where, preparing for the Christmas celebration of the birth of the Christ child seven years ago, Ilse and Helga painted golden stars. Devastation and destruction, rubble, "Trümmer" eclipse the past of two small girls in regulation school sailor's capes, "mit zu kurzen Matrosenmänteln und brennenden Augen." Hand in hand, the twins gaze at the gleaming chandelier behind heavy curtains in a *Palais* overlooking *Schwarzenbergpark*. They argue about which *Palais* would become their dwelling ("Deines und meines – beide glaub ich"), anticipating an illusory future. The shattered wall of *Schwarzenbergpark*, a "halbverfallene Mauer" and the imminent collapse and disintegration, "Einsturzgefahr," darkness, "Finsternis," and the stench of burning, "Brandgeruch" dominate the physical landscape, an external manifestation of emotional and psychological dissolution, isolation and yearning. But even in their separation Ilse and Helga are inured by shared memories and the bond of love, a "kleines Palais im Herzen," and a belief in the "Gute und Tiefe und Wunderbare. [...] Du und ich, wir haben noch beide unser kleines Palais in der Seele – mit dicken, gelben Vorhängen, das sind unsere Träume und ein kleines rotes Licht dahinter, das ist unsere Sehnsucht!"

Aichinger's intensity of vision encapsulates the affective, human trajectories of a war-torn dreamscape. Her *Hohlweggasse* memories embrace the *Aspangbahn* which "fährt daran vorbei, als wäre gar nichts geschehen," but the elderly woman and boy child who waved from the opposite window, an image Aichinger employs in the first chapter of her novel *Die größere*

Hoffnung, have vanished: "Aber sie winkt nicht mehr und es hätte ja auch gar keinen Sinn, einer Ruine winkt man nicht." The sweet vendor, "die Zuckerfrau" and the newspaper woman selling Christmas tinsel, the fragrance of the candle-singed pine needles of the Christmas tree, the glimmer of silver threads, chestnuts, baked plums and nut strudel are no more. Overwhelmingly, the latter discloses the originator of the "Nußstrudeln" who is no longer present. Not only have the "roten heißen Kindergesichter [...] die sich an die kalten Küchenfenster pressen" disappeared, but Aichinger also evokes the intensity of grief, "keine Großmama." She recalls standing with Helga at the icy kitchen window of their grandmother's apartment, noses pressed to the glass as they counted the passing waggons on the railway tracks, the "Schienen," an image which pervades the Aichingerian oeuvre and relentlessly demarcates the deportation and murder of her grandmother and family.

Snow falls endlessly: "[E]s schneit [...] und der Schnee fällt und fällt." While the snowfall elicits the writer's anguish, despair and loss, a sense of reverence subsumes the vista of devastation. Aichinger opens her letter: "[E]s schneit und die Welt wird tief und still und grau, so als wäre sie andächtig und der Schnee fällt und fällt." Thus, the writer manipulates the poetic fallacy, an elemental representation of the human spirit as she unequivocally transposes the snowflakes, "Flocken," storms, "Stürme," layers of darkness, "Dunkelheiten," and mist, "Nebel" into the hope of a destination beyond desperation, oblivion and annihilation. Although she is "krank von Sehnsucht," she dreams of a "Flintertürl," a side door, which will facilitate her reunion with Helga, who is "unser zu Hause und unser Trost. [...] [W]ir wollen weg von hier, wir wollen zu Euch [...] und wenn man im Radio irgendwann *Die Winterreise* von Schubert spielt, schließen wir die Augen und sitzen im Schlitten und fahren zu Euch." Veiled by the defamiliarising effect of falling snow, faces are concealed and lack clarity. In a hairdresser's window display mirror, the writer sees the faces of a woman and child which are transfigured by the distortion of reflection into the face of Helga, "du, mein Geliebtes" and a small child with a

toboggan. Aichinger exclaims: "[E]ine Rodel läuft von irgendwo in mich hinein." The author can believe that the child is
Ruth, Helga's small daughter. In her imagination, Aichinger
grabs the rope and pulls the toboggan for some distance along
the street and as she runs and runs, the velocity is such that the
toboggan transforms into a snow sled and the child, wearing
bobbled cap and red woollen suit, sits behind her. Helga's family, husband and child, give the writer great joy. "Ihr werdet nie
leer und elend sein und das macht mich so froh. Wie eine leise
zitternde Ahnung von Frieden ist dieser Gedanke!"

Where does freedom lie? Aichinger responds by introduc-
ing one of the three tramps, whose golden yellow robes and
silver Christmas tinsel concealed under tattered cloaks in *Die
größere Hoffnung* denote the imperial status of the Magi who
follow the Bethlehem Star to the Christ child. "'Habt Ihr den
Frieden gesehen?' schreit der Landstreicher in dem Weihnachts-
spiel, das ich voriges Jahr geschrieben." The poignant query of
the vulnerable, small cripple Herbert remains unanswered. But,
"obwohl ihm niemand Antwort gibt, [...] er will nach Bet[h]le-
hem, wohin der Stern ihn führt." The Holy Script rewritten, the
tramp and Aichinger co-joined, the writer metamorphoses into
a Holy King, adorned in red, piloting a fighter plane towards
England. "[D]er Stern wird ihm schon zeigen, an welchen Ort!"
Finally, "er ist mitten im Frieden." The cacophony of exploding
time-fused bombs, the droning, the rumours of deportation and
murder subside because Ilse Aichinger's heart is already in England with Helga, her husband, Walter, Ruth and of course,
"Tante Klärchen." The star and Bethlehem, family and England
are powerfully fused into the greater hope.

Gail Wiltshire: By kind permission of Mirjam Eich

The vagabond Wiseman image was created by Aichinger along with
many other images to facilitate the understanding of this letter by
her beloved niece, Ruth, aged 3

Acknowledgements

Cover Portrait

Helga Michie, née Aichinger, and Ruth Rix, daughter of Helga, for the cover portrait of the children of Gisela and Jakob Kremer, Erna (top left), Felix (bottom right) and two unidentified children engaged in the production of a play ("Spiel"), reminiscent of Chapter 6 in *Die größere Hoffnung*. Photo by Gisela and Jakob's eldest daughter Klara, who facilitated Helga's escape from Vienna prior to the Nazi occupation.

General Acknowledgements

This publication has been enhanced by the contribution of photos of the family apartment, the home of Ilse Aichinger's beloved grandmother Gisela, at *Hohlweggasse* 1 in Vienna. Photos courtesy of Ruth and Hugh Rix.

I would like to express my gratitude to Mirjam Eich, daughter of Ilse Aichinger, who was generous with her time in granting interviews, and who graciously gave permission for the publication of quotations, and an image, from the letter in the "*Coda*: Geliebtes Helgilein: *Christmas* 1945."

Collected interviews of Ilse Aichinger, *Es muss gar nichts bleiben*, published by *Edition Korrespondenzen*, provided the foundation for the Afterword.

Gail Wiltshire